"WHAT'S THE MATTER WITH ME? WHAT'S HAPPENING TO ME?"

"Not just you, Charlie. That's what I've been trying to tell you. It's the whole town . . . I don't have the faintest idea why, but if we can find a pattern, something all of you have in common, then maybe we'll get somewhere."

Charlie looked at her. He thought, he really thought, she had something there. He nodded, started to say he'd help any way he could.

Then something struck his shoulder, slammed him back hard into the chair, and he sat there gasping.

"What is it?" Eve said, alarmed. "What's the matter?"

He didn't know. It hurt like hell. He drew the shirt off his shoulder. On it, darkening as they watched, was an angry bruise.

It was only the beginning . . .

THE TOWN WAS BEING SLOWLY, HORRIBLY POSSESSED—AND THERE WAS ONLY ONE UNEARTHLY WAY TO SAVE IT . . .

Also by Stephen Marlowe:

The Shining
The Search For Bruno Heidler
Come Over Red Rover
The Summit
Colossus
The Man with No Shadow
The Cawthorn Journals

TRANSLATION

Stephen Marlowe

BALLANTINE BOOKS • NEW YORK

To
D.P. and J.G.K.

Library of Congress Catalog Card Number: 75-38984

ISBN 0-345-25569-0-195

This edition published by arrangement with Prentice-Hall, Inc.

Manufactured in the United States of America

First Ballantine Books Edition: January 1977

Magic is a great secret wisdom,
just as reason is a great public folly.

—Paracelsus, *De Occulta Philosophia*

translātus, serving as pp of *transferre,* to carry across, to transfer, with derivatives *translātio* (acc *translātiōnem*), a transferring . . . and LL *translātor,* copyist, translator, whence, resp, 'to *translate*' (both senses), *translation* (perh via late MF-F), *translative, translator* (prob via MF *translatour*).

From *Origins* by Eric Partridge

Canvas

1

That early in the morning the Grand' rue was still deserted, its ancient cobblestones slick with mist. Melody limped quickly up the final steep climb and through the archway under the clock tower. It was like leaving the Middle Ages and entering the twentieth century in the blink of an eye.

Behind her were the twisting streets of the Old Town, many of them so narrow that she could spread her arms and touch the walls on either side. Ahead was Place de la Liberté, the central square of the New Town, bordered by shops on three sides and the Route Nationale on the fourth. A large blue bus roared by, making the switch to the twentieth century complete.

"Bonjour, Melody."

It was Madame Vautier, sweeping the sidewalk in front of her grocery shop with a twig broom. The way she said it, Melody's name came out Melo-*dee*.

"Bonjour, madame," Melody said.

"Bonjour, Melo-*dee*." That was the baker Malancourt, carrying an enormous straw basket of baguettes. Melody could smell the yeastiness of the fresh bread.

"Bonjour, monsieur," she said, and with a smile the plump baker gave her one of the long thin breads.

"At your age, mademoiselle," he said, "one is always hungry. Is it not so?"

Well, Melody thought, thanking him, she was certainly hungry now.

She had left the house of the Villières family in the Old Town before breakfast. There wasn't much time. The bus would be leaving Bourg St. Martin for Paris at

3

noon. It was Melody's last day in France; less than twenty-four hours from now she would be back in Connecticut.

She broke off a piece of the crusty bread, still warm from the baker Malancourt's wood-burning oven. The taste, she knew, would always remind her of France. She had already decided to bake her own French bread for her father and herself when she returned home.

"Bonjour, mademoiselle." That was the butcher Trévise, unlocking the corrugated-iron shutter of his shop. It went sliding up with a clatter as he turned to greet Melody.

"Bonjour, monsieur," Melody said, limping quickly along. From the very beginning, the villagers had warmed to her more than to the half-dozen other students who had come from Martinsburg in Connecticut to its sister city of Bourg St. Martin for the summer. She suspected it was the limp rather than the long blond hair, or what they called her gamine grin, or her obvious eagerness to learn everything she could about France and Bourg St. Martin in two short months. Everybody felt sorry for her.

Melody limped along the edge of the Route Nationale. The sun was just coming up over the battlements of the Old Town and the bell in the clock tower struck eight times. It was still early-morning cool here in the foothills of the Massif Central, and a slight breeze tattered the mist that clung to the ground.

Ahead, past the curve in the highway, Melody saw the cinder-block garage, the used-car lot, and the three small trailers that were home to the Piedoie family. The Piedoies had been horse dealers for generations, according to Bibi Tita, the matriarch of the clan, and they had turned to the used-car business after the war. Gypsies— *manouches* in French—were the most fascinating people Melody had ever met, especially old Bibi Tita herself, who sometimes, for twenty francs, read a French-woman's future from the palm of her hand.

Indirectly, she had been introduced to the gypsies by the paintings in the museum, the eerie paintings of

Jean-Baptiste Columbine, three hundred years old and world famous. Columbine had lived with gypsies and painted them, according to Monsieur Taitbout, the curator. One day in the museum a boy Melody's own age had come up to her and said in French:

"You like them?" He was darkly attractive and had an odd, sly-shy smile. He looked, Melody remembered now, both sure of himself and prepared for a rebuff.

"Yes, I do," Melody said.

"What he paints or the way he paints it?" the boy asked swiftly.

"Well, I suppose both." Melody was proud of her fluent French, even if her accent inclined toward third-year high-school American.

"My name's Raoul," the boy said. "At least, that's my French name."

"Your French name?"

"I'm Rom," the boy said. "You know—*manouche.*"

"Huh?" said Melody.

"Gypsy," the boy explained condescendingly. "It means gypsy. Come on, I'll show you."

Melody hesitated, in the musty main room of the museum, surrounded by the paintings of Jean-Baptiste Columbine.

"If you come, maybe I'll tell you my real name. Or one of them anyway."

"One of them?"

"A gypsy has three names," Raoul said. "The first is his secret name. His mother whispers it in his ear the day he's born. The second is his romani name. The third . . ." Raoul shrugged his contempt. "The third is for the *gadje.*"

"The what?"

"Everybody else. The dumb peasants. The *gadje.* The whole world that isn't Rom. You," said Raoul with a sudden enormous smile.

Melody had spent most of her spare time after that with the gypsies. She had learned even more during her summer in Bourg St. Martin about the *manouches,* or at least the Piedoie family, than she had about the French.

Not that Piedoie—Goosefoot—was their real name. The gypsies had a sense of humor. But sometimes they acted—strange. Like the first time she had met Bibi Tita. The old woman looked at her as if she found Melody somehow frightening, almost as if—this was the only way Melody could think of it—Bibi Tita had seen a ghost.

Now Raoul came out of the trailer closest to the road, a steaming mug of coffee in his hand. As Melody had become less shy during the course of the summer, he had become more so. She knew he had a crush on her. She thought of him as a friend to walk with along the river below the town, to drink a glass of wine with at the Café St. Martin, to offer an occasional chaste kiss in response to the plea in his big doleful eyes. It was his grandmother Bibi Tita who intrigued her, after that first meeting. Raoul was practically French, but Bibi Tita was all gypsy.

Melody offered Raoul the rest of the bread. He grinned, shaking his head no. "I'd feel guilty all day," he said. "I know that appetite of yours. You're the only one I know who could starve to death between breakfast and lunch."

Melody was sixteen, five feet two inches tall, and weighed a hundred pounds. She ate like a stevedore and never gained an ounce.

"Is she awake?" Melody asked.

"She hardly sleeps three hours a night," Raoul said. "Of course she's awake. Your last day here, and all you think about is Bibi Tita."

Raoul sighed. "You probably won't even remember my name, back in America."

"What's your name?" Melody asked quickly. "Your real name?"

He was going to tell her, she was sure of it. But then Bibi Tita filled the small doorway at the rear of the trailer and lumbered down the three wooden steps.

She wore a kerchief and gold hoop earrings, a floral-patterned bodice, and Melody didn't know how many full, ankle-length skirts, one over the other. The outside one was a deep blue color.

Bibi Tita—Auntie Tita—must have been at least eighty. Her face was round, walnut-colored and as puckered as a walnut except where the skin stretched taut and smooth over high cheekbones under huge dark eyes.

She spoke peremptorily to Raoul. "Bring chairs behind the garage. Then go."

"Can't I—"

"No. Nor the other Rom." *Rom* meant gypsy in the romani language, but it also meant man. "Just Melody."

Raoul brought the chairs—a pair of them, wooden, straight-backed, and uncomfortable—setting them on the bare earth behind the cinder-block wall of the garage. He waited. "Go," said Bibi Tita in her deep voice, and Raoul went, looking back once over his shoulder at Melody.

"So, little *gadji* with the broken wing," Bibi Tita said. She stuffed her brass pipe with tobacco and lit it. The smoke was harsh. "So you are leaving us today and flying across that enormity of an ocean to your home. The Rom are wanderers, but we have always hated the ocean, feared it. That's odd, isn't it?" She asked abruptly, "And what do you fear, Melody?"

"Me? I don't know. Dying. Or if something happened to my father."

"Not your mother?"

"My mother's dead," Melody said.

She heard a clanging sound from inside the garage and saw a bitter smile on Bibi Tita's face. "What horse dealers we were once!" the old woman said. "The tricks we knew. We would currycomb a flea-ridden nag and tie a scarlet ribbon to its tail and rattle a pail of pebbles under its nose so that later, when someone came to buy, just showing the pail would be enough to make the nag prance and rear like a stallion. But who is to buy horses these days?" The bitter smile became crafty. "Of course one can do wonders with a car too.

Heavy oil in the crankcase, not enough air in the tires, and a wiping of the inside with embalming fluid so that it smells new in the nostrils of the foolish *gadje*. The smell of death, to make a battered old wreck of a Renault seem new." Bibi Tita leaned forward. "Tell me about your father."

"My father? He's like you, like the Rom, in a way. A wanderer all his life, until he bought the newspaper in Connecticut. He's tall and handsome and—I don't know, it's pretty hard to describe him. He's strong, but he's gentle, and—"

"You love him," Bibi Tita said dryly.

She was still leaning forward, and impulsively Melody placed her hand, palm up, on her knee. "Tell my fortune, Bibi Tita."

The request seemed to insult the old woman. She drew back, puffing on her pipe, shaking her head. She removed the hand from her knee as if it were something inanimate, no part of Melody.

"Fortunetelling is not for you. You are my friend. Life is a game that most *gadje* lose. Most times, when I tell their fortunes, they want their fears confirmed, not their hopes realized."

"Then you can't read the future?" Melody asked, disappointed. Often she had seen Frenchwomen come to the trailer behind the garage to have their palms read by Bibi Tita.

The old gypsy woman chuckled. "I am the *phuri dai*, the wise woman, of my people. I can read the past, not the future. But sometimes, in the old days when we traveled, I could learn things of value about a place by pretending to read the future in a *gadji*'s hand."

Bibi Tita's brass pipe went out. She tapped it against the edge of the chair and stuffed more tobacco in it.

"But anybody can read the past," Melody said. "That's history."

"History, written history," she was told, "is what the historian wants to make it. We Rom have no written history. Just tradition, passed down from father to son, mother to daughter. There's truth in that. It makes time go away."

Melody said she didn't understand.

"I can remember what my grandmother remembered, because she told me, and she can remember what *her* grandmother told her, and that one the grandmother before. A few old crones like me," said Bibi Tita, "and you are back in the days of Jean-Baptiste Columbine, who traveled with the Rom and painted them. What has happened to time then? Time does not pass. You pass through time. Did you know that Columbine once had to flee this village for his life? It was just a village then, like the ancient part inside the walls—three hundred years ago. So now of course Columbine is Bourg St. Martin's most famous citizen. Now."

Bibi Tita struck a wooden match and lit her pipe. "Tell me again about the town where you live." Her dark eyes locked on Melody's, held them.

"It's, you know, just a town. A small city, I guess, maybe twenty thousand people. There's a textile mill and—"

"No, child," Bibi Tita said impatiently. Melody had never seen her eyes like that. "The part about your town in the United States and this town here. Martinsburg, that is English for Bourg St. Martin?"

"In the early eighteenth century," Melody said, "some citizens of Bourg St. Martin founded Martinsburg. So naturally, when the sisters-cities program began about twenty years ago—"

"Their names," said Bibi Tita. "Tell me their names." She grasped Melody's wrist and held it hard. Her fingers were dry and strong.

"Their names? Whose names?"

"Those who came from here and founded your city."

"I don't know," Melody said.

"Was there a Ramezay?"

"A what? That doesn't sound like an American name."

"Something like that, then."

The pressure of the dry fingers was removed.

"What is your father's name?"

"Garrick," said Melody. "Robert Garrick."

Bibi Tita's lips narrowed. Her eyes narrowed. She did not seem to be breathing. Melody was suddenly frightened.

"That's a French name too," Bibi Tita said.

"No, you're wrong. My father's family came from England."

"French," said Bibi Tita flatly. "St. Martin is the patron saint of this town; you know that, don't you? Is he the patron saint of your town too?"

The fear receded. "We don't have things like that," Melody said.

"St. Martin's footman is the devil," said Bibi Tita, and the fear went away.

"You believe in the devil?" Melody asked. The question seemed to surprise Bibi Tita.

"Do you believe in God?" she asked.

"Yes."

"Then if there is a God, there is a devil. Otherwise, explain the sorry state of the world." Bibi Tita asked, "They are sending the paintings of Jean-Baptiste Columbine to your home?"

"Yes. In November."

Bibi Tita shut her eyes and whispered, "Then stay here with us. Don't go back."

"Bibi Tita, I'd love to stay. You know that. But I have to go back."

"Stay. Stay with us. You could become one of us—our little blond-haired Romi."

"I'd like that, I really would. But I have to go home."

"There's talk of traveling again. The open road. I could show you places," Bibi Tita said. Melody realized she was pleading. "The shrine of the Black Virgin in Saintes-Maries-de-la-Mer, the horse fair in Seville, the village in the Pays-Bas where Columbine painted in his madness."

"I'll try to come back next summer. Maybe my father will let me come back next summer."

Bibi Tita looked at her. "Next summer may be too late," she said. "Who knows how long I'll live?"

"I'll come back next summer and find you telling fortunes to the stupid *gadje,*" Melody said.

"Yes, of course you will. I did not mean to frighten you." Bibi Tita stood, a large, grandmotherly woman dressed as a gypsy. Not frightening at all. What's the matter with me? Melody thought.

"I have a gift for you," Bibi Tita said. "To take back to America."

Melody waited while she lumbered off to the trailer, climbed the three steps, and went inside. She came back with something wrapped in yellow oilskin. When she unwrapped it, Melody saw a small, leather-bound book.

She thrust it into Melody's hand. The leather binding was stained, cracked along the spine, its corners scuffed.

"Open it," Bibi Tita said, and Melody did. The pages seemed almost leathery too, yellowed with age, a corner missing here and there. Sometimes part of a page was green-stained with what Melody guessed was mildew.

"It belonged to my grandmother," Bibi Tita said. "And her grandmother, and hers—all the way back to the time of Jean-Baptiste Columbine."

Melody looked at a page at random. It was handwritten in a close script, the ink faded frequently into illegibility. She could make out a few words right away, but the handwriting was difficult. She saw the French words for doctor and priest and daughter.

"Promise me you'll read it."

"I don't know if I can. My French really isn't that good. What is it?"

"Promise me," said Bibi Tita.

"All right, yes. And—thank you, Bibi Tita." The last gift Melody would have expected from a gypsy was a book. Gypsies were illiterate, weren't they?

Bibi Tita didn't quite smile. "I know what you're thinking," she said. "Me, I can read French and Magyar and Spanish, but don't you ever tell anyone. It would embarrass me." Melody felt better; this was the old delightful Bibi Tita speaking.

"You've read it?" Melody asked.

"More than once."

"What is it?"

"The Notebook of Jean-Baptiste Columbine, written when he was mad. At least that's what my grandmother said. It could be a forgery, of course. Who knows?"

"Do you think it is a forgery?"

"No," said Bibi Tita.

She came forward and hugged Melody hard. "Come back and see us next summer."

"I'll try."

"Take care of yourself, child."

"Don't worry, I will. Good-bye, Bibi Tita."

Halfway to the trailer, Bibi Tita turned, as Raoul had done. "Little *gadji* with the broken wing," she said.

2

The *manouches* of Bourg St. Martin, like all gypsies, knew a good thing when they saw it.

The Feast of St. Martin, November 11, was decidedly a good thing, and the gypsies had prepared for it for weeks, hammering cheap tin and copper jewelry, knitting lace shawls, producing iron St.-Martin's-head rings on the small forge in the garage, liberating plump geese from various barnyards, which they would offer for sale door-to-door at half the going price in Bourg St. Martin's butcher shop.

Raoul himself had liberated half a dozen geese in as many nights, and he had been so busy working the bellows in the garage that he was hardly aware, until St. Martin's Eve arrived, that Bibi Tita had been retreating more and more into herself. She told no fortunes, sang no old gypsy songs at night in her husky contralto. She spent most of her time, in the cold rainy autumn, among the family icons in the front compartment of the trailer. She watched, on St. Martin's Eve, without interest while the young women prepared hedgehog, Bibi Tita's own specialty, gutting the animal, encasing it in clay, baking it slowly, and then knocking off the clay and with it the spines. The hedgehog was delicious, though not as good as Bibi Tita made it. She hardly ate a bite. Her lustrous blue-black hair was dull, and even showed some gray. She was pallid and listless. In the morning, while all the *manouches* went into town with their wares, she stayed in the trailer.

"Aren't you coming?" Rawl asked.

"No," said Bibi Tita.

13

"You ought to see a doctor," the boy suggested.

"I never saw a doctor in my life. Why start now? When I die, I'll die. Is it St. Martin's Day?"

"Of course," Raoul said.

"Then what are you waiting for? Go sell trinkets to the foolish *gadje*."

"I'll stay if you want."

"I don't want," said Bibi Tita querulously, and Raoul took his suitcase of rings and shawls and hammered copper and tinware and walked along the Route Nationale into town.

Bibi Tita waited half an hour and followed. Parked in the square between Madame Vautier's grocery shop and the gateway to the Old Town, under the clock tower, she saw a small van, a Citroën with Paris plates. Two men appeared in the gateway, carrying a large flat rectangular box. Bibi Tita got between them and the van with Paris plates.

"From the museum?" she asked.

The one facing her, a cigarette pasted to his lips, looked at her as only a Parisian could. He ignored the question. "Gypsy," he told his companion, and carefully they carried the box into the rear of the van. The day was cold, and a blustery wind blew down from the higher mountains of the Massif Central. Only a few people had left the heated terrace of the Café St. Martin to watch the loading of the truck. An *agent de police* stood by, cap set square and low on his head. He rubbed his hands together against the cold. The two men went back through the gateway into the Old Town.

"Hey, Auntie," the *agent* asked, "where's your box of junk? Don't you have anything to sell today?" He smiled cynically for the benefit of the onlookers.

Bibi Tita said nothing. She waited until the men returned with another large flat box, watching them carry it into the van. A second *agent* followed them, and a few children, none of them gypsies, trailed after him.

"Well, that's the lot," said the second *agent*.

"The paintings of Jean-Baptiste Columbine?" Bibi Tita asked.

The second *agent* was a man she knew. He did not have the usual police contempt for gypsies.

"Sure, Auntie," he said. "Those, and half the contents of the museum. *Mon Dieu,* they wouldn't take so much trouble with bars of gold. Waterproof paper and quilted padding for the corners."

"For America?" Bibi Tita asked.

"They'll fly out of Paris this afternoon," the *agent* assured her. "Still be St. Martin's Day when they get there. A five-hour time difference," he explained to the crowd with a pleased little smile in appreciation of his own knowledge.

"Five hours and almost three hundred years," Bibi Tita said, watching the two men from Paris climb into the front of the van.

The van started. It backed a few yards, stopped, then lurched forward, turning to leave the square.

Bibi Tita felt her heart pounding. She lumbered four steps after the van and suddenly pitched forward and down.

That night, even though it was cold, they brought a mattress outside the trailer so that Bibi Tita could die in the open air. It is unlucky for a gypsy to die in bed or indoors. The mystery of death, like the mystery of birth, can pollute a home. They are outdoor things.

Bibi Tita, wrapped in three wool blankets, lay on her side on the mattress. Gasping, she held the back and leg of a chair; Raoul, standing close, held the chair too. That way his own vital flux would pass through the wood to Bibi Tita, cheating death a few minutes, giving her time for her final thoughts. Raoul was not crying yet. The wailing and tearing of clothing would come later. All the gypsies were gathered around a fire which did little to keep Bibi Tita warm.

"You want the doctor, Auntie?" Raoul asked.

"When a Romi is ready to die, she dies."

"The priest, then?"

"Well," said Bibi Tita with a faint smile, "it wouldn't help me but I suppose it would make the priest happy."

She tried to rise, fell back on the mattress. She was shaking all over.

Raoul jerked his head at his cousin Gilbert. Gilbert was not his real name, of course. "Get the *curé*," he said, and Gilbert left the circle of flickering light cast by the fire, running.

The knuckles of Raoul's hand holding the back of the chair were white, he gripped it so hard. Bibi Tita's left hand dropped from the chair. She still held its leg with her right hand. She mumbled something in romani, her eyes wide, her lips trembling. Her grandmother? Raoul found it hard to conceive of the grandmother of a woman past eighty.

"Auntie?" he said.

Bibi Tita gasped something. Raoul's father squatted near her. Bibi Tita's voice grew faint. Her eyes were huge, her face contorted.

"The way she . . . limps," Raoul's father said, shaking his head, perplexed.

Bibi Tita's right hand dropped from the chair leg.

Raoul's father did not have to repeat her final words, although the last words of a *phuri dai,* a wise woman, are meant to be repeated.

Bibi Tita's neck strained, and her head rose up. "The same," she said in a clear, firm voice. "Little *gadji* with the broken wing."

Bibi Tita's head fell back, and she was dead.

Raoul's cousin came with the priest, in the priest's car. The gypsies began their wailing and lamentations.

Painting

3

The big eighteen-wheeled rigs roared by, flatulent in the night, strung with lights like Christmas trees six weeks early—Hemingway, North American, Mayflower, all of them old friends of Matthias Hawley, who was relegated now by age, substandard eyesight, and drink to a five-year-old GMC one-and-a-half-ton truck that rarely left the city limits of Martinsburg, Connecticut.

He slowed in the rain, smelled the sourness of beer bounce back at him from the windshield, and felt a gust of wind take the GMC as he left the Interstate on the exit ramp for U. S. 44.

Might be some ice, he thought. Early for that, second week in November, but it was cold. Twenty miles— figure a half-hour, thirty-five minutes, a night like this—and he'd make the delivery to Mister Garrick waiting with all them VIPs at the Martinsburg Armory, and maybe get back home in time to catch the last few minutes of the Pats-Dolphins game on *Monday Night Football*. A real gent, Mister Garrick. If the GMC left town these days, Matthias Hawley at the wheel so he could feel again the years of highballing it all over the States like a gypsy, it was a job for Mister Garrick at the newspaper.

Matt Hawley was still a teamster in good standing, and he could make bond, and the beer didn't mean much, he told himself, but the way one shot of bourbon led to another these days, that was different. How many times, recently, had he got himself lectured by Ned Revere down at the police station? Stick to beer, beer's okay, he told himself now, although he wished he hadn't

19

had the three beers at the truck stop on the way back from Kennedy Airport, the GMC tucked away outside in the rain between an Old Dominion and a Seven Brothers, almost hidden by their bulk, and Matt Hawley inside lifting a few with Mac and Floyd, Mac that he remembered from before and Floyd a new pimply-faced kid not quite young enough to be Matt Hawley's grandson, but close.

Because when he made the delivery, Mister Garrick would smell the beer as Matt could smell it now bouncing off the windshield at him. Ought to carry one of them breath gizmos like the kid Floyd that drove the Old Dominion on a run up from Virginia, the kid squirting it between his teeth and then opening and shutting his lips like some kind of a dame putting on lipstick. Ought to carry a lot of things—ten pounds less, twenty years less, to name a couple he could think of right away.

He sighed at the windshield, a puff of opacity removed by the defroster, and gave her more gas for the long curve where the two-lane blacktop crossed Frenchman's Creek, which Emmy once had told him was the name of a book *and* a movie. Emmy dead five years now, and maybe that explained the gut and the drink, or maybe it didn't.

No ice yet, anyways, but he could feel the slickness of wet dead leaves pasted like glue to the blacktop as the wind took the GMC again. No traffic, that was for sure, nothing coming or going since he left the Inter-state, just the rain coming down hard in the headlights and clattering, not quite sleet, on the roof of the GMC.

He crossed the creek where the road narrowed into one of those little erector-set bridges, and that meant four miles on the nose to the Armory in downtown Martinsburg on Rivoire Street. The long curve straightened half a mile past the creek, which in some places they would call a river, and the blacktop, still potholed from last year's frost heaves, ran straight then, crossing State 62, blinker red for them, amber for him, and from the crossroad on in, the tract developments began and you were almost in Martinsburg.

"You could drive a wide load, say one of those big house trailers or something, blindfolded all the way from the Interstate into town," Emmy had told him more than once. "I swear you know every inch of the road like you paved it with your own hands."

Emmy, he thought, softly sad inside himself, his eyes behind the glasses filmed over with a sudden surge of tears so that he could tell himself, afterward, there was a split second he didn't look, couldn't see what came up from the south on State 62, ignoring the red stoplight.

But, seeing or not seeing, he still felt the uneasiness. An instinct, what else could you call it if you drove a truck long enough? Something not quite seen, not quite heard, but you leaned forward peering into the darkness, gripping the wheel hard, ready.

The wipers swung, the headlights probed, a rear tire went thump in a pothole, the rain that was almost sleet clattered on the roof, and the uneasiness sharpened into fear.

Pilots would understand. Pilots who stayed alive, anyway.

The amber-yellow light blinked, swaying in the wind on the wire strung over the road. He saw nothing coming toward him, nothing coming up in the rear-view mirror, nothing to right or left on State 62 which had its own erector-set bridge just south of the crossroad where the creek curved and ran parallel to Matt Hawley's route there. But he still felt the dryness in his mouth and the hard, quickened beat of his heart for no damn reason at all, the early warning system playing tricks on him.

He eased up on the gas, said "hell" out loud because there was still nothing to cause the fear and by then if there was he would have known it. So he made a self-contemptuous face and tromped down hard on the gas as the amber warning light swung closer overhead.

Then he braked hard and swerved to the right to

avoid what came into existence at the crossroad in his
headlights in no time, like a movie starting in a drive-in.

He felt the slipping, sliding loss of control as first the
front and then the rear right tire slowed in the mud of the
shoulder. He tried to fight the truck back onto blacktop, but it lurched, front end down, and small pine trees
came at him fast, splintering, brushing the windshield as
he slid, taking out more trees, down the embankment
on two wheels sideways, knowing he would overturn as
surely as he knew he could not have seen what he had.

Looking at the large map of Martinsburg on the wall
inside the Armory, the Frenchman said, "But of course,
Mr. Garrick." He thumbnailed his pencil-line mustache
and adjusted his bifocals higher on the bridge of his
nose. "The beauty of it, the appropriateness."

"Melody's idea, Monsieur Taitbout," Robert Garrick
said, and Melody, standing near them in a crowd near
the map, managed to look modest but pleased with herself at the same time.

"The signs will go up in the morning," Garrick said,
using a rubber-tipped pointer. "Village Commons, that's
easy. That will be Place de la Liberté."

"Magnificent," Monsieur Taitbout said.

"Rivoire Street here gets to be the Grand' rue, Bank
Street the Route de Thiers."

"And we even got permission," Melody said, "to put
up road signs a mile on either side of town calling U.S.
44 the Route Nationale."

"It will be almost like Bourg St. Martin, mademoiselle," Monsieur Taitbout assured her with French gal-
lantry, "thanks to you."

"Permission for a sidewalk café on the Commons,
too," Garrick said. "Outside Nick's, glass enclosed."

"The Café St. Martin," Melody said.

"Of course," said Monsieur Taitbout.

Most of the canapés were gone from the long table
below the map, and the waiters from Nick's were pulling the corks from the last bottles of champagne. Monsieur Taitbout held his goblet out for a refill. His face

went through several delicate Gallic adjustments. "This Connecticut champagne," he said, shutting his eyes in consideration, "it is surprisingly good. Although perhaps the fact that I say 'surprising' demonstrates a certain ignorance."

"New York State," Garrick corrected him with a half smile for Melody's benefit.

"But of course, forgive me. The region of the Hand Lakes, is it not?"

"Finger Lakes," Melody said.

"American names are so . . . poetic," Monsieur Taitbout said. He stole a glance at his watch.

"Should be here pretty soon," Garrick told him. "The driver called from JFK."

"Everything was satisfactory?"

"The truck was loaded not quite four hours ago."

"And you said almost a hundred miles. That is how many kilometers, Mr. Garrick?"

"Pushing a hundred and sixty."

"Four hours ago?"

"Matt Hawley's a good driver."

Monsieur Taitbout looked worried.

"And a careful driver," Garrick comforted him. "He'd take it easy in the rain."

Alvin Waugh, Martinsburg's First Selectman, nodded his bald head, pulled at his earlobe. He was always fidgeting. "Hell of a night out there."

"The Columbines alone are priceless," said Monsieur Taitbout, unconvinced. "Five big canvases from his gypsy period. Five, how do you say, *chefs d'oeuvre*. Priceless. And even the minor works." He ticked them off nervously on his fingers. "A copy of Coysevox's bust of Colbert. The original is at Versailles, of course. A preliminary study for Mignard's 'Cardinal Mazarin.' Three rosewood cabinets by André Charles Boulle. The death mask of the Sieur de Ramezay. And then of course the coins and medals and rare books—I could go on." He went on: "Ours is a small museum in Bourg St. Martin, but over the years we have become proud of its collection."

"I'm sure it's justified," said Alvin Waugh. He looked at his watch too, and at Garrick. He adjusted his shirt and jacket sleeves, just so. He had been surprised when Garrick had sent Matt Hawley to JFK instead of hiring a truck in New York.

Monsieur Taitbout was a small man, his head barely reaching Garrick's shoulder. "You'll hang the Columbines right here in the main hall? Against the red stone it would be most appropriate. A beautiful building," he allowed. "An original concept in architecture."

Garrick exchanged a brief glance with his daughter. Most citizens of Martinsburg considered the Armory a monstrosity. Turreted, crenelated, massive, it stood on one side of the Village Commons, a cut-stone anomaly that spoiled the unity of colonial architecture.

Monsieur Taitbout was now looking at his watch openly. "Eleven-forty," he said, and just then a uniformed policeman came in, his raincoat drenched, water still dripping from the visor of his cap. He looked uncertainly at Alvin Waugh and at Garrick while Melody offered the last of the canapés to Monsieur Taitbout. When the Frenchman declined, Melody ate the two remaining rounds of toast and egg salad. Garrick smiled.

"See you a minute, Mr. Garrick?" the policeman said. He was new on Martinsburg's forty-man force. Garrick didn't remember his name.

"What is it?" Garrick asked, and the young policeman took off his cap and said:

"Well, maybe over here, sir."

Garrick walked a few steps off with him and listened. Then he inclined his head toward the First Selectman, who joined them at the door.

Alvin Waugh frowned, even his bald scalp creasing. He was a spare, lean man, almost as tall as Garrick, and he stood with his weight on one leg, anxiously, like a nervous stork. "Hawley?" he said.

"State police radioed in. Ned Revere's out there," Garrick told him. "Matt Hawley had an accident."

Alvin Waugh didn't quite say "I told you so."

They covered the four miles in just over three minutes, the siren of the police cruiser whooping in short frantic blasts.

"I still can't get used to it," the policeman said. "That's no kind of siren."

"Chief Revere's idea," Garrick told him. "French style, for Bourg St. Martin month."

"Flying the French flag over the Town Hall and the Armory, alongside the Stars and Stripes." The policeman laughed. "I'm supposed to give tickets in French, too?"

"Chief Revere say how bad it was?"

"Driver's okay. The truck slid down an embankment this side of Frenchman's Creek. Overturned. I speak French, you know."

"What?" Garrick asked. He was thinking of the Columbines and the other art treasures.

"Two years in college, Mr. Garrick. I'm Charlie Dahlgren. Hit town about six months ago. Up from the NYPD."

"Sure, I remember."

Dahlgren had a beardless boyish face and blond sideburns down to the lobes of his ears. He looked more like a college student than a cop. "It sure is one quiet town, Martinsburg. After New York, anyway. Not much happens around here, you know? A good place for a cop to raise a family."

"You got one?"

"No," Dahlgren said. He cleared his throat. "How'd she get that limp, anyway?"

"You mean Melody?" Garrick asked.

Dahlgren's voice sounded like he was blushing. "Yes, sir."

Garrick didn't want to talk about it. "Car crash," he said shortly.

"Oh." Dahlgren hit the brake. "There they are."

Ahead through the rain Garrick saw flares on the side of the road and two revolving red dome lights, one on Ned Revere's cruiser, one on the state police car.

Dahlgren cut the siren and pulled off the road behind the chief's car. The front door on the driver's side was open, the courtesy light on, the eight-hundred-candlepower searchlight angled down past the embankment where Matt Hawley's truck had gone over.

Garrick took a look at that first. The powerful beam pinned the truck on its side in the gully. Garrick saw deep skid marks and the trail of broken pine saplings.

"Hey, Rob," Ned Revere called, and Garrick went over to the open door of the chief's car.

"Ned," Robert Garrick said, and "You okay, Matt?"

"Jesus Christ, Mister Garrick, I'm sorry as hell," Matt Hawley said. He sat slumped in the passenger seat, head down, shoulders down, spirits lower.

"You okay?"

"Yeah, but what a dumb goddamn stupid thing."

Ned Revere said, "Grab a chair in back, Rob. They're sending the wrecker from Ghize's garage. It'll be a while yet."

"You been down there?" Garrick asked, getting into the car.

"She split open in back," Ned Revere said. "I hope to hell you had that stuff insured."

"I can make bond," Matt Hawley said.

"It's insured," Garrick said. Past Ned Revere's head he could see Dahlgren climbing into the state police car.

"Horses," Matt Hawley said.

"Now Matt," Revere warned, "let's not have that crap again. You'll only make it worse for yourself."

"Four of the biggest goddamn horses I ever seen," Hawley said.

"Sure," Revere said. "Next thing you'll be telling us pink elephants. How much booze you have?"

"Two beers, maybe three. No booze at all, I swear to God."

"Now Matt," Revere said again.

"Mister Garrick, you'll believe me, won't you?" Hawley said.

"What happened, Matt?"

Ned Revere craned his neck over a burly uniformed shoulder. "Don't say I didn't warn you."

"Up there at the blinker, see? Where State Sixty-two crosses?"

Garrick could see the amber light swaying in the wind.

"I hit it real slow, almost came to a stop. There's nothing coming, but it don't *feel* right. You ever get a feeling like that, Mister Garrick?"

"Sure, we all do. Go on, Matt."

"One second, there's nothing there. The next, I don't know, Mister Garrick. I don't know how to say it."

"You already said it," Revere told him wearily.

"Then," said Hawley in a flat, stubborn voice, "all of a sudden there's this horse-drawn wagon coming right through the red stoplight like it got turned on when you tune in a TV set."

"It was something special in the way of horses," Ned Revere said without any expression in his voice. "Wasn't it, Matt?"

"I'm coming to that, Chief," Matt Hawley said. "I mean, they ain't just pulling the wagon, they're really running. Galloping. I get them in the headlights. They're steaming. And they're *big*. They're big bastards, big as a horse and a half, every one of them. Prancing almost, the way they run. And they got these thick, like, manes of hair around their hooves. You ever seen horses look like that before? I ain't," Matt Hawley said. "I know you figure I was drunk and seeing things, Chief. I look drunk to you, Mister Garrick?"

"No," Garrick said. It was the truth.

"Now he doesn't," Ned Revere said. "Shock can do that."

"I wasn't drunk, I swear. I was just doing my best trying not to hit them horses. I start to skid. I wind up down there. Well, you saw that. Jesus, Mister Garrick. I ain't never been so sorry in my life."

"Where are the horses now, Matt?" Ned Revere asked.

There was a long silence. Finally Hawley said, his voice surly, "They reared, like they seen a snake. The wagon went over on its side, Chief."

"Where is it?" Revere asked.

Hawley sat through a longer silence. He sighed. Garrick could smell the beer faintly. Hawley pointed. "Well, I figure it should be about over there."

"And?" Revere asked him.

"It . . . went . . . away."

"I thought you said it overturned."

"It sure did. I *saw* it overturn."

"Then where is it?"

Hawley said, "A TV set. Just like shutting off a TV set."

Matt Hawley waited for someone to say something. Anything. When that didn't happen, Garrick saw the old man's shoulders move and heard him sobbing.

Ned Revere said, "Here comes the wrecker."

Moments later they were all out in the rain, Dahlgren at the searchlight on his car, Revere at the light on his, impaling the overturned truck with their beams while Harry Ghize scrambled and slid down the embankment.

"Ought to come up all right," he called after a while.

"Will you lose anything?" Revere asked.

"Not if she comes up on the first try."

Garrick heard the drone of the winch and saw Harry Ghize come up for the cable with the big steel hook on the end of it. He saw the glow of a cigarette in the cab of the wrecker, where Ghize's mechanic was operating the winch. He heard a voice, Matt Hawley's.

"Mister Garrick? You believe me, don't you?"

Garrick hardly knew what to say. He remembered the way the old man had sobbed. He put a hand on his shoulder.

"But you *believe* me?"

"It's going to be all right, Matt."

"Yeah, sure. They'll get the truck up. But what about me? Ain't nobody going to give me a load of old tin cans to carry as far as the city dump. Not after this. A car. I should of said a car. You would of believed a car. Except it wasn't no car."

Hawley crossed the road to the other side, and Garrick went with him.

They stood in the rain on the muddy shoulder of the road. Suddenly Hawley pointed. "Sumbitch, look at that. Now who's crazy? Who's crazy drunk now, Mister Garrick?"

In the dim, eerie light at the outer edge of the red glow cast by the flares Ned Revere had lit, Garrick saw deep parallel ruts in the mud, five feet apart.

Across the road the winch groaned, the cable creaked.

"It just disappeared," Matt Hawley said. "Like turning off a TV set."

4

Monsieur Taitbout's head rose slowly out of his cupped hands. "I told them," he said. "I gave specific instructions. Specific. Remove the frames. Pack the frames separately. It is a precaution, you understand? Safer. But did they do this? No, they did not. Heads will roll in Bourg St. Martin."

It was one-forty-five. Charlie Dahlgren and half the Martinsburg Volunteer Fire Department had brought the contents of Matt Hawley's truck into the main hall of the Armory. Monsieur Taitbout himself had used a Phillips-head screwdriver to remove the lid from the most badly damaged crate, a pine-board box four feet by four feet, eight inches deep. One corner was crushed and a raw pine board on the front of the crate had broken, though it was still held in place by screws at top and bottom.

Charlie Dahlgren helping, Monsieur Taitbout had carried the crate to the table, where a space had been made among the empty bottles of New York State, not Connecticut, champagne. Garrick watched them slide out a rectangular package wrapped in glazed paper and padded around the edges with quilting. Monsieur Taitbout used a penknife delicately on the twine that crisscrossed the package, holding the strips of quilting in place.

That was when his head sank into his hands.

"The frame," he said. "Gold leaf, the finest of gold leaf. Have you any idea of the work involved? But no, how could you?" Despite the quilting, the ornate frame had splintered where the corner of the crate was

31

crushed. Bare wood lay exposed. Flecks of gold glinted in the blue material of the quilting.

"You think it is paint the color of gold?" Monsieur Taitbout demanded. "It is not. It is gold itself. Rolled to the thickness of a fortieth of a millimeter. And then beaten. But not just beaten the way I would like to beat those idiots in Bourg St. Martin—no. Wrapped in vellum *and* parchment to withstand the beating. Four separate beatings, and the last two—by then it is very thin—protected by a membrane made from the intestines of an ox. Flattened to one ten-thousandth of a millimeter." Monsieur Taitbout's head disappeared into his cupped hands again, emerged. "And that is only the beginning. Then it must be applied to the frame."

He shut his eyes. Then even more delicately than he had cut the twine, he peeled off the masking tape that held the glazed paper in place. That exposed the painting.

"Jean-Baptiste Columbine's 'Gypsy Camp,'" he said reverently. Standing behind him, Garrick looked at the painting. It was a night scene, trees faintly visible in the background. At the left stood what might have been a circus wagon. A campfire dominated the foreground, a cauldron steaming over it. Gypsies sat close to the fire, hunched over. You could almost feel the cold.

Monseiur Taitbout said: "A perforation." His head bobbed down into his hands and up again. He touched the tiny hole in the center of the canvas delicately.

"Through the paint layers and the ground. Even the canvas," he groaned. "To think of the work of patching alone," he said. "One must cut a patch around the hole, coat it with plasticized polyvinyl acetate, cut another piece of canvas for backing, coat it too with the PVA, join the two patches over the damaged area, heat them, form a bond. . . . then, only then can one fill and retouch."

Monsieur Taitbout took a deep breath and shuddered. "Open the others," he said.

That took some time because Monsieur Taitbout insisted on doing most of the work himself, stopping frequently to catalog in a little notebook the damages he spotted. By then it was after four o'clock. Crates and cartons were scattered on the floor, painting and prints carefully set on the long table, marble and bronze statues and busts wherever there was room.

Monsieur Taitbout sat down. His face was gray, his lips trembling. He removed his gold-rimmed spectacles and blew on them and waved them in the air and replaced them.

"Well, it could have been worse," he said at last. "The copy of Coysevox's bust of Colbert is a disaster. Hopeless. Thank God it is just a copy. For the rest, only the Columbines have been seriously damaged. Have you a cigarette, Mr. Garrick? Me, I have given up smoking."

Garrick gave him a cigarette, lit it. Monsieur Taitbout held it between thumb and forefinger, cupped in the palm of his hand. He did not smoke it. "Only the Columbines," he repeated, shaking his head. "What an odd, tormented, tragic life the man led. But out of torment and tragedy comes great art, is it not so?"

The volunteer firemen sat around, waiting. Charlie Dahlgren looked at Garrick. Ned Revere yawned, stretched, looking at the ceiling.

Garrick said, "Any help you need, Monsieur Taitbout—"

"The irony, the crowning tragedy of the life and *oeuvre* of Jean-Baptiste Columbine, is that his finest painting, his undeniable masterpiece, has been lost to the world." Monsieur Taitbout looked at the dead cigarette. "Provided he ever painted it. We have sketches done by someone else—I can show you tomorrow. Those who knew him in his final period—his so-called black period, in the first decade of the eighteenth century—wrote that he did in fact paint it. Still . . ."

Ned Revere studied the ceiling. Garrick asked, "Can the repairs be made here, Monsieur Taitbout, or will you have to send the paintings out? We'll do it any way you want."

Alvin Waugh fidgeted. "Monsieur Taitbout, I can't tell you how sorry we all are that this had to happen."

"Had to. Precisely," said Monsieur Taitbout. "As I said, torment and tragedy have plagued Jean-Baptiste Columbine. Always." He tilted his head at Garrick. "It is a question of the mountain and Mohammed. *Entendu?* Either the paintings go, or the conservators and their equipment come."

"Well," Alvin Waugh said, his bald scalp furrowed, "we've put a hell of a lot of effort into Bourg St. Martin Month. If the paintings could stay, we'd appreciate it, Monsieur Taitbout."

Unexpectedly, Taitbout smiled. "If they go, perhaps to Boston, perhaps New York, then they are out of my hands. If they stay, I supervise the work myself. *Entendu?* I as well would prefer that they stay. I have had training at the Institut Royal du Patrimoine Artistique in Brussels. But I will need equipment, assistance. I will need a conservator who is an expert on Columbine. Almost as much as I am myself. I will make some calls. Kelly," he said.

"Kelly?" Ned Revere repeated.

"M. A. Kelly, Conservation Center of the Institute of Fine Arts, New York University. We will get Kelly."

"Now that that's settled," Ned Revere suggested, "why don't we call it a night?"

Charlie Dahlgren perked up, but Monsieur Taitbout did not hear the suggestion. He was studying his notebook again.

"Has anyone seen a box?" he asked.

Everyone, Garrick thought, had seen box after box, lids carefully unfastened, contents as carefully removed.

"A wooden box," Monsieur Taitbout elaborated.

Garrick saw Ned Revere glancing around the hall at all the wooden boxes.

"The size of a large *mallette?* What you call a suitcase?" said Monsieur Taitbout. "A veritable box, not one of these packing crates."

It wasn't in the hall. Charlie Dahlgren and one of the firemen went outside and returned to report it wasn't in the truck.

"Coins, costume jewelry, what you would call knickknacks," said Monsieur Taitbout. "The least valuable part of the collection, but nevertheless . . . May we return to the scene of the accident now? It probably fell from the truck."

Ned Revere persuaded the Frenchman to wait until dawn.

"Good lord," Garrick said, taking off his topcoat. "What are you doing still up?"

Melody sat on the sofa, legs tucked under her, long wheat-blond hair hanging almost to her waist. She wore a pink quilted housecoat.

"Homework," she said, closing a large book, getting up on tiptoes and kissing her father.

"At five-thirty in the morning?"

"A history of French art," she said. "I'm really into this Columbine, Daddy. What a strange life he led! You want some hot milk or something? Or I have some soup on the stove."

"A drink, maybe. You go on to bed."

"No, it's okay. I'll have a little snack. How'd it go, Daddy?"

Garrick told her about the night at the Armory while she made him a Scotch and water. He drank half of it and grinned. "I haven't reached the hot-milk-before-bedtime stage yet."

"I didn't mean it that way," Melody said, returning from the kitchen with a Dagwood sandwich. "You hardly look a day over thirty, and you know it."

"Garrick was thirty-nine."

"And handsome," Melody said, chewing. "Did anybody ever tell you you look like Paul Newman, only younger?"

Two of the four years that had passed since the death of her mother, Melody had spent in boarding school. Then Garrick had quit his job with Continental Broadcasting, purchased the Martinsburg *News,* and settled down in the big old house on Rivoire Street. Melody needed a home life, roots. She had become increasingly withdrawn after her mother's death. And there was the limp. "No physiological reason for it," the orthopedist in New York had told Garrick. "The fracture's healed. So it's psychological. In a way she blames herself for what happened."

Garrick's contract with Continental Broadcasting had three more years to run when Catherine died. He was putting in almost as much flying time as Kissinger, and he loved the work. But he remembered the night after Catherine was buried.

"I'll take care of you, doll."

Melody was in the hospital, her shattered leg in traction.

"And I'll take care of you, Daddy."

But of course it had been impossible. He was hardly ever in the Manhattan apartment. Melody hated the series of housekeepers who came and stayed usually no more than a month or six weeks. She neglected her schoolwork. Her limp was severe then, and it embarrassed her to go out. One by one she dropped her friends. She was moody. Garrick might have broken his contract then, quit. He didn't. He was at the top of his profession, and he hadn't got over the shock of Catherine's death. He rationalized his decision: It would be bad for Melody.

"How would you like to go to boarding school?"

"Where?"

"Anywhere you say."

It was an old school near Boston, with a good name and a patient faculty. Melody accepted the limp, made friends because Garrick expected it—and lived for those times he visited her.

The opportunity to buy the Martinsburg *News* came a few months before his contract expired. He surprised her with it, and with the big, pre-Revolutionary War house on Rivoire Street. Her fifteenth birthday. She was so happy she cried.

Less than a year in Martinsburg was enough for Garrick to know he'd made the right decision. He had never seen Melody so delighted with life, and with herself.

He'd had no qualms about sending her to France for the summer, and she returned, if anything, more radiant.

Now Melody asked, "Is Mr. Hawley okay?"

"He wasn't hurt. But he feels like hell."

"I'll go see him in the morning. I baked some bread."

"Aren't you forgetting one little detail? School."

"I'll only miss the first period, Daddy."

"I guess Matt would like to see you."

Garrick finished his drink. He stretched, bunching his shoulders.

"You look like a bear when you do that."

"Yeah, well, this bear is going into a couple of hours of hibernation. Busy day tomorrow."

"I'll put out the lights, Daddy."

Garrick parted the wings of her blond hair and kissed her forehead.

"Oh, by the way," Melody said, drawing away from him. "I almost forgot. Eve Talbot phoned."

Melody had the same look on her face she always got when Eve was mentioned. Eve Talbot was a reporter for Continental Broadcasting, and a good one. Garrick never let himself think how serious he was about her. Melody didn't make it easy.

"She wants to come up later in the week."

"When?"

"She'll call again. She thinks she can get a story out of Bourg St. Martin Month."

"Well, sure she could, doll. Especially after what happened."

"Yeah," Melody said, studying the carpet. "I know. You really like her, don't you?"

"Sure I do."

"She's so . . . I don't know. I just wish she wasn't so obvious about . . . well, you know."

"No, doll, I don't know."

Melody turned away from him. "Don't mind me. Wow, am I ever sleepy! Good night, Daddy."

She went upstairs, limping more than usual.

5

By eight-thirty that morning she didn't feel sleepy at all. She was limping quickly along Rivoire Street toward the Commons. No, she reminded herself, looking at the new blue and white street signs—the Place de la Liberté. She liked the new signs. They made her think of France, of the gypsies and Bibi Tita.

The sky had cleared, and a steady cold wind blew across the big Commons. Melody offered her usual scowl to the cut-stone monstrosity of the Armory, even though she knew she'd be spending a lot of time there watching Monsieur Taitbout repair the Columbine paintings. She thought of the whole collection that had been flown over from France as Columbines. The other works of art didn't matter. She felt a little pang of guilt, though, about the notebook Bibi Tita had given her. She had opened it only once or twice. The handwriting was difficult, many of the words strange. She had compromised by reading whatever she could find about Jean-Baptiste Columbine in the Martinsburg library. One of these days soon, she promised herself, she'd try the notebook again.

Her stride quickened as she approached the white clapboard building that housed the Martinsburg *News*. Her father would be inside now, writing the syndicated weekly column that he said kept him in contact with the outside world. That made her smile. In a way it was the other way around.

More and more his column was concerned with Martinsburg itself. Martinsburg to Rob Garrick was microcosm. It had the old French Huguenot traditions, and of course the early British. Old names like Boybellaud (which had become Ballard) side by side with Hawley. It had the descendants of Italian stoneworkers who had built the dam twenty miles upriver, and a recent influx of Puerto Ricans who worked in the textile mill and the silk-screen printing plant.

It had a downtown area that still looked like something out of the eighteenth century, if you could forget the paved streets and cars. And it had the suburbs with their tract houses, neat lawns, and carefully tended trees. It even had—Melody scowled as she had in front of the Armory—the neon strip that came in from the east, that one section of highway that had been zoned for motels, used-car lots, quick-food restaurants, and shopping centers. It had its share of tourists who came to see one of the oldest stone houses in America, and the many clapboard houses, each with its little historical plaque, that dated from the early eighteenth century.

One thing that set it aside, her father always said, was that it had virtually no crime. Tradition accounted for that, Rob Garrick maintained, and it was a tradition that the newer people in Martinsburg felt as strongly as the old families. If you lived in Martinsburg just a few years you somehow *felt* the generations that had come before, and you felt comfortable inside your own skin. Nothing much happened in Martinsburg except that you had a chance to live the good life. So when Rob Garrick wrote about Martinsburg, he was, he always told Melody, writing about a very fortunate part of America.

Melody heard the hiss and thump of the presses as she went in the back way and upstairs to the small apartment Matt Hawley rented on the third floor. She was carrying a loaf of bread she had baked for Matt. French bread, more or less. Of course, it wasn't stone-ground flour, and Melody had no French baking oven with steam jets to give the bread its crisp, nut-flavored crust. But it was a pretty close approximation. Every Saturday she brought a loaf—long and thin like a baguette—to Matt Hawley. The one she brought now was extra. The poor man, after what he'd been through, and blaming himself . . .

"Miss Melody," he said, standing in the open doorway. Melody could hear voices droning away on a morning TV talk show behind him. "That wouldn't be bread I smell?"

Melody had been holding the bread behind her back, unwrapped like in France. She went past Matt through the clutter of the small living room and put the bread on the kitchen table. The television voices faded and the door shut.

Matt Hawley came into the kitchen. He looked old and tired. He needed a shave. He wore a pair of worn corduroy trousers and a gray sweatshirt. He put coffee up while Melody slit the bread lengthwise and buttered it.

"It ain't Saturday, is it?" Matt Hawley asked.

"I made more dough than I thought."

They ate in companionable silence. The coffee was almost as bad as the bread was good. Matt Hawley just threw some into boiling water with an eggshell and hoped for the best. He lit a cigarette and leaned back.

"Tuesday bread. You know something? It's better than Saturday bread," he told her. "They gonna be able to fix things up okay?"

"Sure, Mr. Hawley," Melody said. "My father said there wasn't all that much damage."

"He tell you what happened? Them horses and all? It just wasn't my fault, I swear to God, Miss Melody."

"Nobody ever said it was."

"The hell they didn't. Chief Revere, he said—"

"Oh, well, the *flics*," Melody said.

"The what?"

"It's French for if you're mad at the cops. You know, like fuzz?"

Matt nodded. "I ain't mad at him. He's mad at me."

"How do you feel?" Melody asked.

The old truckman shrugged. "Last night it was okay. But this morning it's like they beat me all over with hammers. I figure I'll live through."

"You ought to see Dr. Tom."

"Not on your life, Miss Melody. You see a doctor, and he tells you what ails you, and then you get to *feeling* sick. Why ain't you in school?"

"I'll go later. I'm only missing the first period. Math," Melody said with her third scowl of the morning.

"Well, you want to catch the next class, you better go on along now." Matt looked at his watch. "Time for that and the nine o'clock news."

He rose, went inside. Melody heard TV sounds while she swiftly washed the dishes. Matt was standing in front of the color TV when she joined him in the living room and put her coat on.

He turned around, not saying anything. He looked old, nervous. Kissinger, the TV said. China, it said. The Middle East.

"Thanks for the Tuesday bread," Matt Hawley said. His voice sounded odd too. He looked at air over Melody's head. His eyes were empty, like pictures of eyes.

Melody felt herself freeze suddenly. Just freeze. For a few seconds she couldn't move.

Matt Hawley had opened his fly and now stood there, staring past Melody with his blank eyes, exposing his private parts.

Melody turned quickly to the door. She got her hand on the knob and yanked. She heard a sound behind her—a forlorn sobbing. She had to turn around.

Matt Hawley sat slumped in the chair near the TV. Tears were streaming down his cheeks. He wasn't uncovered anymore.

"Miss Melody?"

She didn't know what to say.

"Miss Melody, I swear to God I don't know what come over me. I swear I don't."

All Melody could do was nod.

"Never," he said. "I never did a thing like that before. I knew it was wrong. It was sick. And I couldn't stop. I couldn't stop myself at all."

He gave her an agonized look.

"You won't tell anybody? Your father or anybody? An old man starts in doing things like that, they put him away."

"It didn't happen," Melody said after a while. "Nothing happened. Good-bye, Mr. Hawley. I'll see you Saturday."

"Sure?"

"For sure."

Melody left. Her initial shock had given way to sorrow. She had never felt so sorry for anyone in her life.

It always amused Rob Garrick when Chief Ned Revere came into his office. The office was small, just enough room for Garrick's large desk, a few filing cabinets, two chairs. Garrick, who was six-four and lean, filled it vertically. Revere, half a foot shorter but with huge shoulders and the general dimensions of a barrel, filled it horizontally.

"Come on in, Ned."

Revere took off his visored cap. He had thick, close-cropped graying hair, mild hazel eyes, and an ax blade of a jaw. A bachelor, he was the last of his line in an old Martinsburg family. Most places, Garrick knew, they would have said he had odd interests for a cop. But not in Martinsburg. He liked baroque music, historical novels, and the poetry of Robert Frost. His favorite sport was tennis, which he played with a burly man's stolid, lumbering determination.

"Crazy goddamn day," he said, sitting down. "What was it you told me about summers when you were a cub reporter with the AP?"

"Summers? Oh, sure. The older reporters used to call it the silly season—fifteen, eighteen years ago anyway. The world's got more complicated. No more silly seasons now, Ned. It's too bad. They'd wait for the crazy stories that came in over the wire, or they'd go out looking for them. Nothing ever happened in the summer. Or mostly what did happen was small-time weirdo stuff."

Revere nodded. "We had one of those days today. Silly season. Small-time weirdo stuff, that fits it all right.

Forty men on the force—that's a lot for a town this size, plenty for three shifts, and sometimes a bridge game going on at headquarters." Revere lit a cigar. "Not today."

It was almost four o'clock. The sky was overcast again, threatening more rain.

"Crazy stuff," Revere said. "It kept us pretty busy."

Garrick nodded. "One of those days. I know what you mean, Ned. The staff's been run ragged trying to keep up with it."

"And not one damn bit of it important," Revere said. "That's the funny part. It was if—let me put it this way. Say Martinsburg's a character in a book. It was acting out of character today."

Garrick didn't disagree.

"Item. Stella Lubrano, a little Italian woman who drives an old Chevy and never got ticketed in twenty years for as much as parking on the wrong side of the street. Would you believe sixty miles an hour on Rivoire Street?

"Item. A bunch of high-school kids waltz into Nick's and ask for beer, and he serves them. You know Nick. If you don't look forty-five going on fifty, he asks for an ID. They were sixteen, most of them, and they looked it. When the patrolman walked in and blew the whistle on him, Nick looked as surprised as the cop did. He gets off with a warning. This time.

"Item. Sergeant Whitlock is coming in for the eight-to-four. He passes the rectory garden behind the Congregational Church. And finds Miles Pritchard walking in his sleep."

"Miles? Sleepwalking?"

"Not just sleepwalking. Having some kind of nightmare. He began to shout, wave his arms. Whitlock had to shake him awake.

"Item—well, you get the idea. Twenty-five, maybe thirty things. Silly-season stuff. Two or three a day would be a lot. You figure it out."

Garrick couldn't figure it out. He said, "Like the

whole town decided this would be a good day to kick up its heels? Spring fever, and it isn't even spring."

"Line from a song," Revere said. "Rodgers and—Hart?"

"Hammerstein. *State Fair*. 1945."

Both men smiled.

"Day wasn't all bad," Garrick said. "Look on the bright side. Monsieur Taitbout won't have a nervous breakdown after all."

"Yeah, the box. They found most of the stuff intact. Brought it in half an hour ago. Dahlgren's still out there with that busload of kids from the high school."

"A lot of stuff missing?"

Ned Revere shrugged. "A few old coins, maybe. Nothing important, but that won't stop the kids from having themselves a real old-fashioned treasure hunt."

"Here's the situation," Charlie Dahlgren said, standing at the edge of the road with his hands on his hips and his cap pushed well back on his blond hair. "The truck overturned down there." He pointed. "When it hit, the rear doors got sprung and the box fell out. You can see the broken saplings, right? Okay. And that rock down there, that's where we found the box, smashed open and stuff scattered all around. We got most of it. A few things are still missing. Thick undergrowth, so it won't be easy. But at least it isn't summer. Summer we might have to pull that stuff out by the roots."

Twenty high-school students listened impatiently. They wanted to start the search, the treasure hunt. But then Dahlgren got down to the technique they would use, and suddenly they became interested. This was real police work. Professional.

Dahlgren's delivery was quick and sure, his eyes roving the group of students. The roving would stop frequently on Melody.

"Four basic techniques," Dahlgren explained, looking at Melody and pausing for a moment. "Strip method, zone method, spiral, and wheel. Indoors we usually use the zone or strip. We could use them on flat ground too. Down there we're going to use the wheel. Any questions?"

"A big wheel?" asked Craig Donaldson in an innocent voice. Craig was Melody's more-or-less boyfriend. He used the words "more-or-less" when they spoke of their relationship. She used the words "not-quite."

"Come on, Craig," she whispered, "this is serious. You're not being fair to Officer Dahlgren, anyway."

"Officer Dahlgren," Craig said, "has a crush on you."

Melody shrugged. "Now that you mention it."

"But he's old. He must be twenty-three."

"At least," Melody said, and then Dahlgren was talking again.

"What we do, we all go down there and use the big stone as the hub of the wheel. Then we proceed outward along spokes."

"Radii," Craig said.

"Okay, radii. Figure a hundred feet outward in all directions, that ought to be enough. And you keep your eyes down. You pick apart the undergrowth. You examine every inch. Okay?"

"What happens if we come up with a big fat zero?" Craig asked, and Melody moved a slow, glacial step away from him.

"We begin again at the center. Three times, four. Five. Until it's dark. Any questions?"

Craig looked like he was going to ask one, but saw the expression on Melody's face and said nothing.

"Okay," said Charlie Dahlgren. "Let's give it a try."

A few minutes later they were fanning out from the rock, which was imbedded in earth at the deepest part of the gully fifty feet from and thirty feet below the level of the road. Craig and Melody were following an imaginary spoke up the side of the gully through mud and undergrowth back toward the road. Craig caught Melody's hand, pulled her back. "You're walking too fast," he said.

"No I'm not."

"How do you expect to find anything?"

Melody turned to answer him, but Craig's head was at the level of her knees. He made a whooping sound and came up with a shiny coin in his hand. "Hey, I'm rich," he said. Melody didn't like the smug look on his face. "It's all a question of concentration," he told her condescendingly.

This was definitely not her day to like Craig Donaldson.

Nothing else was uncovered on their first try, and they gathered at the rock again. Melody didn't want to help Craig conduct his search. She stayed at the rock with Dahlgren while the others fanned out again.

"You tired?" he asked her, not quite meeting her eyes.

"Tired? Of course not," Melody said. "Oh, I see what you mean. The limp doesn't bother me."

"It's not much of a limp. You hardly notice it at all." Dahlgren changed the subject: "What's it like over there in France?"

"Neat," Melody said.

"One of these days I'll get there. Just take off and spend a year or so. I want to really explore Europe. Must be the gypsy in me."

"Gypsies," said Melody, "don't want to. They *have* to. It's like a compulsion, or like birds migrating, you know?"

Charlie Dahlgren cleared his throat. He couldn't think of anything else to say. Melody wandered away from him, back up the steep slope toward the road, not really looking for anything. She climbed to the road and turned to watch her classmates bend over, poke at the undergrowth, move slowly along imaginary spokes. She had almost decided to rejoin them when Craig let loose another whoop. She was too far to see what he had found, but he had found something, all right. She turned and stared in the opposite direction. Craig wasn't so bad, really. He was pretty neat most of the time. But now he would be unbearably smug.

A car came up fast, sped by. Melody again considered returning to the gully. Then, for no reason at all, she crossed the road.

She saw two deep ruts in the still-muddy road shoulder. She followed them to a shallower gully and looked down.

There was a faint gleam in the undergrowth and she would remember, afterward, that she didn't go down immediately to find out what it was. She just stared at it. For the first time in months she felt a little twinge of pain in her left leg.

The gleam was still there, waiting down below for her. Waiting—what a funny way to think of it, she told herself, and started down.

Whatever it was had fallen into a patch of wild rose bushes. Thorns scratched her hands as she forced her way through to what looked like a frame of gold bordering something dark. Maybe two feet by two feet. A picture frame?

A single drop of blood fell from her hand to the dark part.

Then she was struggling to get it free of the thorny branches. They fought her, holding, tugging.

When she saw what it was she cried out in delight.

6

"What a clever forgery," said Monsieur Taitbout with a mixture of admiration and Gallic disdain.

The painting lay on a table in the Armory, pinned down by a circle of bright light from a draftsman's lamp clamped to the edge of the table.

"If he were not a specialist in the Dutch Old Masters, especially Vermeer," Monsieur Taitbout said, "I almost might suspect the infamous forger Van Meegeren himself had done it. Most impressive."

"A forgery?" Melody asked.

"But of course, a forgery. What did you expect? Columbine's so-called lost painting, 'St. Martin Sharing His Cloak With a Beggar,' was never in Bourg St. Martin. So how can it be here? It was lost hundreds of years ago."

"Then how did it get here?" Melody asked.

"A clever forgery," Monsieur Taitbout said. "No more."

"Whatever it is, how did it get here, Monsieur Taitbout?"

It was a good question. It was more than a good question, and Garrick found himself waiting for the Frenchman's answer too.

A delicate Gallic shrug, a Gallic pursing of the lips. "I am an art curator, not a detective. Someone is—how does one say?—playing tricks on us."

He studied the painting again. "Ingenious," he said.

"I don't think it's a forgery," Melody said stubbornly. "It's Jean-Baptiste Columbine's lost painting. I know it is."

49

Monsieur Taitbout smiled over her blond head at Garrick. "Come now, mademoiselle," he said.

Garrick studied the painting under the bright lamp. It was square, perhaps half the size of the paintings from Columbine's gypsy period.

In the background, as Melody had already pointed out, was Bourg St. Martin, seen from the south, perched on its high crag. Muted colors, grays and slate blues and pale sienna. Slanting sheets of rain fell across the canvas, touching it with darkness and silver. A single shaft of sunlight pierced the clouds. You could feel the storm, the bitter cold of the day, the icy wind.

As could the two figures dominating the foreground. One, astride a horse and leaning from the saddle, was St. Martin himself, his face a study in—in what? An odd combination. All Garrick could think of was arrogant noblesse oblige. It seemed somehow very French. The second figure was a beggar dressed in rags, which counterpointed St. Martin's finery. St. Martin was leaning from his horse to share a voluminous purple cloak with the shivering beggar. Conflicting emotions fought for control of the beggar's face too. Hatred and gratitude.

The painting was unsigned.

"I will admit," Monsieur Taitbout said, "it is not just a good forgery, not merely competent. It is a magnificent forgery." He took a leather portfolio from one side of the table. "A reproduction of an early sketch for the lost painting," he explained, placing it next to the canvas.

The details, Garrick saw, were almost identical, St. Martin sitting somewhat higher in the saddle, the walled village somewhat farther off and more obscured by rain.

"You can see the differences," Monsieur Taitbout said. "Even your untrained eye, mademoiselle?"

Melody nodded. "But so what?" she asked. "There's no law says he had to paint it exactly the way he sketched it."

Monsieur Taitbout adjusted his spectacles. "On the contrary," he said. "An artist frequently deviates from his original sketch. And in this case the sketch is not even Columbine's. It is a copy made by his friend Vouet. I merely wished to confirm how very fine the forgery is."

"What makes you so sure it is a forgery?" Melody asked.

"My dear, it has to be. When did Jean-Baptiste Columbine die?"

Melody said promptly: "1702," and Garrick looked at her, surprised.

"Tiens, some authorities maintain it was one year later, but that is close enough. And when did he paint 'St. Martin'?"

"A few years before he died," Melody said. "They're not sure. 1695?"

"Give or take a year, mademoiselle, yes. Now look at the painting. How old would you say it is?"

"About two hundred and eighty years," Melody said.

"Of course. If it were the original," Monsieur Taitbout said dryly. "But look at it. What ravages of time might one expect to find—after almost three hundred years? Especially if the painting had been lost, ill cared for?"

Melody shrugged, exasperated.

"One could expect the varnish to be discolored, darkened. Obscuring the colors. The so-called mellow golds and browns of an old painting are usually not that at all. Simply old varnish," Monsieur Taitbout went on. "And what else? If moisture penetrates the varnish, a condition we call bloom is apparent. This results in a blue-white discoloration. *Entendu?"*

It was a rhetorical *entendu.* Monsieur Taitbout continued: "But of course you are thinking the varnish could have been removed, fresh varnish applied. What then? Most times, unless it has been done expertly, a condition known as blanching develops. A gray opaqueness."

Melody's eyes never left the painting. She appeared more and more crestfallen.

"Age also causes crazing and *craquelure,* mademoiselle," Monsieur Taitbout lectured. "Cracks that have penetrated the varnish to the paint layers themselves. Then one must consider wrinkling, blistering, flaking, cleavage, cupping, pentimenti . . ."

Monsieur Taitbout's voice droned on. Finally he asked: "Do you see any of those? Unless the painting had been maintained with meticulous care in a first-rate museum, most of them would be inevitable. Look at it."

Melody had been doing nothing but look at it.

"You are observing a canvas no more than ten or twenty years old. At the outside, thirty. *Eh voilà,*" said Monsieur Taitbout, adjusting his gold-rimmed spectacles again. "But what a formidable forgery! The brushwork, the impasto, I admit it. They seem almost genuine Columbine. And the face of St. Martin—it is a likeness of the Sieur de Ramezay, of course. He sat for Columbine more than once."

Melody felt a surge of hope. "Then maybe—"

"No, mademoiselle,"

"Isn't it possible that—"

"I will tell you what is possible, mademoiselle, if you insist that I assume the role of detective." Monsieur Taitbout made a moue of concentration. "It is no rare occurrence in the world of art. Consider—your father has publicized the arrival of the *oeuvre* of Jean-Baptiste Columbine here in Martinsburg, is it not so?"

Melody admitted it was so.

"Then assume someone—an unrecognized painter, a skilled gut unscrupulous copyist—hears of it. Assume, mademoiselle, he knows of Columbine's so-called lost painting and has access to a copy of the Vouet sketch. *Entendu?* And he thinks, mademoiselle, 'What if I were to paint a forgery of Columbine's lost masterpiece? What if I were to introduce it into the collection en route to Martinsburg? What if, for a time, the painting were considered genuine?' "

"He couldn't get away with it," Garrick said. "Not once an expert got a look at it. Not once you got a look at it, Monsieur Taitbout."

The Frenchman beamed. "Precisely. Now you are

beginning to see. The forger, you must understand, has no intention of, as you put it, getting away with it. He *wants* to be unmasked, Monsieur Garrick. Eventually. And then? Then there are press interviews, television appearances—he becomes an instant celebrity. His career is launched. A harmless forgery makes him a success. You see? I assure you, it is a possibility."

"Isn't it just as possible the painting's real?" Melody said.

Monsieur Taitbout showed her the palms of his hands. "But I have already told you. This painting is perhaps twenty years old, perhaps much less. And consider this, mademoiselle. Assume this unknown forger managed to place his canvas in the collection not in France, but at the airport here in your country. What then? Then it would be packed separately and loaded last, so that when the truck overturned, it would be thrown out first, far from the rest, across the road perhaps. Wouldn't that explain precisely what had happened? As I have said, I am no detective, mademoiselle. But on the other hand, I am no fool. This painting is a forgery, I am absolutely certain."

"Then what are you going to do with it?"

"I? Do with it? Nothing," said Monsieur Taitbout.

"Nothing?"

"Oh, I have a certain interest, of course. To analyze the pigments, for example."

"The pigments?" said Melody.

"Chemical analysis is one way. The forger, did he attempt to approximate Columbine's original palette? Could he find the necessary pigments? They usually don't. Because they can't."

Unexpectedly the Frenchman smiled. "I would like to borrow it for a while. When the equipment I have sent for arrives from the Conservation Center of the Institute of Fine Arts in New York."

At first Melody didn't understand, then she began to smile too. "Borrow it, monsieur?"

"To put it through some tests. For perhaps a week or so. If you will loan it to me."

"You mean I can keep it?"

"Mademoiselle, I have my hands full here. Why complicate matters with an obvious forgery?" Monsieur Taitbout winked at Garrick. "Besides, you found it, didn't you?"

Melody laughed and hugged him hard. "Oh, Monsieur Taitbout!" she cried. His gold-rimmed spectacles almost fell off.

After that she gazed raptly at the painting. Her painting.

Wednesday morning Rob Garrick got up early and made breakfast. Melody was still asleep. He drank two cups of coffee, ate a toasted English muffin, and sat in the kitchen smoking his first cigarette of the day. He allowed himself half a pack.

No wonder Melody was still sleeping. She had spent hours deciding where to hang her painting, finally settling for the obvious. The place of honor in the living room, right over the fireplace mantle. He had offered to help.

"No, Daddy. I'd rather do it myself."

And she had. Carefully, with reverence. Garrick was permitted to hand it to her after she had climbed on a chair with hammer and picture hook and driven the hook into the wall.

The painting was hanging there now, in the darkened living room.

Garrick went inside to open the drapes. He heard Melody coming down just as he pulled the first cord and early-morning sunlight streamed into the living room.

He saw the pink housecoat first, and then her face. Her face looked like every holiday in the world.

Garrick didn't move. He just watched her descending the stairs, walking toward him.

Not limping.

"Don't . . . don't say anything, Daddy. I just . . . feel so . . ."

She was crying and grinning, and then her grin faded and she asked:

"Why'd you do that?"

He saw where Melody was looking—at the painting over the fireplace.

"Hey, quit kidding, doll," he said. If he hadn't done it—and he hadn't—then she had. "I didn't touch it."

The painting was hanging upside down.

7

Dr. Tom Seymour called a vest a waistcoat, and he wore one. He also wore a Phi Beta Kappa key on a thin gold chain, smoked an ancient green-briar pipe, and kept editions of the *National Geographic Magazine* bound in goatskin on teakwood shelves, one volume per year since he had decided to settle permanently in Martinsburg, where he had been born. They went back to the year 1945.

"Why should I go anywhere?" Dr. Tom always asked, pointing at the goatskin volumes. "Whole world comes here, and it's more comfortable than traveling."

He had never dunned a patient, and few had welched on their bills.

Medicine, he pointed out to his younger colleagues, was an art, a most inexact art, not a science. He prescribed placebos as much as wonder drugs, and he always claimed he had a pretty good batting average. He had thin white hair and wild white tufts of eyebrows. His home and office were in the same old clapboard building on Conant Street, now temporarily Rue Napoléon, just off the Commons, now the Place de la Liberté. A bachelor, he set aside a third of his income every year and donated it quietly to various charities, most of them local. Martinsburg was his world, and he wore it comfortably, like a favorite pair of old slippers.

"What do you expect me to say?" he asked gruffly. "Time heals all wounds? Or it's a miracle? Or, young lady, you just got sick and tired of feeling sorry for yourself? Take your pick. I'm not God, I'm just a country doctor. Never was any reason for that limp. Been telling you that ever since you moved here."

"But it just went away," Melody said. "I woke up and it wasn't there anymore."

Dr. Tom blew aromatic pipe tobacco toward the shelves of *Geographics*. "Fine, that's fine. Then what are you doing here? Don't fret. Celebrate."

Garrick said: "One of these days I ought to give you a list of the things they tried in New York. Heat. Whirlpool therapy. Exercises."

"Weights strapped to my ankle," Melody said. "Fifty lifts a morning. Ugh!"

"A neurosurgeon wanted to operate," Garrick said.

"Most surgeons want to operate most of the time," Dr. Tom told him. "Keeping their hand in."

"Will it come back?" Melody asked.

"It never should have been there, so why should it come back?"

They were still in the examining room, Melody on the table, her skirt pulled back.

Dr. Tom shook his white head. His eyes crinkled. "That's a pretty elegant pair of legs you've got there, young lady. So why don't you use them to dance on out of here and enjoy yourself? Not that I mind the view, but there are some sick folks waiting out there."

Melody got up.

"Send the bill over to the paper, Tom," Garrick said.

The white tufts of eyebrows rose, almost to Dr. Tom's receding hairline. "Bill? Just what the devil are you talking about? A whole year, and I couldn't do a thing for her. So she did it herself. Why don't *you* send him a bill, Melody?"

"I will. Right now. Daddy, I demand a four-course lunch at Nick's. I'm so hungry I could eat a—"

"The horse," said Dr. Tom, "is an endangered species with ravenous young ladies like you around. Good day to you both."

It had been barely noon when Nick greeted them and led them through the rapidly filling dining room to a choice corner spot. Seating Melody with his customary flourish, he had whisked away a *Reserved* sign and dropped it on another, less desirable table.

Melody had asked for the antipasto deluxe, lobster bisque, osso bucco with saffron rice, and some of Nick's special goat cheese. She would, she had told Garrick, think about dessert later. The chocolate mousse, or maybe some zabaglione.

"Or maybe both," he said.

Now, the huge serving of osso bucco and the great mound of yellow rice in front of her—Nick had learned to give Melody double portions of everything—she was staring off into space. She'd just picked at the antipasto and had one or two small tastes of the lobster bisque.

"I'm so happy," she said.

"Then eat."

"My Daddy the Jewish mother."

Melody pushed the plate slowly away from her across the starched white tablecloth.

"Think of your reputation," Garrick said. "Think of poor old Nick. He's watching. They'll take the championship away from you by default."

Melody laughed. "It's sort of funny," she said.

"What is?"

"I don't feel like eating. For the first time in my life I'm just not hungry."

Garrick laughed with her. It was an event, all right. As Melody said, sort of funny.

Eve Talbot's voice sounded huskier on the phone than it did in person or filtered through a TV mike. "Rob! I was beginning to think you were out of town. Nobody knew where you went."

"Took the afternoon off. Melody—well, you'll see for yourself later. Where are you?"

"Your office. Is Melody all right?"

"More than all right. I'll pick you up."

"I'd rather walk, Rob. It isn't far. I love your town, especially after New York. What's the big mystery?"

Garrick knew it was no act. Eve really did like Melody, despite Melody's attitude toward her.

"It'll keep," Garrick said. "Fifteen minutes then?"

"I'll send my luggage in a cab. It's so nice to walk the streets where you're not afraid someone's going to mug you. Good old Martinsburg. I really think you made the right decision."

"That makes two of us," Garrick said, and Melody came in as he hung up

"Eve Talbot?" she asked.

"How'd you know?"

"Oh, I can always tell when you're talking to her. Will she be staying long?"

"A few days. Film crew will be here on Friday."

"Will they move in with us too?"

"Doll, that isn't fair. Why shouldn't Eve stay here?"

"No reason, I guess."

Melody decided not to join them for dinner. It wasn't like at Nick's. That was excitement; she had been too excited to eat. This was different. She just didn't feel like eating. She could hear their voices and their laughter downstairs. Her father and Eve. Not that there was anything really wrong with Eve Talbot. She was just so obvious. She wanted to marry Rob Garrick and settle down in Martinsburg and raise little half brothers and sisters of Melody's.

That's not fair, Melody told herself. Give her a chance.

But Melody was jealous, and knowing it didn't change anything.

She sat on her bed, legs crossed under her, Indian fashion. On the bed were several books. *The Seventeenth Century* by Jacques Boulenger, which the librarian had assured Melody was the best available history of the period in France. Durant's *The Age of Louis XIV*, which Melody found easier to read. Cassell's *French-English, English-French Dictionary,* which Melody certainly needed. *Western European Painting of the*

Seventeenth Century by F. J. Berkeley, which devoted an entire chapter to Jean-Baptiste Columbine.

And the old notebook given to Melody by Bibi Tita.

Maybe not wanting to eat now was the same as at Nick's after all, Melody told herself. Walking down Conant Street and across the Commons and into Nick's, not limping, she had been too excited to eat.

The excitement hadn't gone away. Her hands were trembling ever so slightly as she opened the little book Bibi Tita had given her.

"The way to a woman's heart," said Eve Talbot.

Garrick had broiled two Delmonico steaks, thick and rare, baked a couple of potatoes, and let Eve work her magic with the salad. Empty plates and an empty bottle of Nuits-St.-Georges were on the table.

Eve had coppery hair worn in what Garrick thought was called a pageboy. She had green eyes and freckles and, in her late twenties, still had a model's figure that enhanced the elegance of the high-fashion clothes she usually wore. She was really more the jeans and turtle-neck type, Garrick knew, but her TV work dictated her style. Besides, fashion houses like Halston and Oscar de la Renta were pleased to outfit her at cost. She looked superb in their creations, and word got around.

"Sure," Garrick said. "Somebody would think I was trying to seduce you."

"It's been known to happen," Eve said.

They smiled easily at each other. Garrick hadn't seen Eve since July, but it was always like that with them. Easy. Comfortable. Except those times when Melody's resentment became too intrusive.

"You know, you really do look at home here. I mean in this house," Eve told him.

"It's home, all right. It took about ten minutes. Too much bouncing around can do that."

"And not just the house. The whole town. You fit it, Rob. And it fits you."

"It started pretty early. I used to come here when I was a kid. Summers. My father's grandmother had a farm a couple of miles outside of town. Dairy cattle. She ran it with just one hired hand till she was eighty. Quite a gal."

"What was her name?" Eve asked. She was trying not to smile.

"Grandma," Garrick said, and then Eve couldn't help smiling. Old towns, old names, old Americana were her specialty, and none of those things meant a great deal to Garrick. "Well, that's what I called her. I don't have the faintest idea what her name was."

"You'll never be old New England, Rob Garrick."

"Family was, on both sides. For a long way back."

"French or English?"

"French? What do you mean?"

"The Huguenots, of course. Martinsburg was founded by French Huguenot refugees."

"Sure, I know that. But I always figured Garrick was an English name. You know—like the actor?"

"Mmn, sure. But if you studied names you'd find out Garrick's French, if you go back far enough. A lot of Huguenots fled to Holland and England before coming here."

"When was that, anyway?"

"Well, they'd been leaving France ever since the middle of the sixteenth century, but most of the emigration came about the time Louis XIV revoked the Edict of Nantes. That was when the religious persecution hit its peak. 1685?"

"Columbine was painting then," Garrick said.

"*And* he fled to Holland," Eve said. "I think he killed a soldier in Bourg St. Martin and had to run for his life, something like that. There's a gap, though. He turned up in Holland about ten years after that, I think." Eve finished her wine. "As you see, sir, I have done my homework."

"So great-great-something-grandpa was a Frenchman," Garrick said as they went into the living room. Eve stopped in front of the painting over the mantle. It was, Garrick saw, hanging right side up. Melody's little joke.

"That looks like a Columbine."

Garrick explained about the painting while he poured coffee.

"That's . . . weird," Eve said. "Could I have a good look at it?"

Garrick put on the overhead light and dragged a three-way standing lamp closer to the mantle.

"There's a Frenchman named Taitbout you'll meet," he said. "Museum curator from Bourg St. Martin. Even he admits it's a damn good forgery."

"But how'd it get there, where the truck overturned?"

Garrick shook his head. Suddenly he was frowning. "Funny," he said. "This part of the painting."

He touched a finger to the canvas.

"What is it?" Eve asked. "I see a wall and—a door, I guess. And the road coming out."

"It's faded," Garrick said. "The wall. Right over here near the door. See? The damn thing's almost transparent."

"So? Sometimes that happens if a painting's old enough. Sometimes you can even see what was painted underneath, if anything was. A pentimento."

"It's not old enough, according to Taitbout. And it wasn't faded like that before."

"You probably didn't have a really good look at it before."

"Maybe," Garrick said doubtfully. He poured cognac into two snifters, and they touched glasses and sipped. They sat down on the sofa, Garrick still staring at the painting.

"Your great-grandmother's name," Eve said quickly.

"What?"

"Sometimes if you ask like that the answer comes out automatically. It has to be in your memory somewhere."

"No, I really don't think I ever knew it."

"Try Angell. That's old New England, southern New England. No? Conant. Pierce. Seymour."

"Like Dr. Tom Seymour?"

"Well, if you have a Dr. Tom Seymour here, sure.

What Americans don't know about their pasts could fill a shelf of books. A whole library. Take the midnight—"

The phone rang, and Garrick didn't hear the rest of what she said.

He spoke into the receiver: "Garrick."

"It's Ned, Rob. We got a bad one. You better get over to your office. Matt Hawley's killed himself."

Matt Hawley was already in a body bag when Garrick got there. Two cops were carrying it down to an ambulance in the alley behind the Martinsburg *News*.

"Poor damn son of a bitch," Ned Revere said. "No note. No nothing."

"He took the accident pretty hard. The fact that nobody believed him."

"I didn't exactly help," Ned Revere said, blank-faced. "Accusing him of being drunk. Hell, Rob. I don't know what to say."

Both men watched the cops slide the stretcher holding the body bag into the back of the ambulance.

"How'd he do it?"

"You wouldn't want to go up there. He put a gun in his mouth and shot the back of his head off. I didn't even know he had a gun."

"If it was a Luger, he took it off a German during the war."

"It was a Luger, all right."

"Does it have to be suicide, Ned?"

"Door was locked. We had to break it in."

"No, I mean is that what the obit has to say?"

"One of your night men heard the shot. Sam Phillips. When he couldn't open the door, he called us. He was up there with your cleaning woman—that's a Mrs. García, right?—when they got the door open. Too many people for you to write it any other way, Rob."

Garrick nodded, watching the ambulance drive off. He stood in the alley, wondering what he might have done to help Matt Hawley. But by the time you wondered that, he knew, it was always too late.

8

Melody shut the Durant. A dragoon was a soldier, a cavalryman. That was easy. *Dragonnade* was more complicated. It was the billeting of troops, lodging them in houses around France at the expense of the occupants. Sometimes, according to Durant's history, they got boisterous. Sometimes they got more than boisterous, especially the troops of the Maréchal de Marillac, who was a zealous Catholic and abhorred the Huguenot heresy. So the dragoons were free to use a little apostolic zeal to bring the Huguenots back into religious line.

Apostolic zeal soon meant robbing, beating, and raping the Huguenots.

Melody shut the Cassell's dictionary too. That left open only the Notebook of Jean-Baptiste Columbine, and Melody's own notebook, its pages still blank.

Stretched diagonally across her bed, she propped her chin on her left hand. She studied Columbine's difficult handwriting, saw how the ink was faded here and there, how whole sections disappeared under greenish-gray mildew.

It wouldn't be easy, she knew. Big fat understatement, even though her French was pretty good. But she had to try.

Maybe she'd learn something about the painting in the notebook Bibi Tita had given her. That Monsieur Taitbout! He'd probably claim the notebook was a forgery too.

She wrote at the top of the first page of her own

65

book: **From the Notebook of Jean-Baptiste Columbine,**
and made a few dots with her pencil under that, because
the first few words were indecipherable. She heard the
phone ringing downstairs, heard the door shut. She
squinted at Columbine's handwriting and wished they'd
had typewriters back then. She began to write.

. . . cousin of the Maréchal de Marillac. But still,
he was my friend. I painted his portrait more than once,
and that of his child sitting on her pony. They used to
play together, his daughter and mine, and he himself
had taken the Huguenot faith as his own. If there is a
Hell then he will rot in it, the Sieur de Ramezay.

It worried Gaddara. I knew too little, she said, I must
wait. But I had waited almost ten years. It amused her
at first to teach me and only amused her more as I became adept. Her *gadjo* apprentice, she called me.

(Hey! This Gaddara must be a gypsy. Maybe a wise
woman like Bibi Tita? A few lines missing here.)

. . . eventually return west. Besides, I had so much
to learn, and Gaddara considered it a game, the giving
of her knowledge. But that was a long time ago.

The Rom were furious when I returned yesterday
without the stolen wagon. Stolen is their word. I had
borrowed it. And left it in a ditch in France on the road
to Bourg St. Martin. I brought the horses back, though,
and to the Rom the horses are everything. They are *milsoudiers,* those horses (?? Not in the dictionary. And it
doesn't sound romani. Old French maybe? An obsolete
word? Valuable or something I guess. . . . I'm breaking this up into shorter paragraphs. Columbine's idea of
a paragraph was three or four pages.)

I will give an account of the accident in its proper
place. God knows I do not wish to think about it now.
A vision of Hell itself—the most terrifying experience
of my life, save one.

That I must paint it all a second time is nothing. That
I deliver it to Bourg St. Martin is everything. Here in
the Pays-Bas (that's Holland) I am safe.

But I must begin at the beginning, in Bourg St. Martin, Anno Domini . . .

Melody squinted at the date and finally gave up. But it was on the next page, like a heading. Anno Domini 1685.

She rubbed her eyes and tried to focus on the faded handwriting. The slim volume slipped from her lap and fell shut.

It's quiet downstairs, she thought. I wonder whether they're back. I *think* I heard them go out.

Melody fell asleep sprawled across her bed.

"It's called a *croque monsieur*," she told her father and Eve at the breakfast table as she set the hot platter down. "You start with French toast and—not that it's called French toast in France."

"Panama hats don't come from Panama," Eve smiled. "And don't ask an Alaskan for baked Alaska."

"That one's easy," Melody said, beginning to serve. "It's whipped up into snowy peaks."

Garrick was pleased by the easy banter between them, and he added his own observation to keep it going. "If you ask a citizen of Hamburg for a hamburger, he'll give you a blank look."

"They don't have them there?" Melody asked.

"Oh, they have them. That's what a citizen of Hamburg is. A Hamburger."

"Ouch," Melody said. "Anyway, it's French toast, and then you put on a slice of ham and some cheese and broil it till the cheese melts. *Eh voilà,* as Monsieur Taitbout would say. A *croque monsieur.*"

"It's delicious, Melody," said Eve.

Garrick thought so too. He hadn't slept much, and he'd come downstairs ravenous. He couldn't get Matt Hawley off his mind.

When he was on his second cup of coffee he asked Melody: "Hey, what's up? Aren't you feeling well?" He hadn't told her about Matt yet.

"Me? I'm feeling great."

"You haven't touched your breakfast."

"I'd better go get dressed," Melody said. "I'll be late for school." She was wearing her pink quilted housecoat, as she usually did at breakfast.

"When's the last time you had anything to eat?"

Melody looked down at her plate. "Last night when you and Eve went out I raided the fridge."

Eve glanced at Garrick and said nothing until Melody left the kitchen. They heard her going upstairs.

"You figure that one out," Garrick said.

"Well, sixteen. Don't you remember when you were sixteen? So she's not hungry. A very temporary state of affairs if I know anything about your daughter."

"But why bother lying about it?"

"She doesn't want you to nag her, that's all." Eve lit a cigarette. After a while she said: "I waited up for you last night until almost two. You can't have gotten much sleep."

"Not much," he said. He didn't elaborate.

"I'm sorry," Eve said. "He was a friend of yours, wasn't he?"

"He was a nice, harmless old man and he had no real reason to kill himself. Sure, I know, the accident. But still."

"He lived alone?"

"Over the newspaper, yeah."

"Then he got to brooding. Those things happen." Eve crushed out her cigarette. "And I wish *you'd* stop."

Garrick raised an eyebrow.

"Brooding," Eve said.

Melody put the Columbine notebook and her own on the top shelf of her closet, the other books on the shelf under the window. Then she unzipped the pink quilted housecoat and stood in front of the full-length mirror on the closet door.

Had she lost weight? Not much, it was still too soon, but maybe a little.

She turned slowly with her hands on her hips.

She liked the way she looked. Not skinny, not skin and bones, but slender. Small breasts, long legs, and the skin taut over her hip bones.

She caught the flesh at the side of her waist between thumb and forefinger.

Too much there, she thought.

It would be so nice to be *really* slender.

She wondered how long it would take if she kept going easy on eating.

She pirouetted slowly and looked over her shoulder at her slim flanks and thought: Take off a few pounds and you'll be as sexy as one of those models in *Vogue*.

The thought made her feel so good, so self-confident, it would even be easy to learn to like Eve Talbot.

9

Garrick shifted his weight to his front foot and turned his body into the serve, climbing high and hitting the ball squarely, hearing the good, crisp sound as he followed through onto the court, rushing the net. It was unnecessary. The serve rocketed into the corner and Ned Revere's tardy forehand didn't even touch it.

"Game and set," the stocky police chief said. "Where I come from, they call that an ace." He wiped sweat from his forehead and asked, "You had enough?"

Friday afternoons at three they played tennis for an hour at the indoor courts behind the firehouse. Garrick, with his height advantage and what Revere called an indecent serve, usually won. But not this easily. Revere had obviously not concentrated on his game.

They showered and dressed and got Cokes from the machine outside the locker room.

"Look at me," Revere said. "Do I look like a nervous Nellie? I've been a cop all my life, for crying out loud. But it's beginning to get to me. I've got the force working extra strength starting today. First it was that silly-season business. I wouldn't mind some of that now, if that's all we had. Goddamn crazy week. Ten stolen cars. Teen-age joy-ride stuff. That's about nine too many. The last one was a beauty. Would you try Craig Donaldson, Jr.?"

"You're kidding," Garrick said.

"Dr. Tom's venerable old Buick. Doc's a bit absentminded, leaves the key in the ignition. He won't press charges, by the way. So we're dropping it. We," said Ned Revere, "are only too pleased to drop it."

Craig Donaldson, Sr., was president of the Martinsburg Bank and Trust Company.

"The boy wrapped it around a tree out on the Strip.

71

Strained shoulder and nothing else, thank God. But it was his attitude. He acted like he was high on something."

"Was he?" Garrick asked.

"Not according to Dr. Tom. Hell, you know Craig. He dates Melody, doesn't he? He's a pretty straight kid. But that's not the point. You get an instinct for these things. When Charlie Dahlgren brought him in, he looked bewildered. Like he wanted to say, 'Where am I?' Same general setup on four of the other auto thefts. Kids with clean records, from pillar-of-the-community families."

"What about the rest of them?"

"We found the cars abandoned. We're looking. Then there's that fire last night at Hardee's over on the Strip."

"Arson?" Garrick asked.

"I don't think so. Electrical fire. It started in the kitchen. But I've asked Hartford to send the arson squad, just in case."

Garrick shrugged. "Electrical fires happen, Ned. If you're looking for some kind of pattern—"

"I don't know what I'm looking for. All I know is I've got forty cops, and they're good. We sure pay them enough. But this week fifty or sixty wouldn't have been too many."

The fire siren began to wail.

"Here we go again," Ned Revere said. He sounded like a man who had waited in dread for the inevitable and now was almost relieved that it had happened.

It was an old Victorian building on Elm Street, with a picket fence, a garden, a long porch across the white clapboard front. Three stories high, it had a widow's walk as if it had been built in a seacoast town instead of in Martinsburg.

They got there a few seconds before the fire trucks. A crowd had already gathered, and some of them were inside the picket fence. Revere leaped from his car and shouted:

"Everybody back outside, please! Move! Let's go now!"

At first Revere saw no smoke, but he could smell it. He heard a shattering sound as heat inside the building burst some windows on the second floor. Smoke roiled out into the bright autumn afternoon, and flames darted through the broken windows.

"Other side of the street!" Revere shouted. "Give them room, will you?"

Two trucks of the Martinsburg Volunteer Fire Department came slewing around the corner. Firemen were already jumping off and pulling out their hoses before the trucks had braked to a stop.

Flames danced higher then, enveloping the widow's walk. They crackled and roared, feeding on dry old clapboard. Smoke obscured the sign out front that said: *Whalen—Guests.*

Revere spotted a woman in the crowd. Plump and white-haired, she wore a flower-print housedress and carpet slippers. She was kneading her hands.

"Anybody in there, Mrs. Whalen?" Revere asked as Garrick joined them. The fire hoses sent thick streams of water through the open door and windows.

Mrs. Whalen looked vague. "I don't know how it started," she said. "I was in the kitchen baking."

"Anybody still in there?"

"Apple pie. My boarders always expect apple pie Fridays. I smelled smoke." She stared at Revere, as if seeing him for the first time. "I went up to the second floor. There's a room that Larry Applebaum uses for what do you call them, a darkroom. You know Larry, Mr. Garrick?"

Larry Applebaum was the Martinsburg *News* photographer.

"That's where it started," Mrs. Whalen said. "I opened the door and almost got, what do you call it, asphyxiated." She clapped a hand to her cheek. "My apple pies," she said, and made a move to cross the street.

Revere gently restrained her. "Mrs. Whalen," he said, and asked his question again.

"What? No, I don't think so. I'm almost sure. Afternoons I'm usually alone. They all work, young people mostly. I knocked on doors and shouted until I was blue in the face. There's nobody in there, thank the good Lord."

Steam hissed and billowed where streams of water met the flames. The crowd was large now, the clear autumn sky darkened by smoke.

"Mitzie!" Mrs. Whalen wailed suddenly, breaking away from Revere. He ran after her, and so did Garrick. She crossed the street and despite her bulk got past two firemen wielding a hose. Garrick heard her cry, "I never let Mitzie out. She's afraid to go out."

Mrs. Whalen had almost reached the porch when Garrick overtook her. He was not as gentle in restraining her as Revere had been. He couldn't afford to be. She was struggling to get inside.

Garrick heard a yowling sound. A calico cat, back arched, tail swollen, was circling Mrs. Whalen anxiously.

"Mitzie! Darling!" she crooned, and then Garrick heard a splintering, cracking sound, and he looked up just as Ned Revere shouted.

Garrick had no time to think. He shoved Mrs. Whalen away from him as hard as he could.

The widow's walk floated down through the smoke. It seemed to drift toward him, as in a slow-motion film. He could see the charred timbers, could see a section of the railing break clear, and he was moving as slowly as it was.

For an instant he thought he wouldn't make it. Then the widow's walk thudded into the lawn behind him.

Revere and a fireman helped him to his feet.

"You okay, Rob? Jesus, that was close."

The first pair of firemen had gone inside with their hose. Others followed with axes. Soon the fire was under control.

Garrick said he was okay, but then the reaction set in. He could feel the way his legs were trembling.

Melody thought she'd have only some dry toast when she got home from school. She had one slice and spread some raspberry jam on the other. She really was hungry.

She bit a little half-moon out of the slice with jam on it. The jam was too sweet. She wasn't really hungry after all. Those one-a-day capsules, she decided, taking them from the cupboard over the sink. All the vitamins and minerals you need to stay healthy, right? She took one, washing it down with a glass of water.

She had been impatient in school all day long. Not listening. Well, except in French. She wanted to learn all the French she could. Miss Graves's accent was awful, though. How could you teach French unless you'd been to France?

Melody went to her room and locked the door. She got the two notebooks, Columbine's and her own, from the closet, got the dictionary from the shelf under the window. She sat on her bed, caressing the Notebook of Jean-Baptiste Columbine. She loved the way it made her feel.

Like the first time she knew Craig Donaldson was going to kiss her, and she waited, and the waiting made the kissing even better.

This was even more so. Like Alice and the looking glass. Just opening the notebook was like entering another, more exciting world.

From the Notebook of Jean-Baptiste Columbine

Anno Domini 1685

But how can I call it the Year of Our Lord after the events of that night in Bourg St. Martin? If there is a God He is no God I wish to worship, neither in the Papist Church nor my own. Once I thought there was a difference. I expected no help from the Papists, and I sought no help there. But Gavrillac, he was one of us, and he might have helped. He might . . .

(Almost a whole page I can't read.)

If the Sieur de Ramezay had not himself been a Huguenot, I might have understood his perfidy. Not, of course, that he would consider it a betrayal. He was obeying the law of the realm, the law of King Louis, and he was a landowner with more (illegible) than any other. We have suffered the dragonnades before, he told me, even before King Louis revoked the Edict of Nantes that gave us the protection of the Crown. We will suffer them again.

They came in the early afternoon to Bourg St. Martin, riding arrogantly through the gate, the dust of the road on their green and white uniforms and even on their plumed hats. Their captain was a man from the Périgord named Lemaître. They demanded twenty houses for billeting, Huguenot houses, at our expense. A warm November afternoon, but I kept my good wife indoors, and the child: Marie a handsome woman, far from old, and Annique just budding into womanhood, with her walk like a colt and her guileless smile, ready to befriend anyone.

Ours was the house chosen by Lemaître himself. He was young for a captain of dragoons, but he seemed educated. His adjutant and the two mounted troopers were coarse, bearded ruffians. I tried to remain calm. All of them, after all, were answerable to the Sieur de Ramezay, who himself held a commission in the King's Dragoons, and he was my friend.

They drank all afternoon, sending out to the inn for wine. Lemaître showed some interest in my studio. He admired an early portrait of the Sieur de Ramezay and asked if I would paint him.

—I'm no rich man, he said, nor do I have a title. No artist has ever painted my portrait, Monsieur Columbine. He even smiled.

Soon he was seated on the model's throne. I heard laughter downstairs and the sound of glass breaking. I was nervous, and could not produce the effect I desired for the initial charcoal study.

Soon I became aware that Lemaître's attention was

wandering. I saw where he was looking: two recent
sketches and a painting of my daughter Annique on the
wall opposite the model's throne.

—And who is that, Monsieur Columbine? he asked.

I had sent Annique out, through the back door, to
spend the night at the Château de Ramezay.

—A model I use occasionally, captain.

—She lives here in Bourg St. Martin? What a lovely
child!

I continued sketching, listening to the raucous laughter below. Marie had smudged her face, disheveled her
hair, and dressed in her oldest clothing. She was a magnificent model with a mobile face. I could imagine her
downstairs, slackening that fine face into a bovine look.
With luck and God's help, I thought, Marie would be
safe. But Annique?

—Well, does she live here or doesn't she?

—Yes, I said after a while.

—I would like to meet her, this model of yours.

—She isn't here now.

—Then where is she, Monsieur Columbine?

I said, with the Sieur de Ramezay, believing that
would end the matter.

—A model?

I said she was a friend of the Sieur's daughter.

—A model? he said again. How very interesting.
Surely you don't pay a friend of the Sieur de Ramezay's
daughter to pose for you?

He expected an answer, but I didn't want to give him
one.

His eyes, which had been curious, grew hard.

—Monsieur? he said.

I told him no, I did not pay her. He asked how it was
that she posed for me.

I should have lied, but I could think of nothing. Besides, I had no idea how long the dragoons would stay,
and sooner or later Annique would have to come home.

—She's my daughter, I said, and Lemaitre's expressive eyes changed a second time.

—Then fetch her home, monsieur. Let her join us
this evening.

I said that Annique was a guest for several days at
the Château de Ramezay.

—This evening she will spend with us. Fetch her,
monsieur.

She heard a sound downstairs, and then her father's
voice calling:

"Melody? You home?"

Dusk outside. She had been unaware of turning on
the overhead light and the lamp on her bedside table.

"I'm doing homework."

"Come on down, doll. Eve's making dinner."

"I'm studying for a French test, Daddy. I'll have
something later."

"Spaghetti carbonara." It was one of Melody's favorite dishes. Just watching the final preparation at the table in a chafing dish was usually enough to make her
mouth water. Now the thought of it made her feel
queasy.

And she had to find out what would happen to Annique Columbine, didn't she?

"Save some for me, Daddy. I'll heat it up."

Silence for a few seconds. Melody hoped her father
would not come upstairs. The Notebook of Jean-
Baptiste Columbine was hers. Her secret.

"Don't work too late, doll."

"All right."

It was a steep climb up the Grand' rue to the
Château de Ramezay crowning the village behind its
massive walls. I had thought of sending Marie, for I did
not like the way the two dragoons and the adjutant were
looking at her. But how could I send her out that night?
Drunken soldiers were everywhere. I saw a woman
fleeing in terror through the twilight, saw two dragoons
corner her in an alley halfway along the Grand' rue. I
heard her cry out, but I continued on my way. What
else could I do?

They were seated at table when I gained admittance to the Château.

—Jean-Baptiste, said Armand de Ramezay. He asked what brought me there, and I told him.

He stroked his spade-shaped beard with a hand greasy from the roast, considering.

—And what do you wish me to do, my friend? He called me friend then.

—Send a message that you wish her to remain here. His eyes crinkled in a condescending smile.

—I know Lemaître, he said. A civilized man. Annique will be as safe in your house as she is here.

—You don't know what it's like. I've been out.

—Oh, they'll drink, and they'll loot, and it may be that they'll set a fire or two, I know that. It's almost required of them.

—Well, *I* don't require any looting and burning, I said angrily, and I don't know anyone in Bourg St. Martin who does.

—Easy, my friend, said Armand de Ramezay. The King condones it, and so we must accept it.

Like most Huguenots, the Sieur de Ramezay had made his fierce loyalty to the Crown almost an article of the faith. It was a loyalty I no longer shared.

—The King, I retorted, has forfeited all claim to our allegiance.

—Enough! said Armand de Ramezay. He shouted for Annique. She came into the drafty, torch-lit hall, and with her came Dominique, the Sieur de Ramezay's blond-haired daughter, limping (!!) on her club foot.

(The next few lines are illegible. Or maybe it's me. My eyes feel like they're full of sand. I can make out the words "Saint Tortu," but there's no saint of that name listed in the encyclopedia. Better go on.)

The adjutant offered a cup, and I drank sparingly.

—A little Saint Tortuel makes any man feel better, the adjutant told me. (A kind of wine, is that it?)

We heard shouts outside, and the sounds of running footsteps. Far off, a scream. Marie set on the table a fresh loaf of bread and a steaming basin of stewed hare.

The dragoons ignored it, their faces flushed with wine.
Lemaître ate with an almost dainty fastidiousness. His
eyes never left Annique's pale face. An oppressive silence filled the kitchen, heavy like the air before a thun-
derstorm.

When Marie refilled Lemaître's bowl, one of the
dragoons, the more drunk of the two, caught her breast in
his hand. I could see her stiffen before she moved away
from him and back to the stove.

Nothing was said. It was as if it had not happened.
They all devoted themselves to Saint Tortu after that,
even Lemaître.

One of the burly ruffians began to yawn. I thought
then that it would be all right. The heat of the stove had
made me drowsy too.

But then the dragoon who had touched Marie flung
his wine cup against the wall. His face looked mean, his
eyes rheumy.

—You call this wine? It's nothing but *ripopé*. (You
might know it, *ripopé*'s not in the dictionary. Swill, I
guess.)

—My good wife got it at the inn, I assured him. The
best they have to offer.

—Ripopé, he said again. He went to the stove unsteadily and grasped Marie's arm.

—Bruleresse! (Not in the dictionary either.) Are
you good for nothing but the tending of fires? Maybe
good to donoier too, eh? (Damn this dictionary! But
I'm afraid I know what that means. Three more lines
missing.)

. . . nothing to lose. Who would punish them for it?
Who would even be fool enough to oppose them, when
the King himself . . .

(Two lines missing.)

. . . other dragoon and the adjutant held me while
he flung her to the floor and lifted her skirts. She lay
there unmoving while he had his bestial way with her,
breathing through his mouth and nose, snorting like a
pig. I struggled, but they held me fast. Annique sat at

the table, her arms folded on the planks, her head down. She was crying.

And Lemaître? He drank cup after cup of wine. He did not watch the dragoon raping Marie. He was looking steadily at Annique over the rim of the cup.

The dragoon rolled off Marie. When she rose, her eyes were like two glass chips. She thought they would release me then, and the two glass chips looked a warning at me. It is nothing, husband, they seemed to say. It did not happen.

But they would not release me. The wine and what he had seen kindled a fire in Lemaître's blood. He came around the table to Annique.

—And you? he said. You are old enough for *adeser*. (Oh, no!!!) Old enough for *adeser*, but unlike your old *grainte* of a mother, young enough to enjoy it.

Annique clawed and kicked, but he seemed to take pleasure from her resistance. I struggled. I broke loose, but the dragoon who had held me clubbed me a terrible blow on the side of the head and I reeled to the floor.

I saw Marie rush to the stove and return with a knife. The dragoon who had raped her swung his huge arm, striking her across the chest. She hurtled back like a marionette whose strings have been cut, and I heard the awful sound of her head striking the iron stove. She crumpled there, her eyes wide-staring at the beams of the ceiling.

Lemaître had his way with Annique, and after Lemaître the two dragoons. The adjutant sat in a corner, drunk, his head lolling on his chest. He was snoring.

It is difficult to relate what then happened. I saw Marie on the floor near the stove, dead. Saw Annique after the second dragoon had finished with her. She tried to rise. She could not. Her lovely face was contorted, and a stain spread under her, dark in the candlelight—blood.

A man insane with rage and grief is more than himself. How else explain what I could do, and did?

The knife that Marie had seized to protect our daughter I used to slay both dragoons, almost before they realized I was conscious. One the blade took in the throat, slashing sideways. The second in the crotch and then ripping upward through the belly.

Lemaître drew his sword but saw what was in my eyes. He ran to the door and out. I went to Annique. She was moaning and she tried to raise a hand to protect herself. There was so much blood, there on . . .

(A long passage stained and smeared—I think my tears aren't the first to fall on this page.)

. . . carried her in my arms. Screams echoed along the Grand' rue. I stumbled over a body in the moonlight. Smoke poured from the doorway of a house and fire burst the windows, flames darting through.

I reached the doctor's house below the Château, my arms covered with Annique's blood. The doctor was no Huguenot, but still a good man. I thought that then.

He let us in himself and hurried us to the room that contained his medicines. I told him all that had happened. It simply came out of me, like water rushing down a fall. I could not stop myself.

Annique then lay on the table. He did not move to touch her. I was aware of him speaking.

—What? I asked.

His face had no expression. His voice was flat. He said we must leave, and I stared at him foolishly, uncomprehending.

He could not become involved. Or dared not. I had admitted to killing two of the King's dragoons.

I said that Annique would bleed to death. I pleaded with him. He was afraid of me, and he shouted. Soon his two servants came, and one of them went to the table to lift Annique. I thrust him aside and took her in my arms and as I ran out with her I saw the fear on the doctor's face turn to indifference.

I carried Annique up the Grand' rue toward the château of the Sieur de Ramezay.

. . . immediately below the walls of the château in the darkness.

—Jean-Baptiste, he called softly as he stepped from the alley.

It was my friend Jacques Rivoire, the Sieur de Rame-zay's chamberlain. Sometimes for a few sous he sat for me. He was solid as a wine cask and had a face almost as expressive as my poor Marie's.

—Go no farther, he said. They're waiting for you.

I asked him who he meant. Annique was heavy in my arms.

—That bastard I work for, and a captain called Le-maître. They'll arrest you for murder. You can't stay in Bourg St. Martin.

—The child, I said.

One hope remained. Our priest Gavrillac had some knowledge of medicine.

We found him in the presbytère, eating dark bread and cheese, drinking wine. Wordlessly, he led us to his small cell of a bedroom. He lit candles while I placed Annique on the bed. I began to feel hope as he bent over her. Then he straightened slowly and made the sign of the cross.

—The child is dead.

I went to Annique. I smoothed her fine soft hair..

—It is God's will, Gavrillac said, his voice unctuous.

I looked at him but did not see him. I saw the God whose will it was. *Mariole!* I cried. (??)

He sighed, saying, If it will make you feel better, why then curse the Virgin Mary.

Had I been capable of rational thought, that might have warned me. The priest Gavrillac would condone no blasphemy, not under any circumstances.

He placed a heavy hand on my shoulder.

—Stay the night, he said. You're in no condition to run now.

If his acceptance of blasphemy had not warned me, that should have. Neither I nor Rivoire had told him anything of what had happened.

—Rest here. Sleep. In the morning I'll give you provisions.

My friend Rivoire said softly, I think you should leave now, Jean-Baptiste.

Stay, go, it was all one to me. First Marie, then Annique—my life ended in a single night. I did not think of revenge then. It was too soon.

Gavrillac drew the coverlet over Annique's head. I sank to my knees, not praying. I wept.

After a while Gavrillac led us back to the kitchen. He cut bread and cheese for us, but I could not eat.

—Come, Jean-Baptiste, Rivoire said. I know where I can get you a horse.

. . . burial in the morning, said Gavrillac.

Rivoire's face looked anxious. Gavrillac could not sit still. He poked at the logs on the hearth, and they flamed higher. He cut more bread, though none was needed. He went to the window and returned to the hearth again, poking the logs a second time. The fire needed no help. Gavrillac turned and was standing with his fat backside to it when the door burst open.

Lemaître and two dragoons rushed in.

—Here is your man, captain, Gavrillac said.

I sat there an instant, too dazed even to try to save my life. Or perhaps I did not care.

Rivoire leaped to his feet and hurled the heavy chair he had been seated on. It struck the door frame, and one of the dragoons fell.

The second one primed and fired his musket. The ball took Rivoire squarely in the face. Then they came for me.

Lemaître said: You've acted wisely, Gavrillac. He called him that, just the name. Gavrillac was no priest to a Papist soldier.

—I've done my duty as a servant of God and the King, he said.

Lemaître drew his sword.

—Jean-Baptiste Columbine, he said, it is my duty to inform you, in the name of King Louis . . .

—*Encoplez* King Louis! I screamed, and bowled him over with my shoulder and ran. I plunged through the doorway past the fallen dragoon and into the night, aglow now with a dozen fires. There was a roar and something struck my arm, spinning me completely

around. But even with the musket ball in me, even with
my left arm hanging like meat from a butcher's hook, I
could run.

I knew the village, and the dragoons did not. By the
time I worked my way down to the Thiers gate, through
narrow lanes and alleys no wider than a man is tall, the
sounds of pursuit had faded.

The watchman Fouquet emerged from his gatehouse
with a torch. There was a joke in the village about us,
and I remember even then thinking about it. I was a
painter, he a *pinteur*. (What's that—from "pint,"
maybe? A drunkard? The next line seems to confirm
this.)

He came toward me unsteadily, reeking even more
than usual of spirits. No wonder he was no longer a
carter—he was unfit to drive a wagon even as far as
Thiers. If his brother hadn't worked for the Sieur de
Ramezay, they wouldn't have made him a night watchman.

—Columbine? he said, thrusting the torch at me.

I was panting. My arm had begun to ache fiercely.

—Open the gate, Fouquet, I told him. My life depends on it.

He saw the way my arm was hanging, and the blood.

—Some trouble with the dragoons? he cackled.

—I beg you, Fouquet. Open the gate.

He had no love for Huguenots. The wagon master
Guillemard, for whom he had worked, was one of us.
He shook his head, his face red in the light of the torch.

When I pushed past him toward the gatehouse, he
drew his sword and swung it drunkenly. It sliced into
my hanging left arm and clattered to the cobbles. The
pain was already too much. I felt nothing more.

—Huguenot dog! he cried, and ran for the watchman's bell. I reached it first and warded him off. He
shouted once and then I hit him. The torch went flying
and he tumbled to the cobbles. I got the key from its
peg and opened the gate myself, just enough to slip
through between him and the stone portals.

Then I was running again. Suddenly I knew where I was going, the only place I could go.

I reached the encampment in the first light of dawn. A horse whinnied. The campfires had burned down to embers. I went straight to Tita's wagon. (Tita!!!)

The dark eyes in the brown gypsy face looked at me and were instantly alert.

—When are you leaving? I asked.

—Tomorrow, the day after. Who knows?

Again she looked at me.

—Or perhaps today, she said.

Her husband came out of the wagon, yawning. She liked me better than he did, but he liked me well enough. At least I thought so at the time. I was the only *gadjo* in Bourg St. Martin they tolerated. They had always found it amusing that I wished to paint them.

—Strike camp, Tita told her husband. We leave for the South today. It is a good day to begin a journey.

He seemed surprised, but he nodded. After all, she was the *phuri dai* of her people.

It was dawn in Martinsburg too. Melody had spent the entire night translating from the Notebook of Jean-Baptiste Columbine. Dark smudges under her eyes accentuated the gauntness of her cheeks, but she was smiling.

Tita, she thought, how about that? Her name is Tita and she's the *phuri dai*.

What was it Bibi Tita had told her in Bourg St. Martin? Take a few old crones like me and you're back in the time of Jean-Baptiste Columbine. We Rom have no written history. Just tradition, passed down from father to son, mother to daughter. It makes time go away.

But of course it *was* written, and that made it even better. Jean-Baptiste Columbine had put it down in his notebook.

And now Melody owned it, that part of time when Columbine had lived. She had brought it here, across the ocean, to Martinsburg.

She fell asleep with the smile lingering on her face.

10

Ned Revere glanced across the parking lot to the Martinsburg High School marching band, now getting into ragged formation, and frowned. Their tuning up was discordant, and he already had a headache.

As he moved toward his own car, he passed the big white convertible, draped in red and blue bunting, that would lead off the parade. Alvin Waugh was self-consciously helping Governor Maria Stresa mount to her perch above the back seat. It had been quite a coup persuading the busy governor to act as Grand Marshal of the parade, and the First Selectman, duly impressed, was fidgeting more than usual.

Revere looked up at the sky and hoped Governor Stresa did not mind getting wet.

He slid behind the wheel, checking the glove compartment for aspirin without much hope, and started the engine. Flanking the car were two high-school boys struggling with heavy poles, the butts resting in leather slings. As he rolled off, he saw in the rear-view mirror that they had managed to get the twenty-foot banner taut between them. *Bourg St. Martin Month,* it said.

Revere cruised slowly along the parade route, making a final check, trying to ignore the dull pain in his head.

Except for the handful who had worked the graveyard shift, every member of the forty-man force was on duty, and for an extended twelve-hour tour at that. Four patrol cars were manned. A single dispatcher was at headquarters with the switchboard operator. All the rest were stationed along the parade route trying to cope with the crowds.

Must be twice as many as the Committee predicted, Revere thought. That meant twice as many traffic tie-ups, rowdies, lost children. He hoped there wouldn't be anything more serious. With most of the main streets closed to traffic, alternate emergency routes had been set up, but his men couldn't begin to keep the intersections clear with crowds like these.

He pulled to the curb near the Central Pharmacy and asked a patrolman to go in and get him some aspirin.

Melody saw one of the patrol cars on Conant Street just before she entered Health Foods Unlimited. The black-and-white cruiser crawled along, siren whooping, and Charlie Dahlgren took a hand briefly off the wheel to wave. Melody waved back. Blond and boyish, Charlie Dahlgren was cute, and Melody did not mind the innocent attentions of an older man of twenty-three. If it made Craig Donaldson jealous, all the better.

Melody went into the shop and browsed, like browsing in a library. She had decided to go on a health-food kick. After all, she had to eat something, didn't she?

She chose a bag of sunflower seeds and leathery-looking strips of dried apricot.

"Be two forty-nine with tax, miss," said the proprietor, an over-age hippie who wore beads and a linen tunic that looked Mexican.

Melody paid, and the doorbell tinkled, and three boys a little older than Melody came in. She didn't recognize them. Tourists, she thought. They were wearing leather jackets, and their eyes looked funny. Badly painted? She wondered why she thought that.

Just as she opened the door to leave, she heard the over-age hippie cry out. That was followed by a crash.

The three boys had overturned the display rack near the cash register. Jars shattered. Cans rolled across the floor.

The over-age hippie shouted, "What are you doing? What are you doing that for?"

One of the leather-jacketed boys shoved him, and he fell down.

The three boys trashed the shop methodically, pulling down all the display racks, stomping jars and boxes with their boots. They never spoke. They ignored Melody, and after the single attack on him they ignored the proprietor, who wisely remained on the floor.

They walked out calmly, as if they had come in to make a purchase.

The over-age hippie got up, shaking so much he couldn't dial the police number on his phone.

Melody dialed it for him. The line was busy. She tried again. It was still busy.

The switchboard operator tugged off her headset, ripped the top sheet from her pad and shoved it across to the dispatcher.

"Here we go again, Art," she said. "Got any more cars?"

"Mebbe," the dispatcher said laconically. He pulled the microphone closer. "Calling car three, calling car three. Hey, Charlie, where the hell are you?"

Charlie Dahlgren's radioed acknowledgment crackled above the constant buzz from the switchboard.

"Got a domestic disturbance," the dispatcher said. "Out in Greenwood Acres, 519 Laurel. Couple named Joynes. Complainant's the woman next door at 521. Can you handle it?"

"On my way, Art. Over and out."

The operator replaced her headset, looked helplessly at the cluster of winking lights on the switchboard, selected one at random and plugged in.

"Police department," she said.

The main office of the Martinsburg Bank and Trust Company was shut, but the drive-in branch out on the Strip remained open Saturday mornings, even this Saturday morning, as a convenience. Thanks to the parade, the convenience this Saturday proved unnecessary. The two tellers, both young girls, had five thousand dollars in cash to cover banking transactions, and not a single customer until ten-thirty.

One of the tellers was reading a gothic novel, the other filing her nails. They were sorry they had missed the parade. The nail filer minded even more than the gothic reader. It was an exciting story about a young governess in a French château. She always read gothics, but Bourg St. Martin Month had inspired her to select one with a French background.

You could bank at the shopping-center branch of Martinsburg Trust either from your car or by coming into the small office on foot. The teller sat behind heavy glass and, inside and out, transactions were made through a sliding drawer that worked electrically.

The first and only customer came in just after ten-thirty. Neither teller looked up right away. The heroine of the gothic was fleeing through a pine forest for her life, the file was deftly working on a thumbnail.

The gothic reader activated the drawer, receiving a slip of paper the size of a check.

It wasn't a check.

It was plain white paper and on it was printed: HAND OVER ALL YOUR MONEY. DON'T HIT THE ALARM. I KNOW ALL ABOUT THE ALARM.

The gothic reader looked up and screamed. She dropped her book. The man had a gun and no face. She realized he had drawn a stocking down tight over his head.

She opened the cash drawer and, fingers trembling, scooped up a few fifties and tens. She put them in the electric drawer and pressed the button. She did not go near the alarm plate on the floor. The gun and the no-face terrified her.

"Come on," he said, his voice muffled. "I said all of it."

She emptied the cash drawer into the electric drawer and pressed the button again. The no-face was carrying a flight bag, white-lettered TWA on blue plastic. He stuffed the money in that and backed out.

The gothic reader hit the alarm plate.

The alarm buzzed instantly at police headquarters.

"Bank out on the Strip," the dispatcher said.
He tried to locate an available patrol car.
The switchboard kept flashing.

Danny Fassolino was nine years old and the best tree
climber in the fourth grade, maybe in the whole elemen-
tary school.

He sat fifteen feet up in a crotch between two
branches of one of the autumn-bare maples that lined
the Commons. It gave him a great view of the parade. It
gave him a great feeling of being Tarzan or somebody,
sitting way up there with everybody else down below.
The view of the reviewing stand was equally fine, but
pretty soon the speeches bored him and, despite the
windbreaker zipped up to his neck, he was cold. Rain-
water trickled down from branches above. Danny began
to get restless. He got more restless when the Frenchman said something the crowd thought was funny, because he could hear all that laughing, only he didn't get
it. Icy water found its way inside his collar and he said
"shit" out loud and knew his mother would say, "Wash
your mouth out with soap, Danny." Thinking that, he
smiled because his mother couldn't hear him. She stood
fifteen feet below on the sidewalk, alongside his father.
He started to come down. The branch was wet and slip-
pery.

Mrs. Fassolino looked up and screamed, "Danny!"

In New York they had special units to handle domestic squabbles. Teams, often a man and a woman, a patient older cop who was a good listener and a police-
woman who looked like an angel—or a nurse, anyway.

Charlie Dahlgren knew that from his brief stint with
the NYPD.

No such teams existed on the Martinsburg force, of
course, but they generally sent two officers to answer a
domestic disturbance call. It was an unpredictable thing.
Say the husband was drunk and threatening his old lady
with a knife and you took the knife away from him only

to find his old lady all over your back with her finger-nails raking furrows in your cheeks.

Dahlgren answered the call alone. That morning, what with the parade and the mobs of tourists, a single officer manned each of Martinsburg's six patrol cars. No, less than that, Dahlgren reminded himself. Four cars only, and just the drivers. Every other cop was on the streets.

It was a funny neighborhood for that kind of squeal. Middle class, maybe upper middle, halfway out Rivoire Street to Route 44, neat tract houses with manicured lawns. It wasn't down by the mill or the silk-screen printing plant, where the Italians and Puerto Ricans lived.

Charlie Dahlgren was a man pretty much without prejudice, if a cop who had served two years on the NYPD could be that, but still he had come to some conclusions about a domestic disturbance call. Most of the time it meant blacks or Puerto Ricans. So do me something, he thought as he pulled to the curb outside the barn red split-level on Laurel Drive. It's just statistics.

Dahlgren got out of the patrol car and headed up the walk. Only a few people had gathered outside. Dahlgren tried to look like one of the patient middle-aged cops he had seen who handled domestic disturbances for the NYPD.

"They're still going at it," someone said unnecessarily.

Dahlgren could hear the shouting inside.

"They fight like this before?"

No one seemed to think so. Mr. Joynes was the manager of the Food Fair out on the Strip, Mrs. Joynes worked in the welfare office, he was told.

He asked two more brief questions. It was a good idea to know what you were getting into.

"Any children?"

No children.

"There any kind of a drinking problem?"

The Joyneses were known as light social drinkers.

Dahlgren felt better. Children made it tough sometimes. Drinking always made it tough.

He went to the door and rang the bell. He heard a woman cry out and a crashing sound.

"Get the hell away and mind your own goddamn business!" a man's voice shouted.

"Police officer," Dahlgren called, and then he tried the door.

It wasn't locked. He went inside and through a small hallway to the living room, where Mrs. Joynes crouched low behind a coffee table, panting, her face blotched from crying. Her torn flannel bathrobe revealed a plump white breast. She overturned the coffee table in Mr. Joynes's path as he came at her with the fireplace poker. An armchair was also overturned, and the piano bench. They both looked at Dahlgren as if he were another piece of furniture which might or might not be overturned.

Light-social-drinker Joynes lunged for his wife. Mr. Joynes had clearly done more than light social drinking, and it wasn't yet eleven o'clock. In the morning.

". . . playing around," he mumbled and swung the poker so wildly that he almost fell down.

That gave Charlie Dahlgren the opening he needed. He grabbed Mr. Joynes's wrist and jerked it up, sending the poker flying. Mr. Joynes stumbled and fell in a sitting position on the carpet. He sat there swaying like an Indian holy man, and Dahlgren stepped back quickly so he could watch both of them. You never knew about the wife.

The wife looked bewildered.

The husband stopped swaying. He stared up at Dahlgren. "Cops," he said, sounding as bewildered as his wife looked. He got up and Charlie Dahlgren tensed, ready.

Mr. Joynes moved slowly toward his wife, a sheepish look on his face. He hiccuped. Mrs. Joynes made a strangled sound and wrapped the robe around her exposed breast.

"Sweetheart," Mr. Joynes began, with an apologetic

smile. Mrs. Joynes smiled back at him tentatively, and then they both stopped smiling.

They drew apart. Mrs. Joynes raised a hand to her face.

Dahlgren could feel his own face stiffening unnaturally. It was as though he had just snarled and then his face had frozen that way. He could feel it. He knew that was the way he looked.

His arm came up and he felt a weight in his hand.

He was holding his .38 Special, pointing it in the general direction of the Joyneses. Had he cocked the hammer? He had. His finger tightened on the trigger.

Neither Joynes spoke.

Charlie Dahlgren felt his head pounding. He wanted to spray the room with bullets. He wanted to kill them both.

For a long moment he thought he couldn't stop himself. Then he managed to release the hammer. He put the gun in its holster and offered the Joyneses the closest approximation to a smile he could manage.

He felt as confused as they had looked after he had forced the poker from Mr. Joynes's hand.

"Hammer was cocked," he explained, his voice too loud. "I was just releasing it. Sorry I scared you, folks."

Mrs. Joynes let out a long breath and slipped her arm through her husband's. In their mutual relief, the fight was forgotten. Charlie watched as Mr. Joynes helped his wife straighten the furniture.

"You know I wasn't," she said quietly.

"Wasn't what?" Mr. Joynes said.

Mrs. Joynes glanced toward Dahlgren. She was embarrassed. "Playing around," she said finally.

They talked, and he listened. There had been a party last night. A little harmless flirting.

"Officer," they both said, and Dahlgren wished he wasn't there.

"Do you have to—?" began Mrs. Joynes.

"I don't know what the hell got into me," said Mr. Joynes.

They went to each other and put their arms around each other. Mrs. Joynes was trying not to cry.

"You smell like a brewery," she said.

"A distillery," he said.

They remembered Charlie Dahlgren again.

Mrs. Joynes said: "We don't usually . . . we're law-abiding people."

"Give us a break, huh?" said Mr. Joynes. "Do you have to book us or anything?" The enormity of having a cop in their home to break up a fight, their fight, had sobered him.

"No, that's okay," Charlie Dahlgren said. "Forget it."

They chatted a few minutes and shook hands all around.

Charlie Dahlgren felt almost normal when he climbed into the police cruiser. The radio squawked.

The Donaldson house was at the far end of Conant, where Martinsburg gave way to rolling country. It was surrounded by ten acres of lawn, streams, and woodland, part of the property that had long ago belonged to Rob Garrick's great-grandmother. The house itself was the original farmhouse, renovated magnificently. *Better Homes and Gardens* had once done a four-page spread on it.

Craig Donaldson, Jr., sat on the bed in his room upstairs. There were just three decorations on the wall. A life-sized poster of Cher in one of her bizarre costumes, a framed photograph of Melody, and a Yale pennant. Craig wanted to go to Yale. His father had, and his grandfather.

He felt sick. Physically ill. It felt like a big fist had grabbed his stomach and was squeezing it. He broke out in a cold sweat. He rushed into the bathroom and gagged and vomited into the toilet.

Back in the bedroom, he looked at the flight bag on the bed, and the stocking, and the toy gun, and the money. Five thousand dollars. It was exactly five thousand dollars, which meant that there had been no customers at the drive-in branch of the Martinsburg Bank and Trust Company. He knew little details like that. His father was the bank's president.

He wondered if he was going crazy or something. He had just gotten into his car, and driven there, and parked where the car couldn't be seen from the bank, and walked calmly in with the note and the gun. Knowing what he was doing was an insane thing, but he couldn't stop doing it. He sat on the bed and he thought, not really wanting to think, feeling queasy again.

After a while he got up, taking the money into the bathroom and burning it, one bill at a time, flushing the ashes down the toilet.

What else could he do?

Shoot himself, maybe, if the gun was real.

Mrs. Fassolino found Dr. Tom at the reviewing stand and they hurried on foot back to his house because it would have taken longer by car.

Now Dr. Tom was looking at Danny Fassolino's arm in his examining room. The boy had been carried there by his father. He wasn't crying. His teeth were clenched. The Fassolinos hovered close, worried, protective.

"Is it broken?" Mrs. Fassolino asked.

Dr. Tom could see the skin distended in two places on the inside of the boy's right forearm. A nasty break. Compound fracture of the radius. The arm was beginning to swell. Morphine now, Dr. Tom thought quickly, a cage splint, and then a drive to Martinsburg General.

"I'm afraid it is," he said.

He glanced at the cabinet that held the morphine, at the shelf where he kept the disposable hypodermics.

The boy began to moan. The mild shock was wearing off now. That was good. But the boy was beginning to hurt. It must hurt him like hell, Dr. Tom thought.

He did not get the morphine, did not get the disposable needle.

He touched the broken arm and the boy screamed.

Dr. Tom touched the arm again, and the boy fainted.

The pain. It must have been awful. It made Dr. Tom feel powerful, like a malevolent god. He saw the grief-wracked faces of the parents, and that made him feel powerful too.

The feeling went away as quickly as it had come.

Dr. Tom set to work swiftly and expertly after that, fitting the wire cage splint to the broken arm. He did not allow himself to think of the sick thing he had done, nor the feeling it had given him.

He hated pain, other people's pain. Hating it, alleviating it, fighting it, was his life.

11

Melody and Eve were in animated conversation when Garrick got home that evening. He took off his raincoat and tossed it on a chair in the living room.

"Daddy," Melody said in mild reproach. She got up, took his wet raincoat off the chair and hung it in the hall closet.

"Sorry I missed the buffet," Garrick said. "How'd it go?"

"Where were you?" Eve asked.

"I've got a newspaper to run."

"The buffet was news, wasn't it?" Eve asked.

"A few things happened," Garrick said as Melody came back.

"Nothing ever happens in Martinsburg," she said.

"It was a funny kind of day," Garrick told her. He didn't pursue the topic. He said, "Was Taitbout in good form?"

"He's a wonderful TV subject," Eve said, "with those gold-rimmed spectacles of his and that delightful accent. And the equipment! You really missed something. Let's see. Cameras, of course, and something called a directional reflector that makes an ordinary lamp give, uh, raking light. And an ultraviolet lamp to—what did he say, Melody?"

"To make varnish look yellow-green, and overpainting or retouching purple, and so on."

"Then there's infrared," Eve said.

"It penetrates," Melody explained. "You know, through varnish, upper paint layers, even shadows. Monsieur Taitbout said you can see unexpected things in a painting with infrared photography."

99

Garrick glanced at the painting over the hearth. He wondered if Monsieur Taitbout's infrared lamp could explain the unexpected thing that had happened there. If anything beyond Garrick's own imagination had happened.

"And a monocular microscope," Eve said, "for photomicrographs."

"Of course," Melody said.

Garrick smiled. "Of course," he said. "What's that for?"

"To study the pigments," Melody said. "How fine they were ground. It also makes glazes sparkle and impasto look like cliffs."

"You really *were* listening," Eve said.

"I'm interested."

Melody glanced at the painting over the hearth as Garrick had.

"They use a binocular microscope too," Eve said.

"What's the difference between them?" Garrick asked.

Eve waved a hand at Melody. "I yield to our expert."

"Less magnification than the monocular one," Melody said. "It shows the brush strokes and overpainting. Sometimes they use it to spot a forgery. Brush strokes are almost like fingerprints."

"Well," Eve said, "if you want to find out about that painting of yours, why don't you take it down to the Armory?"

Melody shook her head vehemently. "Not on your life. He already said it was a forgery. It's mine, and it's going to stay right here." She moved in front of the fireplace, protectively.

"What if you found out he was wrong?" Eve persisted.

Melody changed the subject. "He wears a headband with a binocular magnifier. It makes him look like a doctor."

"Even I remember what that one was for," Eve said. "So he can keep both hands free for close work."

Garrick suspected that Eve, being Eve, knew what

the other equipment was for too. She wanted to let Melody hold center stage.

"And then he X-rays the painting," Melody said. "It's not much of an X-ray machine, just a tube in a lead-lined box with a glass top. The painting is put over that, face down, and the film goes on top of the painting. Sometimes it doesn't work."

"How come?" Garrick asked.

"Well, some paintings are, you know, X-ray proof. If white lead was used in the ground. Or even a lot of white highlights in the painting itself."

Garrick looked again at the painting Melody had found. This time he didn't have to speak. Melody said, "Leave that alone. It stays here, Daddy. I don't want Monsieur Taitbout putting it through all his tests."

"Why not?"

"He made fun of it."

"That's no reason, doll. As Eve said, he could have been mistaken."

Melody raised her voice. "He's been through enough already!"

Garrick didn't get it. "You mean Monsieur Taitbout?"

"No, I . . ." Melody looked confused. Then she brightened. "You missed a pretty good meal, Daddy. They had all sorts of *charcuterie* and celery rémoulade and *poche de veau farcie aux épinards*. Bottles and bottles of Muscadet, and nobody even bothered to ask how old I was. And the pastries! It really was almost French."

Eve laughed. "And how would you know, Miss Bird? That's what you ate like."

"I did not. I did so eat. I'm stuffed."

Garrick looked a warning at Eve. Why should Melody lie about it? He wondered whether a visit to Dr. Tom was in order.

"I'm going upstairs," Melody said angrily. "Then you can do all the talking about me you want."

"Hey, come on now, Melody!" Garrick said.

She pecked at his forehead dutifully, ignoring Eve, and left the living room, not quite flouncing.

Garrick shook his head. "Beer?" he asked Eve.

"Okay."

He got two Michelobs from the kitchen.

"What's the matter, Rob? I know that look on your face. Still Melody?"

"Yes and no. Well, no, not really. Except that she's acting . . . peculiar, and so's the whole town. Can you hang around a few days?" Eve was level-headed, and a good observer. She had a sharp, intuitive intelligence that could cut through to the heart of things.

"I suppose. I'm not due anyplace special, not for a while yet. Why?"

"Something's going on in Martinsburg. I don't know what, but there's a story here. The cops had their hands full today. More than they could cope with. More than they get in a month."

"No mystery there," Eve said. "A parade, crowds, police all concentrated along the parade route and in the Commons. When the cat's away, Rob. You know."

"Not in Martinsburg. Martinsburg's not that kind of town."

"Even when it's full of tourists?"

Garrick did not reply. He found himself staring at the painting, wishing he could see it better. If Melody's not eating was part of the strangeness he couldn't explain, so was his own attitude toward the painting. The painting bothered him, set up a tension in him. Like what psychologists called an approach-avoidance conflict.

He said: "I had a call from Craig Donaldson today."

"Who's he?"

"Bank president. After Ned and maybe Dr. Tom, he's I guess my closest friend in town. He wanted my advice before he went to Ned—that's Ned Revere, by the way. Chief of police."

"I know. He dropped in at the buffet for a minute."

"Anyway, Donaldson's a man who usually doesn't ask for advice, he gives it. Not today. Craig Jr. had a little talk with his father," Garrick said. "A few days ago he stole a car. This morning he robbed a branch of his father's bank."

"*What?*"

"Stocking mask, toy gun, and five thousand dollars. He burned the money and flushed it down the toilet."

"Why on earth—"

"It was the first question Donaldson asked, after he realized the boy wasn't kidding. Craig said he had to, he couldn't stop himself."

Eve considered that. Garrick could see she was skeptical. "Has he been in any kind of trouble before?" she asked.

Garrick shook his head. "Honor student at the high school. Plans on Yale later. A law degree, he thinks. Also, I know him. He's Melody's boyfriend. He's not the type to take someone else's car for a joy ride—let alone rob a bank, his father's or anyone's."

"What did you tell Mr. Donaldson?"

"To make restitution, see Ned, and then see Dr. Tom."

"Not a psychiatrist?"

"Tom's had psychiatric training. I'd say Dr. Tom and maybe Miles Pritchard. Congregational minister, and a family friend."

"What will Chief Revere do?"

"I'll talk to him. Not that I think I have to. We're a pretty close community here. Besides, to get back: What Craig did is definitely not—unique. Ned called me before I left the office. He tried to make a joke of it. He said, 'Who the hell's been putting what in the drinking water?'—and then he gave me a few choice examples of why he asked. He saved the best for last. One of his cops asked for a leave of absence today, a bright young kid named Dahlgren. College and a couple of years on the NYPD. Ned turned him down."

"Why'd he want a leave of absence?"

"According to Ned, Dahlgren answered a routine squeal this morning. Family fight. Loud, drunk, and it could have gotten violent if Dahlgren didn't break it up. That's part of the pattern, too, by the way. People doing things that are, I don't know, out of character. That's how Ned puts it."

"What was wrong with this Dahlgren breaking up the fight?"

"That's not all he did. He had a crazy impulse. All of a sudden his gun was in his hand. The way he told it to Ned, he wanted to shoot them both."

"My God," Eve said.

They looked at each other.

"If it was just one or two isolated instances," he said. "But it's not. They're all part of the picture. Like Ned Revere said, who the hell put what in the drinking water?"

"Coincidence?" Eve suggested.

"Sure. Maybe."

"Uh-huh. Maybe. I think I'll accept your invitation to stay, Rob. And speaking of pictures, do you know you've spent the past half-hour staring at that thing?"

Garrick got up suddenly and stood before the painting. Eve joined him.

He said nothing. He wanted Eve to say it.

She studied the canvas. "That's funny," she said. "The faded spot. It looks different. You can almost see something there now. Underneath."

Garrick had seen it too. The faintest suggestion of—what, a stairway?

"Yeah, and there's another spot that looks faded now—this window here. But that's not what I meant. Take a look at St. Martin."

They both studied the figure in the foreground, leaning half out of the saddle, sharing his cloak with a beggar. Garrick recalled how he had first interpreted the expression on the face. A look of arrogant noblesse oblige.

"See anything different?" he asked.

"No . . . I don't think so."

"That arrogant son of a bitch," Garrick said, almost as if St. Martin were not on the canvas on the wall but standing with them in the living room, "that arrogant son of a bitch doesn't look so arrogant anymore."

12

Dr. Tom moved the smaller weight on the scale until the balance was suspended.

"I know I lost a few pounds," Melody said. "I wanted to. I was overweight."

"Five-two and a hundred pounds," said Dr. Tom, "is not overweight."

Garrick was surprised by Dr. Tom's appearance. His eyes were red-rimmed, his hands not quite steady. Garrick guessed he'd had trouble sleeping lately. That wasn't like Dr. Tom. "Work hard, keep a clear conscience," he always said. "It's better than any sleeping pill."

Now he said: "Ninety-four pounds including skirt, blouse, and beat-up tennis sneakers. Don't tell me *that's* overweight."

Melody didn't tell him anything. She asked brightly, "Don't I look nice like this?"

Dr. Tom poked at her ribs. "All skin and bones and a lot of long blond hair. How's your appetite?"

"Fine," Melody said quickly.

"What'd you have for breakfast?"

"Tea."

"And?"

"Just a cup of tea. I was late."

"Yesterday?" Dr. Tom asked.

"You mean for breakfast?"

"What did you eat all day?"

Melody got off the scale and smiled. "I'm really into health foods."

Dr. Tom said nothing. He waited for a real answer.

"Well, let's see. Sunflower seeds. And you know that kind of dried apricot that comes in strips that look like orange leather?"

"I asked, what did you *eat?*"

"I had some toasted soybeans too," Melody said.

Dr. Tom caught the flesh of her forearm between thumb and forefinger, and pinched. It left a ridge that faded slowly.

"You're not taking enough liquids either, young lady."

"I'm not?"

"Pain in the tummy or anything?"

"No. I told you I feel fine, Dr. Tom. Honest."

"Heartburn? Nausea?"

Melody shook her head. "I never felt better in my whole life."

There was a mirror on the wall opposite the scale. She was staring at her reflection in it, an expression of suppressed pleasure on her face. She struck a pose with hands on her hips, one hip thrust out.

"Neat," she said.

"Maybe I'm old-fashioned," Dr. Tom told her lightly. "But I like my women with some flesh on 'em."

Melody laughed. "That's okay for an older woman, Dr. Tom."

"I want you to eat, young lady. I mean really eat. The best health-food diet I ever heard of is meat and potatoes. Rare roast beef and—"

"With Yorkshire pudding," Melody cut in enthusiastically, "and thick gravy. Would you like that for dinner tonight, Daddy?"

Garrick said that would be fine.

"Or maybe beef Wellington, if I have the time," Melody continued. "You roast the whole thing in a crust, with ham and paté. It's French," she told Dr. Tom. "Nobody eats like the French. All you have to do is look in the shops and your mouth starts to water. The biggest, reddest tomatoes you ever saw. Five different kinds of salad greens. And the bakeries, the butcher shops—"

"How do you feel right now?" Dr. Tom asked her. "Right this minute?" He was looking at Garrick.

"I'm starving," Melody said.

Dr. Tom filled his green-briar pipe. "I'll want to see you at the end of the week. Four, five pounds heavier. Otherwise you get a malted."

"A malted?"

"Barium. So I can see what's going on inside you. Fluoroscope. If that tells us nothing, you get the whole treatment. It's called a GI series. Nobody likes it," Dr. Tom said. "So gain those four or five pounds. Okay?"

"I'll try," Melody said, her enthusiasm gone as quickly as it had come. She wouldn't meet his eyes. "I guess ninety-eight or so wouldn't be so bad."

"For starters," Dr. Tom said. "Go sit in the waiting room, young lady. You won't find it comfortable," he told her dryly. "Backside's too pointy."

Melody laughed and went out.

Garrick lit a cigarette, Dr. Tom his green-briar pipe.

"You still smoke those things?" the doctor asked.

"Ten a day. Phasing out."

"Better than the pack and a half you used to smoke," Dr. Tom allowed. "Phasing out—the rational approach, is it? Well, sometimes it works. And I figure you're rational with Melody too. Never losing your cool, as I suppose she'd put it."

"What's wrong with her?" Garrick asked, mildly impatient.

"That depends on what you mean by wrong. Fluoroscope won't show anything, I don't think. There's not one damn thing wrong with her physically." Dr. Tom's pipe went out. He relit it with a wooden match. "She doesn't want to eat, but did you see the way her eyes lit up when she discussed food?"

"She loves to cook."

"For you?"

"Sure, for me. So what?"

"I was expecting that," Dr. Tom said. "She's the right age, by the way. Right sex, too."

"For what?"

"For wanting to remain a little girl. For not wanting to grow up. Tell me about her mother."

The question surprised Garrick. "Catherine? They had a good relationship. She was a good mother. She loved Melody."

"Never blew her top? Just like you don't?"

"What are you getting at?"

"Sort of swept arguments under the rug?"

"I guess. I wasn't around much. I guess you could say Catherine was permissive."

"It isn't the same as permissive, but that's close enough. Would you call yourself too permissive?"

Garrick considered. He said: "Melody had a rough time for a while. Boarding school for a couple of years. I was wandering all over the map."

"You went away," Dr. Tom said. "Before that, her mother died. How'd that happen, by the way?"

"Car accident," Garrick said tersely. He didn't want to talk about it, but Dr. Tom remained silent, puffing on his pipe.

"We had a place in the Village then," Garrick told him. "I was in New York a few weeks, anchoring the evening news because old Uncle Will was off in Southeast Asia. But Melody had this friend in Westchester. It rained all day, started turning icy in the afternoon. Catherine wasn't wild about driving, Melody really wanted to go."

"They argued?"

"I don't know. I wasn't there."

"Let's assume they didn't. Let's assume it got swept under the rug."

Garrick shrugged. "Nothing more to say. Car skidded on the Henry Hudson Parkway, jumped the divider. Right into the path of an airport limousine coming south." Garrick's mouth was dry.

"So Melody blamed herself. And at her age then, it wasn't too difficult for her to blame herself for you going away too. In a sensitive child that sort of thing can lead to schizophrenia."

"I won't buy that," Garrick said, not quite angrily.

"I'm not selling it. She's not schizophrenic. There's another way out they take. You want a name for it, I'll give you one. Anorexia nervosa. It's difficult to diagnose early. So let's call it a strong possibility at this point. And if it makes you feel better, Rob, the possibility of an early diagnosis generally means a good, not a bad relationship between parent and child."

Again Garrick shrugged. "That's easy. I'd've had to be blind. She's always been a real chow hound. All of a sudden she won't eat."

"Willful self-starvation," Dr. Tom said. "Anorexia nervosa's a fancy name for that." He shook his head when Garrick was going to interrupt.

"Listen, Rob. A teen-ager, usually female. Usually bright, friendly, industrious, athletic—and obsessed with food. She thinks about it, talks about it, wants to cook for the rest of the family. But she just won't eat, and she has strange ideas about her body. Skinny is good. Skin and bones is beautiful."

"The way she looked at herself in the mirror," Garrick said.

"You noticed that? All right. Was I describing Melody?"

"You know you were."

"Question is, why do they stop eating? It's their way of going back to a safe time, when they weren't being threatened. They're trying desperately not to grow up, trying to keep their body from becoming a woman's body."

"You said threatened, Tom. You were describing Melody until then, we both know that. But nothing's threatening her."

"Well, let's see. Is there something she's afraid of, something that could . . . take you away, like the accident took her mother away?"

Garrick was going to say no. Then he thought of Eve Talbot. He explained the situation to Dr. Tom and asked, "Do I tell Eve she has to leave?"

"Not on your life," the doctor said vehemently. "That's the last thing you do. Melody has to come to terms with it. With an anoretic child you don't avoid conflict, and you don't overaccommodate. You bring it out in the open. Anoretics come from nice families who don't like fights—urbane, civilized people. The anoretic *wants* to avoid conflict," Dr. Tom scowled. "If it didn't sound so Freudian—and you know me and Freud—I'd be tempted to say she wants to return to the womb."

Garrick asked, "How dangerous is it?"

"Depends. Caught early, the prognosis is good. And the treatment has nothing to do with eating. You can't force an anoretic to eat. But you can . . . Put it this way, the family system's broken down. Not from neglect but from what you've called permissiveness. The child's learned not to defend her rights in the usual ways. What she really craves is . . . static. Give her some."

"What kind of static?"

"If she's jealous of this friend of yours, let her be. Let her fight and, if she's going to lose, let her see that—but I'm getting ahead of myself. How serious are you about this woman?"

In a way Dr. Tom was treating him as well as Melody, Garrick realized. "I never let myself think about it," he admitted. "Melody, she—"

"Damn it, Rob, that's the whole point. Father and daughter don't, or shouldn't, exist in a symbiotic relationship. There are two lives there. Separate and apart. When they come into conflict, fighting's normal. If you do marry the girl—does she like Melody?"

"Yes, she does," Garrick said.

"Then Melody has to realize she's gaining a mother, not losing a father."

Garrick lit another cigarette. "You said caught early the prognosis was good. How bad would it be otherwise?"

Dr. Tom said: "The statistics aren't very sound, mostly because a lot of cases are discovered too late, if at all. A severe anoretic will keep on losing weight. An unfeeling parent will try to make her eat. As I said, that never works. Oh, she'll eat. And then go into the bathroom and force herself to vomit."

Dr. Tom's wild tufts of eyebrows went up and he blew pipe smoke at the ceiling. "I'll give it to you straight, Rob. That's not the most severe case. In a really severe case the anoretic child will go on starving herself and thinking she's beautiful when she looks like a concentration-camp victim. It becomes irreversible. She hallucinates, doesn't have the strength to get on her feet. It becomes a simple case of terminal malnutrition then."

"She dies," Garrick said flatly.

"They die, yes. Unless you recognize the problems in time and thrash them out."

"Aren't there any specialists who—"

"Oh, there are treatment centers. Payne Whitney in Philadelphia, for example. The parent of an anoretic who can't cope with the problem is the biggest danger. So you take the child away, hospitalize her. Intravenous feeding, and rewards for plain old-fashioned eating. It takes months."

"Does it work?"

Dr. Tom waited a few seconds before answering. "Usually, no. Once it goes that far, the patient usually finds an excuse to have a relapse when she leaves the hospital." Dr. Tom stood up. "But assuming we're right, we did catch it early, or you did. And you know what you have to do."

Garrick said he knew what he had to do.

Otherwise she starves herself to death, he thought.

13

From the Notebook of Jean-Baptiste Columbine

Gadje believe that the Rom (I almost wrote we Rom) travel where the spirit and the wind move them. It is otherwise. They move with the seasons, like nomads seeking forage and watering places on the great eastern steppes, and they know where they are going.

The clan of Zurka—for that was the name of Tita's loutish husband—journeyed south and east for two years, and they would return to France four years from the month they left Bourg St. Martin. I did not know then that I would not be with them to complete the circuit.

If they traveled like the nomads of the eastern steppes, the watering places they sought were towns and villages where they could work. They were mountebanks and musicians always, and Tita had some regard in the south of France and the Piedmont as a fortuneteller. They became blacksmiths and tinners and silversmiths in the Piedmont, where such occupations were in demand. Farther east, they panned for alluvial gold in the rivers of Serbia. Sometimes they produced counterfeit coins. They stole everywhere, without losing their sense of honor. The whole world was their steppe, and they lived off its meager resources. To steal from the *gadje* was not dishonorable.

I helped in none of these occupations. I was baggage.

Except for Zurka, the others did not mind. Tita liked me and hoped that I would paint them again, as I had in Bourg St. Martin, or at least sketch them. Sometimes she stole charcoal and crayons for me.

—Why don't you work, Jean-Baptiste?

I waved the stump of my left arm at her like the flipper of a fish, and told her I was a cripple. The arm had festered a few days after we left Bourg St. Martin, and I grew feverish. One night they gave me strong spirits to drink until my head reeled and the campfire danced and pulsed and the tambourines roared in my ears. Then Tita and her cousin Kore held me, and with a single stroke of a heavy sword Zurka cut off the swollen arm between elbow and shoulder. I did not scream then. I screamed when Zurka brought hot pitch to cauterize the stump. All the while Zurka smiled. The last thing I saw before I fainted was that smile. It was not that the Rom enjoy inflicting pain, for they do not. Zurka hated me even then.

—I mean, why don't you paint? Tita asked me. We Rom create beauty with a tambourine or a fiddle, with our dancing. Most *gadje* don't understand beauty, but you do. You can paint a bird or a tree or a wagon and it looks more like the thing than the thing itself. I'll dance for you if you'll paint me dancing.

I told her I would never paint again.

Zurka and Tita had no children. He was a big, muscular man with a face dark even for a Rom, and great curving mustaches. Tita was ten years younger, and comely. As he was young to be the *voivode*, the chief of the clan, so she was young to be its wise woman.

—It is because I learned from Gaddara, she told me one day.

—Who is Gaddara?

—You'll meet her near Belgrade.

—Is that where we're going?

—To Belgrade and back. We sell horses in Belgrade.

I asked, Where do you get them? and Tita laughed. We get them, she said.

For two years I neither painted nor sketched nor raised a hand to help with the loading and unloading of the caravan. Nor did I lie with a woman. I ate, and I

slept, and I learned the romani language without trying
to learn it. Where they went I would go. Nothing mattered to me.

The *gadje* believe the Rom are promiscuous, but it is
otherwise. Marriages are usually for life, and the cuck-
olded husband is expected to take his revenge.

The women are bold and, like women anywhere, curious. By the time we passed through the Piedmont and
into the dry, stark hills of Serbia they were wondering
which of them I would choose. I chose none, and this at
first amused and then, in the way of unmarried women,
and some who are married, intrigued them.

My choice would have been simple, had I cared. But
I would not really *ravesquir* (Have sex? I don't think
that's it. Revive, maybe.) until I met Gaddara, although
I did not know that yet.

. . . Tita, certainly. She could not have been more
than thirty, and I knew she liked me. She was comely.
Her *gorjon* (bosom?) was full and firm, and in the
manner of the Rom in fair weather she sometimes exposed it without shame. The Rom women hide their legs,
as these lead to their *armaire*. (Dictionary confusing.
Probably a euphemism for private parts.)

Zurka was proud of Tita's beauty, but jealous. She
danced magnificently at night around the campfire, and
it was a simple matter for her to kindle the desire of the
other Rom while she struck her tambourine and pirouetted from man to man, her dark eyes flashing, her
face gleaming with sweat, her long legs tantalizingly exposed and then hidden under her flowing skirts. It was
all harmless. Tita loved to dance. But Zurka would stare
moodily at the fire, and the more her dancing bothered
him the more Tita danced. This is the way of women
everywhere too.

Sometimes, with little or no provocation, Zurka beat
her.

The nearer we approached Belgrade, the more the
Rom resembled the inhabitants of that country. What
the *gadje* mistakenly regard as Rom clothing is really
the clothing of the East, and soon, in every village we

reached, the men wore pantaloons and loose blouses,
the women earrings and half a dozen colorful skirts, one
over the other. They looked like Rom. Many were even
dark-skinned, like the Rom.

—Do your people come from here? I asked Tita.

—Farther east, she told me. Far across deserts and
mountains. A land called Ind. (India! So there's where
the gypsies come from. I didn't know that.)

. . . for days at a time. When they returned with the
horses, we would break camp quickly and continue
through the wild, desolate country. Our destination was
the horse fair in Belgrade, but I never reached it.

Soon we had a dozen horses, and then fifteen. The
Rom would currycomb them every day, and do something else which I found strange. They would half fill a
bucket with pebbles and shake it close under the horses'
quivering nostrils, making them rear with terror. (Biba
Tita told me why they did that.)

The Rom had hoped to reach Belgrade with twenty
horses to sell, and when we were three days' journey
from that city Zurka took half the men out from camp
one final time. He said he would be gone a minimum of
two days. For some reason this seemed to please Tita.
We were camped near a village of dun-colored hovels,
and the villagers came out to watch the dancing. They
seemed to accept the Rom in a way that we French or
even the Piedmontese don't.

—Aren't they aware that you steal their horses? I
asked Tita.

She laughed.

—Not their horses, she told me. This is the village
where Gaddara lives. Nobody steals horses here.

Tita did not dance that night, though the other
women did. It was warm, and instead of sleeping in the
wagons we had pitched tents. I went to my own tent
early, as the dancing held little interest for me. It was
Tita I liked to see dance.

I lay awake listening to the wild fiddles and the beat
and tinkle of the tambourines, to the shouts and the
stamping of feet. I felt restless, and when I shut my eyes

it was with dread, for I knew I would see again my wife Marie dead on the floor of our kitchen and the dragoons having their way with our daughter. This night was different. When I shut my eyes I saw Tita dancing. Something stirred in me, a reckless desire, a feeling I thought had gone from me as cleanly and permanently as my arm had been severed. I wanted a woman, but not just any woman. I wanted Tita.

It was insane. She had a husband, and he was the *voivode* of their people. She had been kind to me, caring for me, feeding me, placating Zurka when he objected that I did no work. I shut my eyes and saw her dancing again. I smiled at my own foolishness, almost believing that what I suddenly wanted of Tita could make me *ravesquir*. Of course, I told myself bitterly—for one night.

And then Zurka would return and learn of it, and he would kill me.

I willed myself to sleep, but sleep would not come. The music stopped. There were voices, laughter, footsteps, silence. Then I heard a rustling sound and saw moonlight for an instant and then the darkness again.

She came to me swiftly and lay beside me, close against me.

—And if I danced? she said. You would have drunk wine, and more wine. You would have drunk yourself to sleep.

The touch of her hand on me was light.

—I'll leave, if that is what you wish, she said.

I waited, not daring to answer.

—He takes me with his clothing on, quickly, like an animal. There is no love. I am a thing that he uses. The *voivode* and his wise woman. He married me for that. I was *phuri dai* first. But about some things I am not wise.

I felt her tears fall on my cheek. At first I thought she had come to me out of pity, but then I pitied her.

I felt her light touch again. Her hand moved inside my shirt and down.

—I can do things you'd like. Her voice was plaintive. Don't you like this, Jean-Baptiste?

I pushed her hand away gently. (What's the matter with him? What's he waiting for?!!)

—Lie still, I said, and she sighed and did that, while I removed her bodice and the skirts, one by one. Then I took off my shirt and pantaloons, awkwardly with my one hand. We lay a little way apart.

—I wish I could see you, she said. Are you beautiful, are you my beautiful *gadjo*?

—You're beautiful, I said. I don't have to see to know that.

Our lips came together, and our bodies. I thought she wanted gentleness, after her life with Zurka, but I could not be gentle. *Mariole*! It had been so long.

I was mistaken about what she wanted. I felt her nails and her teeth, and then she twisted and cried out under me.

. . . awoke at once and listened to her breathing. Her head was on my shoulder, her long hair across my chest. I touched a finger to her lips and in her sleep she kissed it, and awoke.

—One more night, she said. Two, if we're lucky.

—And then?

There was an emptiness in me. Pity is not love. I would never love again as I had loved Marie and our child. But I would hate. I saw in the darkness the arrogant face of the Sieur de Ramezay.

I said nothing of any of that. I wanted her to speak.

—My people need me. I could not remain *phuri dai* if I left Zurka to live with you. You're no Rom. Do you love me very much, Jean-Baptiste?

—Tonight, I said. I did not mean that to be cruel, and she understood.

She said, Then tonight is what we have.

. . . tent flap parted and silhouetted against the first light of dawn, Zurka.

—Whore! he shouted, and thrust me aside as I rose to hand and knees and tried to get between him and

Tita. He dragged her naked from the tent and flung her to the bare earth of the encampment as I rushed out after them. He began to beat her, and thrust me away again when I tried to stop him. He was strong, and I had but one arm.

Soon the clan came from their tents, one and two at a time, and they watched in a deadly silence. Zurka beat and kicked Tita until she was senseless. Then he spoke to her cousin Kore.

—Get her clothing. Dress her.

Kore, frightened, ducked into the tent and did as she was told. I wet a cloth and bathed Tita's bruised face. Kore tapped my shoulder. She was blushing. She had brought my own clothing. The Rom just watched. They neither approved nor disapproved of what Zurka had done. They were waiting.

Zurka sat with his back against a wheel of the wagon he shared with Tita, drinking wine. He stared straight ahead, looking at no one, seeing nothing.

Tita's eyes opened. She took in everything at once.

—Jean-Baptiste, she whispered, listen to me. He is quick in anger but slow in thought. No harm will come to me. He needs me to govern the people, he knows that. Without me they would choose a new *voivode*.

She spoke those words quickly. Then she said, You must flee at once, before he . . .

Zurka smashed the wine cup against the side of the wagon.

—Give the *gadjo* a knife, he said.

No one moved.

—Run, Jean-Baptiste, Tita said.

But I stood there. How far could I go? Where would I go?

Zurka smoothed his long mustaches and smiled.

—Kore will bring the *gadjo* a knife. Unless she would rather see the *gadjo*'s throat slit because the *gadjo* cannot defend himself.

I knew I could not defend myself against Zurka, knife or no knife. He approached us slowly, a long-bladed dagger in his hand. He was proud of that weapon—Toledo steel, taken from a southern Rom, a *gitane,* in the south of France.

Tita was sitting up. Kore looked at her. Slowly Tita nodded, and Kore climbed the steps into one of the wagons. She returned with a knife, its blade as long as Zurka's.

—Strike fast, Tita told me in an urgent whisper. He'll want to play cat and mouse. That is your one chance.

But I had no chance. The clan gathered in a circle, and it was over very swiftly. Zurka crouched low, teeth gleaming under his mustaches, the *gitane* knife moving in tight circles low at his side. I tried to do what Tita had told me, but I was no knife fighter. I lunged once, awkwardly, and Zurka's left hand caught my wrist and twisted. The knife Kore had brought me dropped from my fingers.

Zurka remained in his crouch. Pick it up, *gadjo,* he said. We are only beginning.

I stooped, and his boot lashed out, catching me on the side of the head. I landed on my back and heard Tita cry out. Then Zurka straddled me and pinned my one arm to the ground with his knee. The point of his knife touched my throat.

The people muttered among themselves, but Zurka said, I have the right. The right is mine.

I could feel the point of the knife pricking my skin. Zurka was in no hurry. He drew a line across my throat with the knife, delicately, almost like an etcher using his burin on a copper plate. I waited to die. His eyes told me I would die. And then I did not see Zurka, I saw the Sieur de Ramezay. I knew ironically in what I thought the final instant of my life that I had something to live for—to make the Sieur de Ramezay pay.

—What, have you no prayers? Zurka asked.

I remained mute. The point of the blade dug at my throat.

—Won't you beg for your life, *gadjo?*

I heard a crackling sound, and Zurka leaped off me. He rolled over and over on the ground.

On all sides I heard shouting, a single word. Gaddara.

I sat up and saw, inside the circle of the people, a coal-black horse, and on the horse what I at first took to be a slender boy dressed in black and holding a bull-whip in his hand.

The end of the whip was coiled about Zurka's neck. He tugged at the rawhide that was strangling him. The horse reared and Zurka was dragged through the dust. Then the rider's arm lowered and Zurka could free himself.

—Gaddara, he said hoarsely.

The rider said, Take your nags to the horse fair in Belgrade. Then leave Serbia. If you harm Tita, if you even beat her, you will die. I promise you this, no matter where you are.

The rider's voice was a woman's. I saw her long black hair. She dismounted and came to me. The Rom cleared a path for her. Even Tita edged away.

The woman named Gaddara walked haughtily, and she was beautiful, her face fine-boned, her skin fair against the jet of her hair, her eyes a deep violet.

—Have you possessions, Jean-Baptiste Columbine? she asked me.

It was impossible that she could know my name, but she knew it. I shook my head.

—Then come with me at once.

I looked at Tita.

—No harm will come to the woman of Zurka, Gaddara told me.

The violet eyes gazed into my eyes, and suddenly I knew I had to go with her, had come this far with the Rom so that I could.

She reached down a hand and caught my hand and helped me to my feet. We walked together toward her horse, and again the Rom made way for her. They were frightened. They would not meet the steady gaze of those violet eyes.

Gaddara swung up lightly into the saddle, telling me

to mount behind her. I did that awkwardly, with her help. She kicked her heels into the flanks of the coal-black horse, and it began to trot.

I did not look back at any of them. Not Zurka, not Kore, not even Tita. I had traveled two years to reach my destiny.

Melody shut the notebook. She was too tired to go on, even though she wanted to. How could Gaddara have known Columbine's name? she wondered. How had she known—she *must* have known—he would be there?

God, what a woman, Melody told herself. Riding into the encampment like that, with a bullwhip, saving Columbine's life, the way they all were terrified of her. . . .

And she was slender. Melody opened the notebook again to look at that part. So slender that at first Columbine thought her a boy.

Melody would be slender like that soon too.

14

Half an hour with M. A. Kelly was enough to convince Monsieur Taitbout that he should have sent for another art restorer, any other art restorer.

Kelly, indisputably the world's foremost expert on the work of Jean-Baptiste Columbine, was also a perfectionist.

And arrogant, opinionated, domineering.

But with her dark hair drawn back severely in a bun, her indifferently cut tweed suit, her plain face, how could she expect to get away with the attitude of calculated aloofness she affected? A woman needed beauty for that.

And yet, thought Monsieur Taitbout, reassessing her with his expert Gallic eye, there was something about her, a *je ne sais quoi,* waiting to emerge, like a butterfly from a cocoon—

M. A. Kelly confused and irritated Monsieur Taitbout.

It had begun with "The Gypsy Camp." Monsieur Taitbout had set the painting on the easel, adjusted the lighting, stood back. "You see?" he chirped. "Or rather, you don't see?"

They stood close. She smelled of soap, not perfume. Tall, angular, she was younger than he had expected. He offered her his binocular magnifier, and she adjusted its headband with deft fingers.

He was proud of the patch he had made, proud of the way he had cut canvas to the contours of the hole after trimming the frayed threads, proud of the thinness

123

of the polyvinyl-acetate coating, proud of filling, retouching, revarnishing.

"As good as new," he said. "Or," with a small Gallic
laugh, "as good as old."

M. A. Kelly stood, unmoving and unmoved, studying
the canvas through the binocular magnifier.

"Not bad," she said. Monsieur Taitbout smiled. "But
not good," she went on. "The problem is the backing
canvas. Too much PVA on the backing patch. It's a
common enough mistake."

Monsieur Taitbout cleared his throat and adjusted his
face. M. A. Kelly raised the binocular magnifier to her
forehead. "But more than good enough," she admitted.

"Ahh," said Monsieur Taitbout.

"If all you wanted to do was repair the hole."

Monsieur Taitbout bristled at her arrogance. "It's as
good as new," he said.

"It's not a new painting. It's almost three hundred
years old. Look at the varnish, for starters."

The varnish was dim, not entirely transparent. But of
course thought Monsieur Taitbout. The painting had always looked like that.

"Remove it," said M. A. Kelly. "From all of them.
You'll want to mix some acetone or methanol with the
rectified paraffin. You agree?"

Monsieur Taitbout had not even agreed to remove
the varnish from the five Columbine canvases. He said
nothing.

"Well? Are you an art conservator or aren't you?"

Taitbout was a curator with some fair knowledge of
the art restorer's skills.

"Tell me, monsieur—" M. A. Kelly was speaking
rapid accentless French, "do you clean a painting to examine it, or examine a painting to clean it?"

"I—"

"One should think in terms of both, monsieur."

Three tourists entered through the door on Monsieur
Taitbout's left—a man, a woman, a child. The man
stood, his legs wide, leaning forward, a camera in front

of his face. The flashcube caught Monsieur Taitbout
with his mouth open. The tourists left.

"Just who the hell was that?" M. A. Kelly demanded
in English.

"Visitors. Tourists. This is all part of Bourg St. Martin Month."

"I," said M. A. Kelly, "am not going to work for the
amusement of tourists. Keep them out of here."

That was when Taitbout's head began to throb. "You
will have to see Mr. Garrick at the newspaper," he said.

"What does this have to do with a newspaper?"

Taitbout tried to explain, but was interrupted.

"I'll see Garrick. Don't let it trouble you."

It had not been troubling Monsieur Taitbout. It had
even given him some pleasure to work in front of the
tourists, no mere technician but in a way a performing
artist.

"Meanwhile," M. A. Kelly said, switching to French
again, "we have a marvelous opportunity—these paintings are old, monsieur, and they have been subjected to
the usual ravages of time and inept curators. We will
restore them. How much time have you?"

Monsieur Taitbout's stay in Martinsburg was open-
ended. Still, he hesitated before answering her question.
He had always dreamed of working with a restorer like
M. A. Kelly. Who wouldn't? Only the great conservator
Stravros Mihalarias was her technical equal, and Mihalarias would not share his expertise or his secrets. But
Taitbout knew, if he knew anything, that she would not
be easy to work with. He was a sensitive man. A day or
two of her and the headache would be nothing. He'd
wind up with a *crise de foie*.

"That depends, madame," he said.

"Mademoiselle. I will draw up a schedule. Cleaning.
Varnish removal. Chemical analysis. Pigment analysis.
Permanency testing. When can you begin?"

Monsieur Taitbout's head was pounding.

"Before you know it, these paintings will look like
they just came from Columbine's easel." She said that

in English, the arrogant tone of voice gone. "Think of them hanging in Bourg St. Martin—totally restored."

The possibility of that, headache or no, *crise de foie* or no, was too much to resist.

"I am ready to begin whenever you wish," he said.

It took Margriet Kelly less than five minutes to unpack her suitcase at the Martinsburg Motor Lodge. Three smocks, a parka, a topcoat, just two dresses, functional underclothes. No makeup. No nightgown or pajamas. They were unnecessary in an overheated motel room.

Swiftly she undressed, hanging the severely cut tweed suit in the closet. She could use a shower and nap after the long drive, she told herself, and certainly after her first meeting with Monsieur Taitbout. She was always younger than they expected, and it was worse with an aging sexist like Taitbout. She hoped she hadn't been too abrupt with him; they'd have to work together, after all.

Barely over thirty and just six years out of the Institut Royal de Patrimoine Artistique in Brussels, Margriet knew her reputation was already considerable. Only the almost legendary Greek conservator Stavros Mihalarias commanded more respect in museums on three continents. His reputation was based on a method he had developed to separate and preserve paintings that had been executed one atop the other on the same canvas. The technique, Margriet was aware, required the skill and patience of a neurosurgeon. Still, Mihalarias was a technician, period. The undeniable dean of art conservators, but limited.

Margriet had earned a degree in psychology before studying at the Institut, and had combined the two disciplines in her doctoral dissertation, a comparison of the insanity of Goya and the insanity of Columbine during both painters' so-called black periods. If insanity was the right word. Goya had been comparatively simple. His gradual descent into madness was historically documented. But Columbine was more complex. The trauma of the death of his wife and child, the years of wandering with the gypsies—but no historical documentation of mental illness, no political involvement like Goya's, no hermit's retreat like Goya's, no misanthropy like Goya's. No old age, Margriet thought as she stepped into the shower and turned it on full force. Columbine had died in his early fifties and, unlike Goya, he had lived a very private life. Further, since his fame grew after his lifetime, not during it as in Goya's case, even less was known about him.

The one extant letter written in his own hand and considered authentic by most scholars posed more questions than it answered. Columbine had written it shortly before his death to the young French painter Denis Vouet, and in it he unexpectedly discoursed on the subject of black magic, knowledgeably and with passionate conviction. He had, according to the letter, read the *grimoires,* those compilations of magic used by sorcerers in medieval times, and he believed that the artist, in a way a magician himself, could learn from them. Learn what, he never made clear, but his knowledge of the *Key of Solomon, the Lemegeton,* the *Grimoire of Honorius,* the *Arbatel of Magic,* the *Grimorium Verum,* and the *Black Pullet* was considerable.

Two pages of the letter were missing and with them most of a key passage. She knew the intriguing remnant by heart. "I have seen such things, my dear Vouet. I have seen the inexplicable conflagration even in a church of God, I have heard the sinister astral bell, and with my own eyes I have seen the wasting away of a man so cursed. But of course I do not expect to convince you, and I only suggest all this in a spirit of rational inquiry."

Rational? Margriet wondered again, soaping herself, rinsing, and turning the water cold for a moment before shutting it off.

She toweled herself dry, slid between the crisp, cool sheets of the king-sized bed in the overheated room, and was asleep in three minutes.

She dreamed that a one-armed man was making love to her.

The one-armed man, his face so like the self-portrait hanging in the Louvre and the Rijksmuseum, was Jean-Baptiste Columbine.

When she awoke, the vividness of her dream at first amused her. She loved her work, after all, didn't she? Talk about obvious symbolism. . . .

The dream had also been disturbingly erotic, and its effects lingered. She dressed slowly, finding even the touch of her own hands stimulating. Picking up her hairbrush, she smiled wryly at herself in the mirror.

The eyes that smiled back at her looked different, darker. Her face, enhanced by the smile, seemed oddly feline.

She dropped the hairbrush and whirled suddenly, experiencing a moment of acute terror.

Someone was in the room with her.

She saw the bed, the motel-modern chair and table, the dresser, the print of a covered bridge on the wall, the styleless drapes covering the window.

She was alone in the room, the door locked, the chain in place.

What's gotten into you? she thought. The next thing you know, you'll be looking under the bed. She turned back to the mirror, her face pale, her hand unsteady as she retrieved the brush and ran it through her hair.

She was pale—of course, that was it. That was why her eyes seemed darker, her face somehow different.

Melody and Craig rode their bikes to Nick's after school. The glassed-in terrace was crowded, but they found a table against the wall in back. Nick's was the only restaurant on the Commons and this time of day it was taken over by Martinsburg's small Puerto Rican population. They would drink beer and promenade around the Commons and drink more beer, jabbering away in Spanish all the time. Melody liked to hear them talk—it was foreign, even if it wasn't French.

"How do I look?" she asked.

"Is that a new sweater or something? It's pretty sharp," Craig said.

"No, Silly. I'd had this old thing for years. I mean me. My diet."

"I still don't know what you're on a diet for," Craig said.

"Why does anybody go on a diet? To lose weight."

"You're too skinny already," Craig said.

"So's Cher, and you've got a poster of her on your wall."

"That's different. She's sexy."

"Thank you very much," Melody said elaborately.

The waitress came over. Craig ordered a pizza with the works. Melody asked for a diet cola.

"I didn't mean it that way," Craig said.

"I'm not much skinnier than Cher, am I?"

"Well, one thing about her, she's not flat-chested," Craig said. "A diet Coke. What's with you, anyway?"

"I told you I'm on a diet. Besides, I'm not in the mood for a pizza. I'm not *that* flat-chested, am I?"

Craig smiled and blushed. "Maybe you're a slow starter," he said.

"I don't want to get any bigger there."

"The way you're eating—*not* eating—you don't have to worry about getting bigger anywhere. Keep it up and you'll look like someone they just rescued off a lifeboat in the South Pacific."

"I'm not underweight," Melody protested. "I've got small bones."

The waitress came with her cola and Craig's pizza. Craig picked up a wedge and stuffed half of it into his mouth. Melody stirred her cola with a straw, the ice tinkling. The pizza smelled delicious.

Melody's mouth was watering. She watched him chewing. She said, "Mushroom and green pepper and Italian sausage and anchovies. It smells yummy."

"There's Italian sausage *and* pepperoni," Craig said, picking up another wedge. "Also black olives."

"Can I have a bite?"

Craig offered her what was left of the second wedge. Melody took a nibble and returned it.

"Don't stuff yourself," Craig said.

"I just wanted to see what it tasted like with both kinds of sausage," Melody told him.

But Craig was no longer listening. A car came slowly along Commons Avenue South. It braked to a stop outside Nick's and a voice shouted: "That's him! There he is!"

Both front doors and one rear door opened and three men came out, moving fast. They entered the enclosed terrace and headed straight for a corner table to Melody's left, the big man who led the way, stony-faced, intent.

"All right, on your goddamn feet," he said, his voice loud.

The two young men at the table looked up. One of them placed a restraining hand on the other's shoulder.

"I said on your feet."

The two young men raised their heavy glass mugs and drank beer ostentatiously.

"Get your ass out of that chair," the big man said.

One of the young men started to rise. The other held his shoulder hard.

"Ahh, I might have known. They always told me spics were yellow."

A hand made a tossing motion, and half a mug of beer found its mark. The big man shouted, knuckled his eyes, grabbed the front of the young man's windbreaker and yanked him to his feet, slapping the empty beer mug from his hand and knocking him down with a hard clubbing blow of his right fist.

Then things happened almost too fast for Melody to follow.

The young man got up, backhanding his bloody lips, spitting out a tooth. He swung ineffectually and the big man hit him again and he crashed backwards against a table, overturning it. Someone shouted; someone else came up behind the big man, trying to hold him, just as

Nick emerged from the interior of the restaurant, waving his arms.

The young man propelled himself away from the overturned table, collided with Nick, and stumbled toward the big man, who had just succeeded in breaking loose.

Melody heard someone cry: "Look out, Harry, he's got a knife!"

The man named Harry and the young man lurched toward each other awkwardly, both of them off balance. Melody saw the glint of the knife, and then the big man named Harry was bent over, clutching his side, and the young man stared in amazement at the knife in his hand.

"Jesus," he said, and he ran.

He was gone before anyone could stop him.

Garrick stood in the doorway, the expectant smile fading on his face.

"Mr. Garrick?" the woman said. "Mr. Robert Garrick?"

He nodded. "Come on in. It's cold out there."

She entered the hall, collar of a black coat turned up around her neck. Garrick caught a glimpse of a severely plain hairdo, a severely plain face. She was tall and slender, the exposed skin of her face red from the sudden cold that had come with late afternoon.

Garrick had been waiting for Eve Talbot, who was out with her camera crew shooting some of the old houses in town that dated back to its Huguenot founders. He helped the woman remove her coat.

"I'm Margriet Kelly," she said.

They entered the living room together, Garrick draping her coat over the back of a chair instead of hanging it in the closet, the socially accepted way of suggesting a short visit. He had an editorial to write.

"Have a seat, Miss Kelly. What can I do for you?"

She sat primly on the edge of the sofa. "You don't know who I am, do you?"

Garrick shook his head, offering a small social smile. "No, I'm afraid not."

"Maybe if I said M. A. Kelly."

And then he remembered. "Oh, sure. Monsieur Taitbout's art restorer. Glad you could finally make it, Miss Kelly."

"I'd prefer the word 'conservator.' If you think 'restorer' you get the idea you can take liberties with the original work. That's a mistake in my profession. You *do* see the difference?"

Garrick said he thought he saw the difference. He remained standing. "Drink?"

"No, thank you. I won't stay long." Margriet Kelly folded her hands in her lap. "I'd like you to do me a favor, Mr. Garrick." She explained about the tourists. "A conservator is a technician, not a performing artist, despite what Monsieur Taitbout thinks," she told Garrick.

"Why don't you compromise?" he suggested. "Work out a schedule. You mornings and no tourists, Taitbout afternoons and the Armory open to visitors."

"Yes, I suppose we—"

Her voice didn't trail off. It just stopped dead. She was staring past Garrick's shoulder.

"That painting," she said.

She got up and went past Garrick as if he weren't there. She stood before the hearth. "Good God," she said. "Do you know what this is?"

"I know what it's a copy of," Garrick told her. "Columbine's so-called lost painting. A first-rate forgery, according to Taitbout."

Her back still turned, Margriet Kelly said: "That's no forgery. It can't be. It's too good. It's too perfect."

"And too new," Garrick said, sorry to disappoint her. "Twenty years old, Taitbout said. Thirty at the most."

As she turned slowly, Garrick's eyes were still on the painting. "I don't care how new it looks. It's genuine." Her voice had been thin. It was throaty with excitement now. "It's the lost painting of Jean-Baptiste Columbine."

Garrick was facing her by then. He remembered afterward that he tried not to gape. It wasn't possible.

Lustrous black hair drawn back tight acccentuated the fine high cheekbones and the shadowed hollows under them, the feline look of her face. Her tweed suit, far from being dowdy, as he'd judged when he helped her off with her coat, was very Abercrombie & Fitch, stylish in an understated way, and although she was slender, as he had at first thought, the tweedy fabric couldn't quite hide her lithe curves.

Plain? Dowdy? She had walked in like that. She was beautiful now.

As if—the thought came suddenly—seeing the painting had changed her.

He became aware that she was talking. ". . . certain tests, of course, but believe me, they won't be necessary. No forger, no matter how good, can duplicate another man's work. An artist's style is as unique as a fingerprint. The brush strokes, the use of impasto, the highlighting, it's pure Columbine. . . . What's the matter?"

"What? Nothing," Garrick said.

He realized he'd been staring at her the way she'd stared at the painting.

The door burst open and Melody came rushing in.

"There was a fight down at Nick's," she cried. "A man got stabbed, Daddy. It was awful. He just—Oh, hello."

"Hello," Margriet Kelly said.

"This is my daughter Melody," Garrick said. "Melody, Miss Kelly. She's the art restorer who—"

"Conservator," Margriet Kelly corrected him, smiling at Melody.

"What's this about a fight?" Garrick asked.

"A fight ain't no race riot," Sergeant Whitlock told Charlie Dahlgren as they drove along Mill Street. "What's the matter with the chief, anyway?"

"He just said be careful how we bring him in, that's all."

Charlie could understand Ned Revere's concern,

even if Whitlock couldn't. Whitlock had been born in
Martinsburg and spent twenty years on the force, earn-
ing his sergeant's stripes. Fewer than three hundred
Puerto Ricans lived in town, most of them employed by
the textile mill near Riverside Park. West of the mill
stood two eight-story brick apartment buildings, as
anomalous in Martinsburg as the Armory was. Many of
the Puerto Ricans rented apartments there. Except for
the river and the narrow curving wedge of park, it reminded Charlie Dahlgren of one of the rare good neighborhoods in Spanish Harlem.

"You know the guy?" Whitlock asked as they drove
past the chain-link fence of the mill. It was dusk, and
the street lights had just come on. A few men walked
along the sidewalk, moving fast. Charlie could see their
breath. It was the first really cold night of the year.

"García?" Charlie said, shaking his head. "You've
got to be kidding. It's like Smith."

Whitlock laughed. "And spics, they're like Chinamen, right? All Chinamen look alike. You New York
guys make me laugh."

The New York police precinct where Charlie had
been assigned had a large Puerto Rican population. He
had picked up some Spanish, just street Spanish, but
that was more than anyone else on the Martinsburg
force had. Charlie was Ned Revere's expert on Puerto
Ricans.

He slowed the patrol car in front of the apartment
building and drove half a block farther before pulling to
the curb. He almost wished that Angel García had had
a record—if not in Martinsburg then in New York
where, according to the personnel man at the mill, he
had grown up. But he was clean here in Martinsburg
and a phone check of New York revealed no yellow
sheet on him. Three witnesses at Nick's had identified
him. He was twenty-three years old, Charlie's age. The
man he'd stabbed, Harry Mauriello, was in the
intensive-care unit at Martinsburg General right now.
They had collapsed one lung to stop the hemorrhaging.

"I still don't get what the chief's so worried about,"

Whitlock said. "A guy knifes someone, you bring him in."

"Sure, okay," Charlie said, getting out of the patrol car. He knew what was worrying Ned Revere.

Charlie Dahlgren was worrying Ned Revere, which was why he had sent the placid Cal Whitlock with him. Charlie had done office work since that morning last week when he'd handled the Joynes case out on Laurel Drive. Ned figured, as Ned would, that it was time Charlie got his confidence back. "I don't want to hear about it anymore," he'd told Charlie half an hour ago. "It never happened. Understand?"

Charlie had nodded, wishing he was as sure of himself as Ned was of him. Ned hadn't felt the insane compulsion to kill.

Sergeant Whitlock had come in, and Ned told the heavy, balding man, "Handle it with kid gloves. Puerto Ricans, they're clannish, and they come up here with a chip on their shoulder. That's not Martinsburg's fault, but it's your classic race-riot situation."

"Race riot?" Whitlock had repeated. "What the hell, Ned."

"He lives with his mother out there. Say she doesn't want to see her boy collared. It's happened before."

"Not in Martinsburg," Whitlock said.

Revere ignored that. "So she starts screaming police brutality, and the neighbors remember what it was like in New York. Play it cool, that's all I'm saying, Cal."

Whitlock had almost sounded insulted when he said: "I've collared a few guys in my time, Ned."

"Charlie here'll go along in case you need some Spanish."

Whitlock grinned. "Say something in Spanish," he told Charlie.

"Besa mi culo," Charlie said.

"Hey, watch your lip, even I know what that means," Whitlock said, still grinning.

Charlie wondered now, as they got out of the patrol car, if Whitlock knew what had happened last week. He doubted it. He didn't think Ned would have told him.

Not that that changed anything. Ned was giving Charlie a chance to prove himself, and Ned was a little worried about it.

Don't cause any race riots, Charlie. Don't shoot anybody, Charlie.

Charlie Dahlgren was determined to vindicate himself. He liked police work. He wouldn't let Ned Revere down.

He would let himself down.

"Cold," Whitlock said. The street was deserted. They started to walk back.

"In New York," Charlie told him, feeling the need to talk, "you'd leave a guy with the bus so the street people didn't trash it."

"That must be one great town to work in," Whitlock said, and they went into the vestibule of the apartment building.

It was clean. It even smelled clean, there was no graffiti on the walls, and nobody had knocked out the overhead light. Whitlock's laugh was more a grunt. "Still thinking of New York?" he wanted to know.

Charlie shook his head.

The name García was in the first row of the tenant directory. Apartment 2-C. Charlie was about to thumb the bell.

"Hold it, kid," Whitlock told him. "I don't expect trouble, but I don't go manufacturing it."

Charlie felt foolish. He knew Whitlock was right. It was routine, like parking half a block away. He watched the older man get out a ring of keys; his second try opened the vestibule door.

The stairs were clean and well lighted too, as was the second-floor hallway. They passed one door and heard muted music with a Latin rhythm. They passed a second door and reached 2-C.

Whitlock mouthed the word silently: "Ready?"

He went flat against the wall on one side of the door, Charlie on the other. That was routine, too, probably overcautious under the circumstances, but still . . .

Whitlock rang the bell, and a woman's voice called at

once, "Yes, who is it?" as if she had been expecting them.

"Mrs. García?" Whitlock said. "We're the police."

Her sigh was loud enough for Charlie to hear. The door swung in slowly and both men came away from the wall. The door had not been locked.

Mrs. García was plump, dark-haired, sad-eyed. "He din' run," she said. "He came righ' home."

"Is he here now, ma'am?" Whitlock asked gently.

"It was an accident," she said. "Angel, he was defen' himself," she amended.

Neither Whitlock nor Charlie said anything.

"The man, he din' . . . die?"

"No, Mrs. García. He's still alive."

Mrs. García crossed herself. She called softly, "Angel, the police have come."

They stood in a small, pleasantly furnished living room which, Charlie saw, would have a view across the park to the river. A door beyond the sofa opened. Mrs. García said quickly, hopefully, "He's a good boy, he ain't in no trouble his whole life," and Angel García came out. He wore a jacket and a tie. His face was pale, his lips quivering. He looked at Whitlock and Charlie, took a deep breath and said, louder then he had intended: "Okay, I'm ready."

"Will he need anything?" Mrs. García asked. "Toothbrush, razor, you know. Maybe some sandwiches?" she asked, her voice breaking.

Whitlock said, "We'll take care of all that, Mrs. García."

They all waited an awkward moment. It was Angel García who went to the door and said, "Then Jesus, let's just get out of here, okay?"

Charlie touched the handcuffs clipped to his belt. Whitlock shook his head no, almost imperceptibly. Charlie went into the hall with Angel García, Whitlock a few steps behind them. Mrs. García waited in the doorway.

"I'll be all right, Mama. Don't worry."

The door didn't shut until they reached the stairs.

They went down and outside the same way, Charlie and Angel García together, Whitlock behind them. Charlie had to walk fast to keep up with Angel García, who had squared his shoulders and strode rapidly along the sidewalk.

Charlie had parked the patrol car under a street lamp. In the spill of light, two kids were standing alongside it, staring in at the dashboard. They looked up and backed off when they heard footsteps, and one of them said, "How do they work the siren? I can't see nothin' to work the siren with."

Something snapped in Charlie. The first instant he told himself it was like what had happened out on Laurel Drive, but he could control it, it was going to be all right, and the next instant he convinced himself it wasn't the same thing at all, it was different, these kids were trouble, you could see it on their goddamn spic faces under the street light, you could see it in their eyes, shifty-eyed bastards, the next thing he knew one of them would pull a knife or a gun or something and Whitlock wouldn't be ready for it.

"Okay!" Charlie shouted. "Hands flat against the roof of the car, both of you!"

They didn't move. He was aware of Whitlock coming up swiftly behind him and he said, "I told you hands against the roof of the car, then take two steps back and hold it. Now!"

"Hey, officer, we—"

"Move, goddamn you!"

They got into frisk position, as Charlie had commanded them, while Whitlock stood there with a perplexed look on his face. Charlie frisked the first one swiftly and felt the flat knife in his back pocket right away, only when he drew it out he discovered it wasn't a knife but a comb.

Which didn't stop him from swinging the kid around by one shoulder and slamming his fist in the kid's face, knocking his head back against the door of the car and drawing a cry from him as he slid to the sidewalk, where Charlie kicked him and kept on kicking him until he heard someone, it was Angel García, shout, "What's the matter, you crazy?" at the top of his voice while Charlie drew his revolver.

Angel García ran, and Charlie profiled and extended his arm, getting off one shot before Whitlock could grab his arm and twist it to one side.

Whitlock said something, his voice outraged. Charlie didn't hear what he said. He heard people shouting. A dozen men had gathered, more were running along the sidewalk. Charlie just stood there until Whitlock said, for his benefit and the benefit of the crowd, "Get in the cage, you stupid New York shit."

The rear door had been opened, and Charlie got in. The boy he had kicked was helped into the front seat while Whitlock spoke to the crowd or tried to speak to them while they shouted at Whitlock.

Whitlock got in and started the motor. Hands rocked the patrol car. It lurched away from the curb. Charlie heard a rock clang on the roof. He heard how the boy he had kicked was moaning.

Charlie started to cry.

15

Melody could hear their muted voices downstairs. She had waited a polite fifteen minutes after Eve returned, then excused herself. Oh, she thought now, Eve really wasn't so bad, it was just that she had a way of barging in at the wrong time, of intruding. Almost as if she were part of the family.

Melody wondered what it would be like to have Eve Talbot for a stepmother. Then she told herself that wasn't really important. The important thing was her father. If he married Eve, and if Eve made him happy, that was what mattered.

If.

Until tonight, Melody had regarded it as a distinct possibility. Now she wasn't so sure.

She had never seen her father so taken by anyone as by that Margriet Kelly. The way he kept looking at her, hanging on her every word—even Eve had noticed it.

Melody was pretty impressed by Margriet Kelly too. How a woman could dress like that, and wear her hair like that, and still make Eve Talbot look drab by comparison, Melody didn't understand, but she'd seen it with her own eyes.

Melody had instinctively liked and trusted Margriet Kelly until they'd talked about the painting. Melody's painting. They always want something, Melody thought now. Eve wants my father; Margriet Kelly wants my painting so she can study it and laugh at me like Monsieur Taitbout. Or would she laugh? She had sounded serious enough.

"Masterpieces have turned up in some pretty odd

141

places—a Fragonard in the flea market in Paris, a Rembrandt in a thatch-roofed cottage in England. So why not a Columbine here?"

Melody was almost tempted.

What if it really was real? As real as the notebook she held in her hands now?

It was still early. She'd have hours and hours with Jean-Baptiste Columbine tonight.

From the Notebook of Jean-Baptiste Columbine

I was free to come and go in the village, but I rarely ventured forth alone. It was as if Gaddara had *faé* me. (Bewitched?) I wanted to spend every waking moment with her, even if sometimes she terrified me.

I asked her once, after I had seen some of the things she could do, why one wished to be a practitioner of the black arts, a magician.

—To achieve power, she said. To achieve as much power over the universe as God has.

It did not sound blasphemous when she said it, or perhaps she had already taken me beyond such bourgeois ideas as blasphemy.

—Like a gypsy wise woman? I asked. Like Tita?

Gaddara laughed.

—Oh, Tita knows a few things I've taught her. But her magic is that of a child.

—I have seen her use toad amulets to heal a sick horse, I said. I have seen her find coins of gold given up for lost.

—And how did she do that?

I was trying to impress Gaddara. I hadn't actually seen that, but once Tita's cousin Kore had told me about it. I had not believed it then.

—She made a hole in the ground, at a crossroads, and she stole holy water from a church and poured it in the hole while she recited the Lord's Prayer backwards. Soon the coins appeared in the hole.

—Tita is a good pupil, Gaddara admitted. Holy water can have magic power. So can a crossing, and anything backwards or especially upside down. I taught her those things. But Tita does not possess the key to real power.

—Power to do what?

—Tita's husband Zurka died last night, Gaddara told me suddenly.

I stared at her. The caravan was long gone from the horse fair in Belgrade, well on the road to France.

—You couldn't know that, I protested.

—He was drunk, and he beat Tita, and soon after he beat her he had a seizure. I warned him. It happened while they were in camp outside Turin below the Alps. It is a simple matter to put a curse on a man if you have the key.

—It's a long way from here to Turin, I said.

—Distance is of no consequence, or time.

—What is the key? I asked her.

—You are not ready to understand that yet.

Still, I asked her to tell me.

—Very well. To use the strength of something you love against something you hate. Then there are no barriers to what you may accomplish.

—I don't understand.

—Perhaps it will help if I tell you what Zurka was doing when he had his fatal seizure. He was asleep, and dreaming. I had shamed him. You saw that. A man does not like being shamed by a woman. Tell me, what is the thing I like best in the world?

We had been three months together when she asked that. By then I knew. Not to know, I would have had to be an idiot. Sometimes Gaddara exhausted me.

I said, making love.

Gaddara laughed.

—Especially with my Frenchman, she said. As for Zurka, he dreamed he was violating me when he had his seizure and died.

That drew a laugh from me. I could not imagine any man violating Gaddara. To make love with her was to *margauder*. (Damn!) Gaddara was truly like a cat then, all claws and fangs and supple feline strength.

Often I wondered why she had chosen me. Even in our small village there were men who could satisfy her appetites more. I was no longer a virile youth, nor particularly strong, and I had but one arm.

—You have depths of feeling, she said. Of pain, of the pain that breeds a monstrous hatred. You have suffered.

—Is that what it takes to master the black arts?

—Who said you will master them?

—You're teaching me.

—It amuses me to teach you—some things.

I never learned where Gaddara came from. At first I thought her a gypsy, but she smiled when I told her that.

—I am to the gypsies, she said, as the gypsies are to the *gadje*.

A wainwright of the village with whom I had a slight acquaintance told me once that Gaddara just appeared one day, ten years before, alone, dressed in black, and riding a black horse. She came from the East. She rode the black horse straight to the gates of the one fine house in the village, and was admitted. A man named Boro lived there alone then. She stayed three nights with Boro, who owned much of the farmland around the village, and at the end of the three nights Boro was dead. Gaddara, her eyes bright, her cheeks rosy with health, emerged with the papers that deeded Boro's lands and house and servants to her.

The wainwright only spoke of this when he had much to drink, and even then he sounded afraid.

There was an ornate bronze knocker in the shape of a lion's head on the front gate. When Gaddara emerged with the papers—the wainwright swore to this—the lion's head was upside down. I believed him. It was what I would expect of Gaddara—the terrible power, and then the playful touch.

Gaddara spoke the language of Serbia fluently but with an accent. Her romani was the same, and sometimes she spoke French with me. I asked her if she had ever visited my country.

—Visited? In a manner of speaking.

I have seen her do things. *Mariole*! There came a time when I . . .

(Half a page missing.)

Once a tax collector came to the village from Belgrade. He was to stay two weeks and visit every house, every mud-brick hovel, no matter how mean, to adjudge the wealth of its owner and so levy a tax. The village had a bad harvest that year, Gaddara told me, and the villagers could afford to pay no taxes. Even so, the tax collector began his rounds. A deputation came to Gaddara, forgetting their fear of her in their greater fear of the tax collector, and asked for her help.

—His name is Boro, like the man who owned this house, she told me. That will make it easy.

I asked her why.

—To control a name is to have power over the thing the name stands for.

I did not understand, and she tried to explain.

—A name is a miniature image of a thing, and in the working of a curse it may be substituted for the thing itself. Why do you think the gypsies have secret names unknown to any but themselves? So no one can injure them by injuring their name. Why do you think the angel of God who wrestled with Jacob refused to reveal his name? Or the angel who visited Manoah, the father of Samson? Why do you think no child of a Jew is named for a living relative, why but that if the child owns the name the relative will die?

The name of the thing is the thing, Gaddara told me, but still I doubted.

She said, And what of God Himself? We know Him by the Tetragrammaton, the Hebrew letters YHVH. But that is no more than a form of 'to be.' It means that He exists. We pronounce it Jehovah, but that is not God's name, no more than Adonai is, or Elohim. The one means Lord, the other God. You see, even the God of the Hebrews and Christians feared to reveal His name.

Suddenly Gaddara smiled.

—Anyway, we shall use Boro's name against him. You and I.

I was afraid when she spoke those words. I? I echoed.

—Certainly. It will be easy, as you will be using something you love.

From somewhere she procured a lead tablet the size of a brick but flatter. She gave me a knife.

—Draw his name. Boro. Draw it in a way that I could not. Draw it beautifully.

I simply stared at her.

—You're an artist, aren't you?

I became more afraid. I said, This is your village, not mine.

—My village? It is no more my home than it is yours.

I hoped to divert her from what she had in mind. I asked, Why do you live here?

—It is neither East nor West. It is a crossroads, Jean-Baptiste. Now draw his name beautifully for me.

I scratched the name Boro onto the lead with the blade of the knife, indifferently.

—Anyone could do it that way, Gaddara scolded me.

So finally I scratched the name Boro in high Gothic style onto the lead tablet. Gaddara examined it and nodded. She brought a spade.

—Now we must dig a hole in the courtyard.

—A hole?

—You can understand French, can't you? A deep hole, to bury the tablet in.

She dug the hole that evening, while I watched. When she considered it deep enough, she said:

—Bury the tablet.

I did that, and Gaddara said: Now repeat these words after me. As this lead grows cold, so shall the blood of Boro.

I repeated the words, and Gaddara laughed.

—Don't just say the words, think them. Believe them.

—How will you know if I think them or not?

She patted my hand, whether condescendingly or reassuringly I could not tell.

—I will know.

She had me intone the words repeatedly while she stared into my eyes. Her own violet eyes grew large. They seemed to fill all space. I almost believed I could cast a spell. (She's hypnotizing him!)

I heard her chant: *By o pouro Del and o Bengh, by goodness and by evil, by love and by hatred, let it be so.* My own intonation rang in my ears, until suddenly she bade me stop.

—The thing is done, she said.

How else can I write this except to set down as simply as I can what happened? The next day on the outskirts of the village the tax collector Boro was bitten by a viper and died. The people buried him in an unmarked grave, and a deputation came to Gaddara again to thank her.

Later, when Belgrade sent someone to learn what had transpired, the people would tell him that Boro had come, had assessed, had left the village with the levied tax. Collectors had done that before, after all.

But had I really done anything? Vipers are not rare in the rocky hills above the village.

"Get out of here!" Melody shouted. "What are you doing here?"

She was still in the Notebook.

O pouro Del and o Bengh, goodness and evil, love and hatred, a lead tablet buried in the courtyard . . .

"Keep away from it! Don't touch it! What are you doing?"

A hand shook her shoulder. It was her father.

"Hey, take it easy, doll. I just wanted to kiss you goodnight."

Her voice sounded strange in her own ears. It was hard to focus her eyes. "I'm sorry, Daddy. I must have . . . drifted off. I was having a bad dream."

"What's that book there?"

She shut the Notebook. "About Columbine."

"That's some binding. You mean they had it in the library?"

"They . . . got it for me from the state library system."

He reached out for the book, but she drew it away. "I'm really zonked, Daddy."

That made the look of concern leave his face. He even smiled. "You're what?"

"Zonked. So sleepy I can hardly keep my eyes open."

She offered her cheek for his kiss. After he left, she locked the door and returned to the Notebook.

. . . dolls molded of melted candle wax, and nail parings or a hair from the victim's pubes. Then there was sickness, and sometimes death. Once for nine days, every day, I saw her water a branch of weeping willow and pour the water at night on the door of the victim's house.

I have seen her cause abortion with a brew of aloes, ginger, nutmeg, sage, rue, *grateron* (?), and other herbs, strained through the apron of a woman in her monthly time. I have watched her cure a festering wound with moldy bread crumbs. Or a headache with water from nine different places drunk from a phallus-shaped gourd while the Lord's Prayer was recited, not in Greek as they do it here, but in Latin.

I helped her collect the herbs, prepare the brews, find the springs of pure water.

She knew the name of every person in the village, and of his ancestors back to the fifth generation. Names are power, she told me often enough.

She would attempt no curse, no cure, without first making love with me.

But once I had spent the day high in the hills seeking *grateron* and other herbs, and when I returned, exhausted, I could not do as she wished. She looked at me contemptuously, and she was gone all the night.

For three days we did not speak. I thought she would send me away, and the thought was frightening. Where would I go, so far from the world I knew?

She read the thought in my eyes and said: Then don't fail me again, Jean-Baptiste. There is strength for me in the torment you have experienced.

—What torment? I asked her.

—Why, the rape and death of your wife and child, of course.

—*Mariole!* Do I talk of it in my sleep?

—No.

—Then how do you know of it?

—I know, she told me. But there is another here in the village who has known suffering. He experiences it vicariously, every day of his life.

This surely was the man she had gone to, and I had to ask the question.

—Who?

—Think, Jean-Baptiste. Who is it that experiences vicarious suffering?

I stared at her incredulously.

—That's right, the village priest, Father Vasili.

She looked into my eyes and laughed. He loved me for it, she said. O pouro del and o Bengh, both at the same time. There is power there for me. But it makes him hate me as well. O Bengh cannot exist for a priest of the Orthodox persuasion, or of your own for that matter.

I remembered Bourg St. Martin.

—If o Bengh is evil, I said, then it exists in every priest who ever lived!

—You are a great help to me in my work, Jean-Baptiste. And much safer than Father Vasili. One day the conflict in him will destroy his reason. He will try to kill me.

Shocked, I asked, her, What will you do?

Her face smiled, but not her violet eyes.

—Why, I shall kill him first, of course.

Melody shut both notebooks, Jean-Baptiste Columbine's and her own. Her hands were unsteady, her eyes gritty.

Had her father come in earlier? She thought he had, but wasn't sure.

She'd have to be careful with the Notebook. It was hers, like the painting, and nobody had any right to . . .

The painting. They had talked of taking it to the Armory, and she had almost agreed to that.

She got up quickly, and a wave of dizziness swept over her. She sat down on the edge of the bed. Her vision blurred. She thought she was going to faint.

When the dizziness left her, she tiptoed downstairs in the darkness. She was ravenously hungry. She went into the kitchen and opened the refrigerator.

It was dazzling white inside, the small bulb shining on bright beautiful cans of fruit juice, jars of jam, a container of milk, half a roast chicken—

She ripped off a chicken leg.

Mustn't.

Just one bite.

She had one bite, and another. Soon her teeth were scraping gristle and bone. She looked at the bare, naked bone in her hand, felt the greasiness on her lips. She thought she'd be sick.

Mustn't.

She went barefoot into the living room, turned on a small lamp. The painting was still there.

Did it look different?

That Monsieur Taitbout, insisting it wasn't old enough. Just look at those faded places. What were they called, pentimenti? Anybody could tell it was old enough. It takes years and years for the fading to happen.

Melody turned on another light. She felt better, the nausea gone.

The beggar in the foreground, huddled under a fold of St. Martin's cloak, didn't he look different? Younger?

Or the faded place near the gateway. Hadn't that changed too? Grown lighter, more transparent? Melody could almost see—could vaguely see—figures underneath, a painting under a painting.

Suddenly she felt a pang of sorrow. Matt Hawley—he was dead. Her father had told her. When? She didn't remember. She was vague lately. She lived for her nights with the Notebook.

Poor Matt Hawley. No matter what they said, it had to have been an accident.

Then Melody remembered how her father had turned the painting upside down the first night she'd hung it. A funny kind of joke. She wondered now why he'd done it.

16

Ned Revere caught a couple hours' sleep on a cot in the day room at police headquarters. He never could understand why it was called a day room. Like in the army. Well, it made a little more sense than in the army. In the army a company day room was, more or less, off limits during duty hours—meaning, mostly, during the day. Off duty, mostly at night, you could play cards in the day room, or shoot the breeze or some pool maybe, or watch TV. So why not call the damn thing the night room?

The force worked three eight-hour shifts in Martinsburg. Pretty standard, Revere thought. Eight to four, four to midnight, midnight to eight. There was a Ping-Pong table in the day room, a card table, a soft drink machine, some comfortable old chairs courtesy of the Elks Club, a few shelves of paperbound books, a color TV, three cots, and Revere's stereo set.

Sergeant Whitlock's call from Martinsburg General came in on Revere's private line, not through the switchboard. Switchboard personnel were civilian, not police, and Revere was inclined to think what they didn't know wouldn't hurt them.

"Ned," Sergeant Whitlock said, on the private line, "I don't know how to say this, but here goes. I'm at the hospital. We got a kid here named Herbert López. Seventeen. Fractured jaw, three broken ribs. Maybe he'll lose an eye."

Ned Revere said: "The García kid do that? I don't get it, Cal."

153

"Your goddamn New York hotshot did it. He knocked the López kid down and stomped him."

"Explain," Revere barked into the phone, and Whitlock explained, or tried to.

"It was like he was nuts or something. At first I figured what the hell, maybe he saw something I didn't see. By the time I realized he was off his nut, it was too late. I'm sorry, Ned."

"Where's Dahlgren now?"

Two patrolmen had arrived at the hospital with a D&D who'd put his hand through a plate-glass window. Whitlock had just sent Charlie Dahlgren back to headquarters with them.

"What about García?" Revere asked.

"When he saw what your boy was doing, he took off."

Ned Revere was seated at his desk sucking at a bottle of Tab and wishing it were Scotch when Charlie Dahlgren came in. He looked even younger than usual, his visored cap in his hand, his blond hair mussed, his fair complexion mottled. Revere thought he'd been crying.

Blame who—Charlie? Himself? Charlie had asked to be suspended.

"Sit down, kid. Tell me about it."

Charlie Dahlgren remained standing. He tried to talk but his voice caught and he began to sob.

"Pull yourself together," Revere said gruffly. "It's off the record. For now."

Comb his hair, straighten his shoulders, and Charlie would still look like one of those rookies on a TV cop show, straight out of the police academy.

"What did López do to make you act like that?" Revere asked.

Charlie blinked. "Who's López?"

"The kid. The kid you kicked."

"I couldn't stop myself," Charlie said. He was still sobbing.

Revere had harbored the faint hope that Whitlock had missed something, that even if he'd overreacted,

Charlie Dahlgren had been acting in self-defense. The hope vanished now.

"There was no provocation?"

"He was just standing there."

"Not even verbal provocation?" Revere asked. Give me something, kid, he pleaded silently. Give me something I can help you with.

Charlie shook his head. "It was just like out on Laurel all over again."

Ned Revere didn't know what to do. He'd never been faced with a cop who'd gone off his nut before.

The worst part of it was Charlie looked quite sane now. Broken up, sure, but sane.

"Listen, kid," Revere told him, "I want you to check into the hospital." Revere waited a moment. "Psychiatric ward," he said.

Dahlgren made a sound halfway between a sob and a laugh. "I hope they've got a padded cell."

"Go easy on yourself, kid. A nervous breakdown doesn't mean you're nuts."

"Sure, okay," Charlie said. "I'm not nuts. I just get this compulsion to shoot people, or kick them in the head. Jesus." He shook his head. "Lock me up and throw the key away, chief."

A few minutes later, two patrolmen drove Charlie back to the hospital. Revere called Dr. Tom and got the answering service. Dr. Tom was at the hospital, and Revere finally got through to him there. He explained the situation briefly, then said: "Way back, didn't you get a degree in psychiatry?"

"Studied it some. Don't practice it. Bunch of witchcraft. They have a resident in psychiatry, Ned. He'll run a battery of tests on young Dahlgren. I'll look in if you'd like."

"That's what I meant. I'm no more of a psychiatry buff than you are, Tom. Charlie's got no family here. He'll need all the sympathy he can get. You'll understand why when you see him."

"It's going to take a while," Dr. Tom said.

"What is?"

"Psychiatric evaluation. The resident—young fellow named Brooke—has his hands full."

"Yeah?" Revere asked. He wasn't really listening. He was thinking of what they'd hand him in the morning: a charge of police brutality for starters. He'd have to call Rob Garrick, ask him to play it down in the paper until they had time to evaluate Charlie's condition. Meanwhile, get a departmental investigation going. Whitlock's testimony and maybe get in touch with those people out on Laurel. Or maybe just Whitlock, leave well enough alone.

If the diagnosis was nervous breakdown or some kind of psychiatric disorder, maybe Charlie wouldn't face a criminal trial.

"—two days, at least," Dr. Tom was saying.

"Isn't that pretty long, Tom?"

"Ordinarily, yes. But the psychiatric ward's had fifteen commitments today. People committing themselves, or their families doing it. I doubt Brooke's had fifteen a month since he's been here."

"Well, I'd appreciate it if you could speed things up, Tom. Not just for the department, though I figure you can see the need there. But for Charlie. This is the second time he's gone off the deep end like that. He knocks an innocent kid down, kicks him in the head. No reason to. Then the compulsion, if that's what it is, leaves him and he stands there on the sidewalk looking down at the kid and crying. But I already explained that. He's pretty broken up."

There was a pause. Then Dr. Tom said, "That's odd. Those fifteen commitments I told you about, Ned. Except for the degree of violence, they followed the same pattern. An ungovernable impulse, what the French call a gratuitous act, and then the contrition. Your Officer Dahlgren wasn't the only one."

No more than Martinsburg was that kind of town, Ned Revere thought as he hung up. The pressures for a compulsion to do violence just weren't there.

Well, not normally. There were all those tourists now

and the inevitable increase in petty crime, like the trashing of Health Foods Unlimited or the nuisance that motorcycle gang was making out on the Strip. But that didn't account for everything.

Like the fight at Nick's. Revere had the preliminary report on that. Mauriello, in Martinsburg General now with a collapsed lung but, thank God, off the critical list, worked at Specialty Textiles. So did the kid García who'd knifed him. So did a girl named Corelli. Mauriello dated her, García dated her. Nothing serious. Maybe she slept with Mauriello, maybe she slept with García, these were pretty permissive times, there was no law against that. The two guys who'd come busting into Nick's with Mauriello were her brothers. They weren't drunk, but they'd been drinking. All of a sudden they didn't want a dirty spic making time with their sister.

They'd volunteered that information sheepishly to the desk sergeant fifteen minutes after the fight. Sheepishly because they didn't consider García a dirty spic. Until that afternoon García had been their friend as much as Mauriello.

Puerto Ricans up from New York had a good thing going for them in Martinsburg. It was a prosperous town, a growing town, and its older residents felt comfortable inside their own skins. The only large minority group was of Italian extraction, the children and grandchildren of Sicilian stonemasons who'd built the dam up Frenchman's Creek. They resolved their differences with those of English and French Huguenot stock, the original settlers, and with the Irish and Jews who had come later, at the ballot box, at the town meeting, at the P.T.A. They were accepted, and they treated the Puerto Ricans as those of English and Huguenot descent had treated them.

Martinsburg had an Episcopal church, a Baptist and a Methodist church, a Congregational church, a Catholic church, and a synagogue. There were no far-out groups to either initiate or attract religious strife.

People, Ned Revere thought, drifting at the edge of

sleep on a cot in the misnamed day room, the stereo
playing Mozart softly, got along with each other in
Martinsburg.

Then why had he used the words "race riot" earlier?
And why was he still thinking "race riot" now?

Almost as if he was hoping it would happen.

He didn't go home that night. He prowled headquarters—his own office, the muster room, the squad room,
the communications center. He went outside a couple of
times to walk briskly around the Commons through the
softly falling snow. His were the only footsteps.

Race riot, Ned Revere thought, shaking his head.
Not very goddamn likely in Martinsburg. But it didn't
have to be a race riot, did it? He could almost see the
crowds running wild in the streets, fighting, looting,
burning, as if Martinsburg had escaped too long what
had afflicted other cities in other times, other places,
like some kind of a medieval plague that moved relent-
lessly, unseen, across the countryside, the hills, the val-
leys, the rivers of France, from walled village to walled
village, leaving terror and death behind.

Funny damn thought. Well, Bourg St. Martin Month,
he told himself, and returned to the day room, where he
played Mozart louder, an old recording by Dennis
Brain of the Horn Concertos. He still felt restless.

"Everything okay, sarge?"

"No squawk for half an hour. Quite as a tomb."

The Jupiter Symphony, and that didn't help either.

"How's it going, sarge?"

"Pretty good night to catch up on your sleep."

Another turn around the Commons, through the
softly falling snow.

He glanced up at the high white spire of the Congregational Church and wondered what it would look like
burning.

A torch against the darkness, the frenzied shouting,
the wail and scream of sirens, and maybe Miles Pritchard trapped inside.

Jesus!

Ned Revere no longer wondered about Charlie Dahlgren's sanity.

He wondered about his own.

Dr. Tom was drinking a cup of coffee, smoking his green-briar pipe. He hadn't shaved yet, and the white stubble startled Garrick. It made Dr. Tom look ten years older. No, Garrick realized, it wasn't only that. Dr. Tom's face was drawn, his eyes dull. His hand shook slightly when he poured coffee from the silex.

"Hell of a night," he said. "A man my age can't keep those hours. Didn't get home from the hospital until four A.M. Psychiatric ward, believe it or not."

He told Garrick about the fifteen commitments. "Don't ask me to explain it," he said. "Don't ask me to explain anything right now. I can hardly keep my eyes open."

Garrick sipped his coffee. It was strong and black, and he needed it. He hadn't done much sleeping last night either.

The way Dr. Tom studied his face made Garrick wonder if he looked ten years older too.

"Melody?" the doctor asked.

Garrick nodded. "It was pretty late when I went upstairs last night. There was a light under her door. I knocked. No answer, so I went in. She was sitting up in bed, reading. I kissed her goodnight. Nothing."

"What do you mean, nothing?"

"She just sat there, went on reading."

"Must have been a pretty good book," Dr. Tom observed mildly.

"I shook her shoulder—no response. About ten seconds, and then she came out of it. Startled. She—this is hard to explain. You'd have to have seen her. She didn't recognize me. Her eyes looked strange. Empty is the only word I can think of. She did some shouting. Don't touch her, don't touch it, something like that."

"What did you do?"

"I didn't have time to do anything. Her eyes looked

normal suddenly and—" Garrick paused "—it was all right. She was Melody again."

"Has she been eating?"

"I thought I wasn't supposed to push that."

"That's right, you're not. But has she?"

"She's still losing weight," Garrick said. "She hasn't eaten a square meal in I don't know how long."

Dr. Tom tapped dottle from his pipe. "The word you used to describe her eyes. Empty. Would 'vague' do as well?"

Garrick thought a moment. "Maybe," he said.

"It's difficult for an anoretic to concentrate. It's difficult for anybody who's starving to concentrate. They become vague, light-headed. Eventually they hallucinate."

"Then what?"

Dr. Tom stuffed tobacco in his pipe, relit it. "They're pretty far along by then, Rob."

"You want to see her again?"

"No, I don't think so. Not yet. How's the girl friend?"

"She's in and out of the house as much as I am. No flareups with Melody, if that's what you mean."

"That's what I mean, and it's a shame there aren't. Be better if you could bring things out in the open. How are you on the generation gap, Rob?"

Garrick found himself smiling. "Once Melody had a party for some of her friends. We played an impromptu game for their benefit, just Melody and me. Arguing about politics, women's lib, communes, things like that. The other kids stayed out of it but even so we couldn't keep it up. Inside of five minutes Melody burst out laughing. I couldn't keep a straight face either."

"I'm not sure I follow," Dr. Tom said.

"We were playing what Melody called the Great Generation Gap Flap. It didn't work, Tom. No gap."

"That's typical too, I'm afraid. Harmony no matter what."

"It's not sweeping anything under the rug," Garrick said, remembering their last conversation. "It's just the way we are. What do you want me to do, invent conflict that isn't there?"

"There's always emotional conflict between parent and child, Rob. Stop playacting."

"Oh, Christ," Garrick said a little angrily, "that was just a game we—"

"Of course. Very civilized. Urbane. And just maybe, under the circumstances, the worst possible thing for Melody."

Garrick calmed down. He'd spent a lot of time away from Melody. How well did he really know her? Perhaps their impromptu game, so natural to him, had been a symptom of something he didn't quite understand. "What do you want me to do?"

"We'll give it a few more days."

"Then what?"

"Then we put her in the hospital and tell her she has to eat. There's a system of rewards, you see. She gets to watch TV, use the lounge, gets to have visitors, only if she does eat. But it doesn't work unless you root out the causes. We may have to try deep analysis." Dr. Tom shook his head, stood up. "Let's hope it doesn't come to that."

"It's crazy, Tom. She has everything to live for," Garrick said. "Except for that business last night, she's been happy and warm and—"

"I know," Dr. Tom cut him off. "They always are."

"Martinsburg Senior High School, good morning."

"Is this the high school?"

"Yes, sir."

"I'll say this once. There's a bomb in there. Set to go off in half an hour."

"What? Hello? Hello!"

The line was dead.

In moments the fire-drill bell sounded and the school's two thousand students were evacuated in a swift, orderly fashion, marching double file through the melting snow away from the low brick building.

Three police cars pulled up in front, followed by all the rolling stock of the Martinsburg Volunteer Fire Department. Police and firemen searched until the half-hour was almost up. Then they too withdrew.

They waited five minutes, then ten and fifteen. No bomb went off.

"Five minutes into the first period," Melody said. "What a weird time to pull a fire drill, you know?"

Craig squinted at her. The snow-reflected sunlight dazzled his eyes. "That's the whole point," he said. "You never know when a fire's going to break out."

Craig had called from a phone booth in the high-school lobby. He thought that was pretty funny. Poe's purloined letter.

That, and the Boy Who Cried Wolf.

Call two, three more places. The Martinsburg Department Store, maybe Nick's. The textile mill, or even the bank. All false alarms, and pretty soon they'd have to decide it was some kind of a harmless crank.

His father was removing stumps, preparing part of the wood lot behind the big house out on Conant for some gentleman farming.

To blow the stumps his father was using dynamite.

Craig wondered whether he would really use some himself. That was part of the fun, not knowing yet.

Painting

the M   rg News. A   administered
e of mo   sulphate last night claimed the life

17

From the Notebook of Jean-Baptiste Columbine

. . . a bright day, and hot, the leaves of the olive trees stirred by no wind, the donkey carts dragging dust along the road, the brown and black goats, their udders swollen, seeking shade wherever they could find it, the wife of the wainwright seated in the shadow cast by their hut, nursing her child.

I found a stick of charcoal and a flat board, and began to sketch. A few lines, a smudge, a few more lines. My fingers were stiff, so stiff, as if I had never held charcoal before, never done a preliminary sketch.

The wainwright came to watch. A line here and there, another smudge—they meant nothing to him at first.

But soon my fingers began to remember. I had the likeness of it, the angle of the mud-brick wall, the woman, the suckling child.

I had them, and they were no longer there for me. They were on the board, where I had given them a different kind of life. Only the board was real.

The wainwright began to shout at me, and made the sign against the evil eye.

Then he took the board in his two hands, and broke it across his knee. He broke the pieces of it. In a frenzy he smashed the wood against a rock. He was panting, sweating. When he looked at me as he had at the charcoal sketch of his wife and child, I fled.

The incident amused Gaddara.

—Well, what did you expect? she asked me. To them

163

it is magic, black magic no different from the arts I practice. A likeness of his wife takes something away from her, part of herself. He believes that gives you power over her, as a gypsy would believe you have power over him if you learn his secret name. He believed you could use the picture like an image made from melted candle wax, to cast a spell, Jean-Baptiste.

I laughed.

—You don't believe that.

—No, it is a more subtle thing. But then so is the use of melted wax, or a lead plate, as you have seen. He believed the picture would give you dominance over his wife. He won't permit that. He would kill you first.

—I want to paint, I told her. I have to paint again.

—Naturally, Jean-Baptiste. It is the thing you love most. Paint the olive groves, paint the hills and the hovels of the village. Paint the goats foraging on the edge of a dry riverbed. Dominate them and no one will object. Where will you find paints to use?

I told her I would find them. I knew then that I had to, and so did Gaddara.

(A few lines missing.)

. . . inorganic pigments were the simplest to find. Red and yellow ochre, and *terre verte*. Olive oil, even a first pressing, would make the pigments muddy, but would still suffice. As for the organic pigments, rose madder was no problem, nor buckthorn. The plants grew in clefts on the steep hillsides above the village. I almost wept when I found azurite, which would substitute for lapis lazuli.

All that hot summer I was gone with the rising sun and returned exhausted at nightfall with my treasures. I believe the villagers thought me insane.

I went to work with mortar and pestle. Goat hair, I hoped, would prove adequate for brushes.

—You look like a gypsy among gypsies, Jean-Baptiste. The sun has burned you black.

I barely heard Gaddara's words.

—You're happy, Jean-Baptiste.

I heard that. It was as if she had scolded me.

—The torment, the suffering have gone from you.

So consumed was I with my activities that Gaddara and I had not slept together for weeks.

Still, she looked satisfied, like a cat licking clean a bowl of cream.

When all three of them could make it, Garrick had lunch on Thursdays at Nick's with Dr. Tom and Miles Pritchard. Pritchard, minister of the Congregational Church, was a few years older than Garrick, and almost as tall. With his craggy good looks and trim, athletic build, he could be taken for a football or basketball coach rather than a minister.

Dr. Tom's wryly cynical approach to the world was a good foil for Miles Pritchard's relentless optimism, and Garrick ordinarily looked forward to their weekly lunches. Today he'd almost begged off. Melody had been worse this morning, vague and listless until he'd mentioned the painting. She'd complained of a sore throat, hadn't dressed for school.

Garrick had wanted to say, almost had said, "Well, what do you expect, letting yourself run down like that?" What he'd told her instead was: "Okay, doll. The rest'll do you good."

"I don't need any rest. I just have a sore throat, that's all. I'm not tired or anything." Melody's voice had taken on an uncharacteristic whining note. "It's going around. Everybody has it."

"Miss Kelly called me about the painting yesterday."

"I changed my mind," Melody said.

"How'll you find out if it's a genuine Columbine unless you—"

"I don't care. I found it. It's mine."

Eve came downstairs and into the kitchen. She glanced at Melody, then at Garrick, concern in her eyes.

"How would you like to go on television?" she asked Melody.

"Me?"

"I heard what Rob was saying. Even if the painting

doesn't turn out to be genuine, there's still the odd way you found it, the mystery of how it got there."

"It is so genuine!" Melody cried.

"Why don't you let Miss Kelly find out for sure?" Garrick suggested.

"It would be a big help to me," Eve said. "Just what I need to round out the program."

"I don't want to talk about it anymore," Melody told her. "I'm going back to bed."

"Did it ever occur to you, young lady," Garrick said, "that you have a responsibility to find out if that painting's real?"

"I said I don't want to talk about it."

"I think we ought to."

"Talk to Eve then," Melody said rudely, "not me." She stood up. "I'm sorry, Daddy. Blame it on my sore throat, okay?"

"Okay." Garrick felt her forehead; she had no fever. He watched her slouch out of the kitchen and looked at Eve, shaking his head.

Now at Nick's he joined Miles Pritchard at their usual table in the rear. "They make the best martini in town here," Pritchard said, sipping from his old-fashioned glass. "Every man of the cloth ought to have a secret vice." Pritchard had a deep voice and a contagious bonhomie. "What's yours, Rob?"

"Vice or drink? I'll have a Scotch and soda, please," he told the waiter.

"Tom called. He'll be late."

"He's been working too hard," Garrick said.

"Doesn't he always?" Pritchard shrugged. Off duty— he referred to it as off duty—he affected mod clothing. Today he wore a British delta jacket in a bright plaid and a darker shirt open at the collar. "The last of the old style GP's. And standing room at the psychiatric ward doesn't exactly help. Fifteen commitments—no, sixteen, if you count that young policeman."

"Who told you about him, Miles?"

"Ned did. We had a long talk, Ned and I," Pritchard

said. "My idea, after that obfuscation you passed off as a newspaper story."

"That's the way Ned wanted it." Garrick's drink came, and so did Dr. Tom.

"Just a tomato juice," he told the waiter. He couldn't keep his hands still. He moved his plate an inch or so closer to the edge of the table, then back; he rearranged the silverware, picked up and unfolded his napkin, then folded it and put it back on the table. He tugged at his collar. The flesh of his throat was flabby, wrinkled. I wasn't imagining it, Garrick thought. He's aged ten years.

"How's that blond beauty of yours?" Dr. Tom asked.

Garrick didn't want to bother him with it now. "No real change," he said. "She had a little to eat this morning."

Dr. Tom moved his plate again, an inch or so to the left, then back. "Four more commitments yesterday," he said, his voice flat. "And three so far today. Not to mention another call by that false-alarm bomber, but I imagine you know that."

Garrick nodded. The call had gone to the Martinsburg Department Store. It had been evacuated. There had been no bomb.

"There's someone who *ought* to be committed," Dr. Tom said. "If they can find him."

"Meaning the others shouldn't have been?" Garrick asked.

"You tell me. We have a preliminary evaluation of the Rorschachs, the TAT's. Try this for a composite of the patients: Without any warning, no history of any neurosis, they feel impelled to do something they find totally reprehensible. Here's an example. Housewife. Three children, happy marriage, never any trouble. She's in the kitchen carving a roast, and her husband comes in. She wants to use the knife on him. No reason whatever, and of course everything in her fights against the compulsion. She can't cope with it, becomes hysterical.

"Some of them go further, act out their compulsions. Dahlgren's an example of that. Or get this one: a professional man, young, family-oriented, child-oriented, and he doesn't just read Spock, he reads Piaget. He comes home from work and with no provocation beats his children. Really beats them. And he's not the only one to get that violent. Until we went over the tests, it looked like we had an epidemic of psychos on our hands."

"But what did the tests show?" Garrick asked.

"I'm getting to that. The Rorschach and TAT are statistically reliable, both for psychosis and neurosis. There were no psychotics in the group, not even incipiently. Neurosis—well, that's more of a gray area, but even there nothing really showed up. Of course there were the usual mild neurotic responses, but no more than you'd find in any group selected at random. Our composite is a more or less normal individual who, without any motivation, was compelled to the one type of behavior he ordinarily would have found totally unthinkable. As if you, Miles, were to wake up tomorrow morning and know with absolute certainty that you no longer believed in God."

"I think I see what you mean," Pritchard said. "As if you, Tom, were to decide that killing your patients, not curing them, was your real vocation."

The waiter appeared with menus, startling Dr. Tom. His pipe dropped with a clatter on the plate, dottle and sparks scattering on the tablecloth. He brushed at them awkwardly, his hands unsteady, and pushed his chair back. "Little boys' room," he mumbled, and hurried off. His face was shiny with sweat.

Garrick finished his Scotch. After a while he said: "Are you thinking what I'm thinking? I'm worried about him."

"Well, he's been under a strain. And he's not exactly young, after all."

Garrick shook his head. "A man doesn't change like that overnight, not someone like Dr. Tom. All of a sudden he's a nervous wreck."

Pritchard, as ever, was optimistic. "Nothing that a good night's sleep wouldn't . . . here he comes."

Dr. Tom returned, striding almost jauntily. His eyes were brighter, the expression on his face relaxed. He sat, picked up his menu. "What's Nick's favorite poison today?" he said.

He had been gone less than five minutes. The change was startling.

After they ordered, he said: "Luncheon crowd's dull today, isn't it? Just take a look at them, will you? Grim sons of bitches. Know what I think?" Dr. Tom's voice was light, almost jocular. "Those psychiatric commitments are only the tip of the iceberg. Nervous breakdown's becoming endemic in Martinsburg. Did I order the chicken or the veal?"

Conversation was desultory after that and Garrick became aware with a sense of shock that Dr. Tom couldn't hold up his end of what there was of it.

If he didn't know his friend better, he would have thought Dr. Tom was high on something.

Melody stood nude in front of the mirror, hands on hips, breathing deeply, sucking her belly in. Not that she had to. It was board-flat, beautiful. She could feel the sharpness of her hipbones, the skin drawn taut over them. Not a trace of fat on her ribs. That made her small, high breasts stand out too much, and she wished they were smaller still. But she couldn't help that. Her legs were good. Really neat. Not an extra ounce of flesh on them. Were her knees too bony? No, not exactly. She turned in a slow half-pirouette. It depended on the angle. Same as her face did. Look at those dark sexy hollows. You're a regular femme fatale, Melody Garrick.

A little weak, though, and if you stand up suddenly the room goes around and around and you see those black spots.

You don't really have a sore throat. Oh, maybe a scratch and a tickle, that's all. It doesn't even hurt when you swallow, does it? Who are you kidding?

Well, you don't have to go to school *every* day, do you? What's more important anyway, trigonometry or Jean-Baptiste Columbine?

Melody admired her slenderness once more, making a full pirouette before the mirror. She got back into her warm pajamas. She had to draw the string so tight it made the flannel bunch up in front.

You *are* hungry.

You are *not!*

She opened the notebook. Just touching its pages made her feel better, the weakness and dizziness gone.

A few days after I had finished grinding the pigments, I went into the courtyard to draw water from the well and found Gaddara nude on the hard stones under the bright sunlight, in a trance.

I have already written of how sometimes prior to practicing her arts she would go into a trance and seem as one dead. (It must have been some of those missing sections. When the tax collector was killed, maybe?) Often I asked her the reason for this, but she always put me off, saying it was beyond my comprehension.

In the courtyard she was on her knees, resting back on her heels, her spine rigid, her hands on her thighs, her bare breasts high, the column of her throat arched so that her head was back, her sightless eyes staring up at the sky.

Though I had seen her like that before, I had never remained to see what might transpire. But I had grown bold in her company, and this time I waited. I touched the bare skin of her shoulder. The sun had warmed it. The flesh was rigid. I could see no sign of her breathing and for a moment grew alarmed. But I placed my hand on her breast and could feel the slow strong beat of her heart. Still I waited, while the afternoon shadows lengthened across the courtyard. I could hear the sounds of the village beyond the walls—the bray of a donkey, a man's shout, the rumble of cart wheels. In late afternoon a wind sprang up and clouds rushed overhead to obscure the sun. Thunder rumbled far off. The storm came quickly, the rain driving down in sheets, but still Gaddara kneeled there, unmoving. She might as well have been carved from stone.

Shortly before dusk her head slumped, the rigidity left her back, she rocked forward off her heels and opened her dark eyes. The rain had stopped, the air smelled sweet, but she looked at me with anger.

—How long have you been here?

—Most of the afternoon, I admitted.

—I am vulnerable like that. The gate is closed, the villagers would not dare enter here, but you . . .

—I will never harm you, Gaddara, I said.

Slowly the anger left her.

—No, you wouldn't.

—Could you teach me to do that?

She asked me to fetch her robe. When I had done so, she asked:

—And what would you do when you left your terrestrial body?

—Whatever it is that you do, I said boldly.

She laughed.

—It is no simple thing, Jean-Baptiste. I enter my astral body to travel along the paths of the Tree of Life. I enter my astral body to attain power, to use that power.

—Use it for what? I asked.

—How do you think I knew of Zurka's death?

Zurka, I remembered, had died in far-off Turin.

—You were there? I gasped.

—In a manner of speaking. Gaddara patted my arm, a gesture both patronizing and reassuring. Very well, Jean-Baptiste, she said. If you really want to learn, it will amuse me to teach you.

So for a time my laboriously gathered pigments were forgotten, and I became her pupil as I had never been before.

To begin, she brought some twigs of thyme, fresh from the hillside. She held them under my nose, asked me to breathe deeply.

—You like the scent? Concentrate on it to the exclusion of all else. The scent of thyme, the feel of velvet, the shape of a wheel, of a triangle, it does not matter. You must concentrate on it and make all else go away.

I tried, that day and the next, for hours at a time. But still I heard the sounds of the village and saw clouds drifting across the sky.

Gaddara was patient with me. On the third day she led me out to the courtyard.

—Remove your clothing. It encumbers you.

When I had stripped, Gaddara commanded me to stand on one foot, my right foot, holding my left ankle with my hand. In moments I lost my balance and tumbled awkwardly to the ground.

—You must learn to do that for hours on end. Think of a word, Jean-Baptiste.

—What word?

—Any word you wish. Think of it to the exclusion of all else, like smelling the thyme.

I looked at Gaddara and selected the word *margauder*. Her smile was patronizing.

—No, that won't do. It means you are thinking of my body, desiring it, concerning yourself with an external thing.

I selected the word *priest*.

—Are you jealous, Jean-Baptiste? That won't do either.

So finally I selected the word *stone,* and to that Gaddara had no objections.

—Now think of stone. Not just any stone, but the essence of stone. To the exclusion of all else. And, when you achieve that, stop thinking of it.

—And think of what?

—Nothing, Gaddara said. Absolutely nothing.

I could not do that, no more than I could make the scent of thyme obscure the world. But as the days passed I acquired a little of Gaddara's ability. A time came when the scent of the herb was overpowering and made my vision blur. A time came when I could stand like a stork for hours all through the heat of the afternoon. A time came when I could concentrate on the thought of stone almost to the exclusion of all else.

—Are you hungry? Gaddara asked me.

I said no, I was not hungry.

—That is a good thing. To submit to the cravings of the terrestrial body is a weakness. The astral body has no cravings.

A month after Gaddara began her tutelage of me in earnest, I could fall to my knees, sit back on my heels and sleep without really sleeping, the scent of thyme filling the world though no thyme was there. A month after that, I felt a wrenching shudder pass through my body, and for the smallest of instants I imagined I stood to one side and saw myself kneeling on the stones of the courtyard. When it passed I was trembling and bathed in sweat.

—You went out, Gaddara told me.

I nodded mutely.

—What did you see?

—Myself.

—A time will come when you will see other things.

Days I practiced the exercises Gaddara taught me. Nights she discussed the touchstones of her magic. Of the use of names I already knew, and of objects like a doll of melted candle wax or a lead tablet. How could I forget the tax collector Boro?

—That is sympathetic magic, Gaddara told me. It depends for power on the duality of things—the use of something you love to destroy something you hate. Everywhere there exists duality, you understand that, Jean-Baptiste?

I said no, I did not understand.

Gaddara explained: You already know of o Del and o Bengh, the forces of good and evil, the two Gods who contend for power over the world. There are lower manifestations of them to be found on the paths of the Tree of Life. These you must learn to control. They will give you power to change the world, a power as real as this house, or this village . . . as real as your hatred for the Sieur de Ramezay.

—How do you know that name? I cried.

Gaddara laughed harshly, and her face seemed almost ugly then.

—To have power over you I must have power of what you hate as well as what you love. And what is it that you love, Jean-Baptiste?

—You know that. My work. My painting.

Gaddara spoke no more of the duality of the world that night.

I have arranged for you to meet with Father Vasili, she told me.

—Why? I asked.

—The church needs a new icon. You will paint it for him.

I merely stared at her.

—Do you understand, Jean-Baptiste?

—No.

—Father Vasili's guilt will destroy him, or it will destroy me. Need I tell you my preference?

18

A pianist was playing a melody of old fifties tunes in the almost empty cocktail lounge of the Martinsburg Motor Lodge when Garrick got there.

"Sorry I'm late," he said, slipping into the booth.

"I half expected you would be. Out of character for a newspaperman to be on time." Margriet Kelly smiled. "Isn't there always a last-minute story?"

"Something like that," Garrick told her.

He ordered Scotch on the rocks for both of them.

"Not exactly standing room only," Margriet said, looking around the almost deserted cocktail lounge.

"Well, sure. There were two more bomb scares this afternoon, one of them right here. It sort of puts a damper on the festivities, even though by now the police are convinced it's just a harmless crank."

Their drinks came, and Garrick raised his old-fashioned glass. "To the girl with the odd name," he said lightly.

"It really isn't so odd. Kelly's about as ordinary as you can get. The Margriet part's Dutch. One of the routes the Huguenots took back in—what, the seventeenth century?—was France to Holland to Ireland to the colonies. So I have a Dutch first name. It's been in the family for ages."

Her voice was throaty, the way it had been when she'd seen the painting. Her jet-black hair hung free to her shoulders, framing her fine-boned face, giving her violet eyes an exotic look. Garrick wondered again how he had ever found her dowdy.

"You knew Martinsburg was settled by Huguenots, didn't you?" he asked.

"It's just about all I've been hearing—Bourg St. Martin Month."

"Things going okay with Taitbout?" Garrick asked.

"Well, under the circumstances it hardly matters. No more tourists to speak of. But he had no objection to your compromise. Anyway, he'll be leaving in a day or so."

"He will?"

"You haven't seen him lately, have you? He looks awful. His liver, he says. I think the problem's really me."

"You? It was his idea to call you in the first place."

"Oh, let's say we have some basic differences about art conservation. Which brings me to the point, Rob. I have to get my hands on that painting in your house. That's what I wanted to see you about."

The cocktail pianist bowed off with a small frozen smile, and Muzak replaced her.

"Did you get a chance to talk to Taitbout about it?" Garrick asked.

"I didn't see any point in it."

"He's convinced it's a forgery, you know."

"You told me. I'm convinced he's wrong."

"Then tell me how it got here."

"Why don't *you* tell *me*?"

Garrick did.

"That doesn't make any sense at all," Margriet said impatiently. "Paintings just don't turn up in ditches alongside highways in Connecticut or—what's the matter? You look upset."

Garrick finished the rest of his drink. He knew what he wanted to say, and it made him feel foolish. But it was Margriet Kelly's line of work, wasn't it?

"Where it turned up isn't the only thing that doesn't make any sense. There's something weird about that painting."

"What do you mean, weird?"

Garrick said nothing for a moment. How would she react? A condescending smile? The suggestion that he'd been working too hard?

"Well, let's say Columbine, or the forger, or whoever it was—"

"It's Columbine's 'St. Martin.' It's no forgery."

"Let's say it's a painting over a painting, whoever painted it, okay?"

"Sure, that's common enough. And I did see one obvious pentimento and another faint one."

Garrick said, "They weren't there when I first saw the painting."

"That's impossible. It doesn't happen overnight, it takes years, centuries. Did Taitbout clean it or anything? Sometimes cleaning lightens the darkened overpaint, and you can see what's underneath."

"He didn't clean it," Garrick said. "But I saw it, I'm telling you."

For an instant Margriet looked almost prim, as he'd first seen her. "There's no way that could happen."

Well, Garrick thought, no condescending smile, anyway, no suggestion that he'd been working too hard.

"I'm sorry, Rob. I didn't mean to snap at you. There's got to be some explanation. The most obvious one is that you're mistaken, that's all."

Garrick decided that since he'd gone this far he might as well let her have the rest of it. "Then there's the expression on St. Martin's face," he said.

That seemed to surprise her. "Have you seen Vouet's sketch of the painting? You know more about it than I thought. The face of St. Martin troubled me too. Everything about the canvas is authentic Columbine, except for that. Of course Columbine could have changed his mind after making his preliminary sketch. And even that no longer exists. All we have is the copy made by his friend Denis Vouet. Vouet was a kind of sounding board for Columbine in his later years when he got interested in black magic."

"I didn't know he was."

"Oh, sure. It's well documented. In fact, a letter Columbine wrote to Vouet establishes the age of a *grimoire* originally thought to have been compiled later."

"You lost me there," Garrick said. "What's a *grimoire*?"

"A handbook for sorcerers, witches. Magicians. And I don't mean the kind who pull rabbits out of hats. Black magic was no laughing matter in Columbine's day. Anyway, the *grimoire* is called the *Black Pullet*. At first scholars thought it was written in Egypt in 1740, then they decided it probably wasn't compiled until at least twenty years later, and in France. And then a mention of it turned up in a letter to Vouet, the only authenticated Columbine letter we have, dated 1698. Which makes the *Black Pullet* much older than anyone thought."

The tract on black magic interested Garrick less than the painting. "You said everything about the canvas was Columbine except St. Martin's face. What's wrong with it?"

"It's not at all like Vouet's copy of the sketch. But as I said, Columbine could have changed his original concept. Or the fault could have been Vouet's. In the sketch St. Martin's all arrogance, almost a classic study in arrogance. And you've seen the painting. How would you describe the expression on his face in the painting?"

Garrick shook his head. "You tell me," he said.

Margriet told him. "St. Martin looks scared out of his wits."

From the Notebook of Jean-Baptiste Columbine

. . . is perhaps a measure of the evil of religion that the Catholic faith of the West and the Orthodox faith of the East could consider each other *escomenjableté* (oh well, here we go again) on the basis of a difference in doctrine which affects neither the goodness, nor the love, nor even the omnipotence of God in the slightest. Rome maintains that the Holy Ghost rises from God the Father and the Son, the metropolitans in Moscow insist the Holy Ghost rises from the Father but *through* the Son. The distinction is minimal, yet neither can peel the other's chestnut. (??) When I mentioned this to Gaddara she asked me:

—And which do you Huguenots believe?

—I am a Huguenot no longer. I believe in nothing, least of all a God who is goodness and love.

—Then it will be no problem for you to do what I wish, Jean-Baptiste.

Father Vasili was a plump, black-bearded, illiterate little man whose wife—unlike Catholic priests, those of the Orthodox faith must marry—was the most superstitious member of his flock. It was nothing for her to repeat a short prayer five or six hundred times a day, like a magic incantation, fingering her rosary all the while. As for Father Vasili himself, he followed Gaddara about the village like a dog its master, his deep-set eyes never leaving her.

But the expression in those eyes was not simple lust. They burned with hatred too. Whether this was because Gaddara had begun to repulse him or because he was ridden with guilt for coupling with her, I never learned.

When I asked Gaddara, she merely said:

—That filthy beard, and the stink of garlic, and the way he ogles me in the streets or brushes against young girls when he can! Tell me, Jean-Baptiste, are all priests *rokerels*? (A guess: dirty old men?)

In the small domed church of the village was an icon painted on wood depicting the entry of Christ into Jerusalem. Father Vasili claimed it had been done by a monk from distant Novgorod generations ago. The varnish was so dark it was almost black, and deep cracks marred the paint.

—The woman who lives in Boro's house tells me you are a painter, Father Vasili said one day.

By then I had some success in speaking and understanding the language of the village. I had been commiserating with the priest on the sorry state of the cracked, blackened icon. Father Vasili, strangely, showed no hostility to me. Perhaps he thought I had lost my manhood with my arm. He did not suspect I was both lover and apprentice to Gaddara. Besides, he assumed I was a heretic of the Roman persuasion, and he was fishing for my soul.

—We could not pay you much. We are a poor village. What you do you would be doing for the love of God.

We haggled about the price, because haggling was the accepted thing in the village.

—Then it is agreed?

I said it was agreed, and Father Vasili's yellow teeth smiled through his beard.

—My right eye will see a masterpiece, I am sure, he said.

It seemed a strange way to say it. Your right eye? I asked.

—I was injured when I was a child. There is no vision in my left eye.

We decided that I would paint an icon of the Crown of Thorns, and I returned home to tell Gaddara.

—The Crown of Thorns will do as well as anything, Jean-Baptiste. It is the other painting that matters.

—I am to do two paintings for the icon?

—One for the icon, and one hidden underneath.

Then Gaddara asked an odd question:

—What do you know of the Black Mass, Jean-Baptiste?

From habit, I almost crossed myself. Then I shrugged.

—What everyone else knows. It is a mockery of Holy Mass.

—Beneath the icon of the Crown of Thorns you will paint Father Vasili celebrating a Black Mass.

Melody slipped a bookmark between the fragile pages and hurried to the extension phone in her father's bedroom.

"Hello?"

"Melody?" She didn't recognize his voice at first, he sounded so subdued. "This is Charlie Dahlgren."

"Oh, hi, Charlie."

"Look, is your father home?"

Melody glanced at the clock on the dresser. It was almost seven. "He said he wouldn't be home for dinner. Did you try the paper?"

"He isn't there. Could you have him call me when he gets in? I'll be home."

Melody vaguely remembered reading about Charlie in the paper. He was in some kind of trouble, but she couldn't recall what it was.

"I'll tell him, Charlie. What's the matter, anyway? You sound funny."

"There's something I've got to talk to your dad about, that's all," Charlie said. "Well, take it easy, kid."

"Yeah, you too, Charlie. S'long."

"So long."

Charlie Dahlgren rented the second floor of a two-family white clapboard house on Bank Street. There was a plaque out front from the Historical Society that said the house had been built in 1760. Charlie had been lucky to get the upstairs apartment with its sloping, beamed ceilings, leaded-glass windows, and living-room fireplace.

Charlie hung up the phone, not feeling lucky now. At the hospital he'd told Dr. Tom Seymour all the things he saw in those inkblots, and he made up stories about the pictures in the other test, the TAT, and a young doctor named Brooke had tried word association on him. After two days they said he could leave, and Ned Revere took him back to police headquarters and arrested him, then said, "All right, get out of here. I talked the judge into releasing you on your own recognizance. Don't make me regret it, Charlie."

Now Charlie sat in the living room, shoes off, feet up, sipping a strong bourbon and water and, despite Dr. Tom's assurances to the contrary, convinced he was going crazy.

Maybe he shouldn't have talked to those other guys in the hospital. Three of them had shared a room with

him. They'd taken the same tests he'd taken, and since
they'd been released when he was, he figured they'd got
the same clean bill of health. Well, all but one. A guy
named Huntington, a vice-president at the textile mill,
and when they told him he could leave he broke down
and started in screaming, so they let him stay. The others left, same as Charlie.

All of them had these crazy impulses, but unlike him
they'd stopped short of acting on them. They'd even
been able to joke about it a little, or say it was strain,
the pressures of their jobs.

None of them had kicked a Puerto Rican kid in the
head for no goddamn reason at all.

I'll do something like it again, Charlie had kept telling himself in the hospital. I know I will, what's the
matter with them and their stupid tests, anyway?

The vice-president from the textile mill kept screaming about the bells. He heard bells like church bells
ringing somewhere, except that they were inside his
head. The others had looked at one another anxiously.
Charlie didn't know if they heard the bells or not; they
never said.

Now he gulped at his bourbon. When he let his mind
sort of slide away from him, he was sure he could
hear—well, something. Would he have thought of bells,
except for the textile mill vice-president?

There was just this noise inside his head when he let
his mind wander. A sort of flat, metallic click repeated
over and over, faint and far away yet deep inside him.
A bell without any resonance?

Something. Some goddamn thing, and it was driving
him nuts. That and the certainty that he would do
something violent again.

Leaving headquarters, he'd thought of going over to
Dr. Tom's, but didn't. In the first place, he couldn't just
walk in and tell Dr. Tom he was hearing things, and
was scared because of what he knew would happen
when he didn't know what it was, only that it would be
bad. And besides, there was Dr. Tom himself.

There wasn't anyone in town he respected more than Dr. Tom. So it didn't make sense. A guy nearing seventy, an M.D., almost as much a landmark in town as this house with its bronze plaque from the Historical Society. Charlie had seen him on and off two days in the hospital, and he knew the symptoms because he'd seen enough of them in New York.

Mainlining symptoms. Dr. Tom was shooting horse, Charlie was sure of it.

He'd wrestled with that one a while, and then he'd called the Garrick house. Maybe just a little suggestion that Garrick ought to look in on Dr. Tom, let Garrick take it from there. He'd know how to handle it. Only Garrick hadn't been home.

Charlie winced and put his hands over his ears. The fucking bells again.

Then he realized just how close to the breaking point he'd come. It was only the doorbell.

He thought he recognized the redhead from somewhere. Pretty, with a snub nose, green eyes, freckles.

"Mr. Dahlgren? Or do you prefer Officer Dahlgren?"

The moment he heard her voice he knew who she was. He'd seen the Continental Broadcasting truck in town, seen the TV crew shooting all over the place.

"They suspended me, Miss Talbot," he said, managing half a smile. "But I sure would prefer it."

"Can I come in and talk?"

She had an easy, relaxed way about her, just like she did on TV. But still Charlie hesitated. She was a professional, and once she started asking questions, Charlie knew he wouldn't be able to stop talking. It would all come spilling out of him, and he wasn't sure he wanted that.

He said, "If it's about the trouble I—"

"It's about Martinsburg," Eve said. "Not just you. Do I really have to stand out here on the landing, Mr. Dahlgren?"

He returned her smile and said, "What the hell, make it Charlie and come on in."

They sat in facing wing chairs in front of the fire-place. She declined a drink. "But you go ahead," she told him.

He refilled his glass, heavy on the bourbon, a splash of water, and sat down again. He felt uncomfortable when, instead of firing a salvo of questions at him, she said, "This is a nice place you have here."

"Look," he said defensively, "let's get this part of it over with. I guess you know what I did. Right? And you want to know why I did it. Well, believe it or not, I just don't know."

"Oh, I believe you, Charlie," Eve said, no longer smiling. "I spent the afternoon interviewing a few people who got out of the hospital when you did. They made me start wondering."

"Yeah? What about?" Charlie asked.

"About those who never went to the hospital."

"I don't get you."

"Look, you're from New York, aren't you? Then picture this. It's night, a deserted street in a bad neighborhood. Two men walk along the sidewalk toward each other, both strangers in that neighborhood and maybe a little uneasy that time of night."

Charlie nodded. "Just about any neighborhood you could name in New York these days would qualify."

"They're approaching each other, and the closer they get the more frightened they become. Each one's sure the other's a mugger. They pass each other, and both of them look back over their shoulders, and by then they're walking fast, almost running."

"Sure, that's the way it is in New York," Charlie agreed.

"That's the way it's been in Martinsburg today, all day, any street you walk on. The furtive glance, the wide berth, the feeling that—something's going to happen. If you want to give it a name, it's almost as if some sort of mass hysteria's hit Martinsburg. Did it occur to you that if two dozen people went to the hospital for observation, there might be hundreds of others who experienced the same symptoms? It isn't just my idea, by the way. Chief Revere's thinking along the same lines."

"He told you that?"

"Without even being asked, Charlie." Eve said quickly, "You're afraid you'll do something else, aren't you?"

Charlie looked into his glass, then drained the rest of the bourbon. He didn't answer.

"I interviewed five people who'd been released by Dr. Brooke. I asked them the same question I asked you. Three of them said yes. The other two looked just as nervous as you did. Tell me about the bells, Charlie."

He could feel his face flushing. "I don't know what you're talking about."

"Sure you do."

"All right, then you tell me!" Charlie cried. "What's the matter with me? What's happening to me?"

"Not just you, Charlie. That's what I've been trying to tell you. It's the whole town."

"Sure, the whole town's haunted or we're all under a spell or something," Charlie said, calming down. "Come on, Miss Talbot."

"There was a town in France after the war," Eve said. "Without any warning a few people became violent, and then pretty soon everybody started acting insane. Not just mass hysteria. Mass paranoia."

"That really happened somewhere like that?"

"There was an explanation. There had to be an explanation. There always is."

"What was it?"

"I forget all the details, but it was the bread—something got into the bread, a grain fungus that acted like a hallucinogen. When it wore off, the town went back to normal."

"You're trying to say something like that's going on in Martinsburg?"

"I'm trying to say that whatever's affecting you is affecting a lot of people. I don't have the faintest idea why, but if we can find a pattern, something all of you have in common, then maybe we'll get somewhere."

"Something we ate?" Charlie laughed.

"That's not as funny as it sounds. Ate, or came into contact with, or a shared experience of some kind. I don't know. As I said, there has to be a rational explanation. I want to find it and I need your cooperation."

Charlie looked at her. He thought, he really thought, she had something there. It made him feel better. It wasn't just him. The whole town, like that place in France. He nodded, started to say he'd help any way he could.

Then something struck his shoulder, slammed him back hard into the chair, and he sat there gasping, tears stinging his eyes.

"What is it?" Eve said, alarmed. "What's the matter?"

He didn't know. It hurt like hell. He fumbled with his shirt buttons, drew the shirt off his shoulder.

On it, darkening as they watched, was an angry bruise.

19

By the time they'd had three rounds of drinks and finished dinner at the motor-lodge restaurant, it was almost eleven.

"Good Lord, will you look at the time?" Margriet said.

Garrick had found himself using her as a sounding board for his concern about Melody and Dr. Tom. He hadn't realized how tense he'd been, but she was easy to talk to, and he hadn't felt so relaxed in days. By the time he called home to check on Melody he was no longer thinking about the painting.

"I'm fine, Daddy," Melody said. "My throat's all better. It was just a little scratchy, that's all."

"Eve get back?"

"Not yet. Charlie Dahlgren called. He wants you to call him."

"Right. I won't be late, doll. I might drop in on Dr. Tom first."

Margriet was waiting outside the booth. "How is she?"

"No more sore throat, anyway."

The parking area was brightly lit. Garrick had parked halfway along the east wing, between the entrance and Margriet's room.

"Look at it," Margriet said. "It could be anyplace in the whole country. Same restaurant, same cocktail lounge, same motel-modern decor. Outside, the same neon jungle on the highway, the same sea of asphalt for a parking lot. It's a darned shame when it happens to a town like Martinsburg."

187

"We're better off than most places," Garrick said. "At least our zoning is—*what the goddamn hell!*"

Garrick stood in front of his car, a Porsche 911S. All four tires were flat.

"Yours?" Margriet said. "Oh, no."

Garrick crouched near the front left wheel. The air hadn't just been let out, the tire had been slashed. There had been an epidemic of that in Martinsburg too, the last couple of weeks, to add to everything else.

"What'll you do?"

"Get a cab, phone a garage in the morning," he said, the anger leaving him, but not the bewilderment. Why Martinsburg?

He locked the car, walked Margriet to her room at the end of the wing. She held out her key. "Here we are. You can call from the room if you'd like."

The room was as Margriet had indicated—motel-modern, functional, without any real style.

As he helped her out of her coat, he saw that Margriet was appraising him, the violet eyes studying him, and then he had the odd impression that she was appraising both of them, as if she could somehow get outside herself.

"You don't stay mad very long."

"What's the point?"

"I'd yell my head off."

"That wouldn't fix your tires."

"No, but it would make me feel better." Margriet sat down on the foot of the bed.

"How tall are you, anyway?" she asked, looking up at him. Her voice was different, edged with tension. It took Garrick a moment to realize why. Drinks, dinner, and then the inevitable motel room, the obvious prospect of that drabbest of American dreams, the one-night stand.

"Six-four," he said.

"I'll bet you played basketball in college."

"Nope, football scholarship. But I never made the varsity." Garrick grinned down at her. "I was too busy discovering girls to keep in training."

"Like your friend—is it Eve?"

"I met her much later, in New York."

"But she must have been the type. You know, megaphone on a white sweater. Cheerleader, fraternity sweetheart," Margriet said. "I wasn't. I was the girl who sat in the library Saturday afternoon boning up on Jean-Baptiste Columbine because nobody took me to the game."

"That's not the way you look now," Garrick said lightly. He wondered again how he could ever have thought her unattractive, the drab little mouse with a degree in art conservation. She had an exotic and very distinctive style that Garrick found provocative.

He backed away from it, not certain why. Eve, sure—but Eve wasn't the only reason. The predictability of the situation? That too, but there was something else, an odd feeling that his desire for Margriet had nothing to do with her, or with him, that it wasn't just predictable, it was almost compulsive.

He went to the phone quickly, disturbed by the thought, and asked the switchboard girl to call him a cab.

When he hung up, Margriet was standing. "Thanks for the dinner. I enjoyed it." The tension had left her voice. "You'll let me know about the painting?"

"Well, I told you how Melody feels about it."

"Why don't you tell her she could help me? I think she'd find the work interesting."

"I know she would," Garrick said. "It's worth a try. I'll be in touch."

She went with him to the door. "Don't wait too long. Okay?"

"Okay," he said, and she tilted her face up at him for a chaste good-night kiss.

"Them bulletproof screens, you know what I mean?" the cabdriver said. "And there's a kind of drawer where you put the dough in and I make change the same way. We voted on it today."

"What? Who did?"

"The guys here in town. Gonna install them as soon as we can. Three cabs robbed this week, a couple last, that's too fucking much, excuse me, Mr. Garrick. But it was all in the paper, about the robberies. You read the paper, don'tcha, Mr. Garrick?" The driver laughed at his own little joke, then became serious again. "Say, maybe you can tell me what the hell's the matter with this town. All of a sudden it's different, you know what I mean? Like these nights the little woman stays home, period, unless I'm with her. It's almost like it ain't Martinsburg no more. Fifteen years ago we come up from Philly to get away from that kind of crap, streets that weren't safe at night, especially in Nicetown. You ever been to that part of Philly? It ain't what you'd really call nice." Again the driver laughed, and again he grew serious. "Okay, Nicetown's a slum. In a slum, you expect things like that, you know what I mean. But now we got it here. A bunch of the guys, we've set up a schedule to patrol the neighborhood at night. Anybody looks for trouble, he'll get his head handed to him." The cab slowed, slid toward the curb. "Well, here we are. Look at all them lights on. Don't the doc ever sleep?"

"Keep the change, Vinny."

"Yeah, well, thanks, Mr. Garrick."

The cab rumbled away on abused shocks, senile springs.

The windows in the office wing of the Seymour house were dark, the L of the office barely visible so that the house looked like what it had originally been, two stories, square, under a steeply pitched roof, three hundred years old, home for how many generations of Seymours?

The entire first floor was ablaze with light, the second floor dark, as far as Garrick could see, except for a single window at front left. He raised the wrought-iron door knocker, let it fall. No response. He waited, tried again. A midnight car followed its headlights along the street. He'd have heard the thud of the door knocker by now. Or would he?

It wasn't any longer a question of half-suspecting.

The more he recalled the scene at the luncheon table, the more he was sure of it. Dr. Tom wouldn't be the first overworked physician to find relaxation in his own pharmacopeia.

Unless, Garrick thought with a sudden surge of relief, he'd been called out. Garrick went along the driveway. He only had to go halfway, because the garage door was open and in the garage he could see the gleam of Dr. Tom's new car.

He debated what to do next. Call it a night, drop by first thing in the morning?

He felt an odd, intuitive unease and returned to the front of the house. He tried the door.

It wasn't locked, which meant nothing because Dr. Tom rarely locked his door.

Again Garrick debated, then he opened the door a few inches and called, "Tom? Dr. Tom?"

No response to that either. He opened the door wider, went inside. Louder now, with the door shut behind him: "Tom? It's Rob Garrick."

Living room brightly lit, the faint lingering aroma of Dr. Tom's pipe tobacco, the expected bachelor untidiness—pillows piled on one end of the long sofa, where Dr. Tom sometimes read reclining, a couple of oversized ashtrays, pipes on them, a pair of ancient leather slippers on the floor, a pile of books and pamphlets scattered on the low table. Kitchen, by contrast, tidy—no indication that a meal had been prepared there, or eaten there, or in the dining room for that matter. The sense of unease sharpened momentarily. A drug habit usually made you indifferent to food, didn't it?

Don't jump to conclusions, Garrick told himself. Dr. Tom took most of his meals out, after all.

Library next. Big fireplace, dead ashes to the level of the firedogs, one wall with two large windows and three walls of books. "Medical books are in the office," Garrick could almost hear Dr. Tom say. "This is where I do my *serious* reading."

He had books, Garrick knew, on a wide range of subjects. Dr. Tom's intellectual interests were catholic, and he had added to his library over a long lifetime. A couple of thousand volumes anyway, Garrick figured, not counting those in the living-room shelves.

Dr. Tom's latest serious reading could be seen on the big teakwood desk—a stack of four books, one open and face down, a yellow legal pad, a few pencils. Again Garrick felt the unease, the reporter's sixth sense. He crossed to the desk and read the titles of the books.

The Secret Lore of Magic, Essentials of Demonology, Materials Towards a History of Witchcraft, The Black Arts. Garrick registered mild surprise. He had never known Dr. Tom was interested in the occult.

He picked up the yellow legal pad, saw two columns of words pencil-written in Dr. Tom's crabbed, difficult handwriting.

Symptoms of "psychic attack"	*Brooke's patients*
1. anxiety, mental distress	all
2. smell of decomposing flesh	none
3. body bruises, sometimes in shape of goat hoof or ace of clubs	none
4. poltergeist phenomena & inexplicable outbreaks of fire	debatable; check fires with Ned
5. smears of slime with/without footprints	none
6. sound of "astral bell"	more than 50%
7. convulsion, tearing pain near heart, heavy pulse, spasms of neck or stomach, impotence, sweating, gummy eyelids	some evidence of one or more of these symptoms in all
8. gradual emaciation, concomitant mental lassitude; ultimately death	(Melody Garrick???)

The two columns ended there, with Melody's name in parentheses, followed by three question marks. The parentheses, Garrick assumed, were because Melody was no patient of Dr. Brooke's, the question marks because Dr. Tom already had diagnosed her symptoms in accordance with his medical training, not his small library on the occult.

Hold on now, Garrick told himself, Tom Seymour doesn't believe in that sort of business any more than you do. Psychic attack? Poltergeist phenomena? Smears of slime with/without footprints?

Still, something had led Dr. Tom to consider the occult.

Garrick checked the columns again. Items six and seven, possibly item four, could have pushed him in that direction. Item eight would have offered him the excuse for an intuitive leap, in this case from medicine to magic.

Item eight was Melody. Gradual emaciation, concomitant mental lassitude. Melody wrapped in parentheses, Melody followed by question marks.

Ultimately death. Dr. Tom's handwriting less crabbed, less difficult there, as if he were certain of those two words.

Calm down, Garrick told himself. Nothing's changed because Dr. Tom jotted some far-out speculations on a yellow legal pad.

Garrick could almost hear him saying, "What the devil do I, or any doctor for that matter, really know about the human body, or the relationship between the body and the mind? Can I tell you why one patient lives, why one dies—and, come to think of it, why one dies slowly in great pain and another eases off through untroubled sleep? It's the *art* of medicine, my friend, and a lot of trial and error, and every now and then, if you're lucky, what some people call miracles."

Garrick left the pad, the books, the desk. For the first time since opening the unlocked door and entering the house he began to feel like an intruder. He doubted that Dr. Tom would have approved of anyone reading what he had written. It was hardly the sort of speculation an M.D. put into a learned paper to read before the state medical society.

Heading for the front door, Garrick recalled that from outside he'd seen a single light upstairs. He debated going up there. If Tom had simply been asleep, Garrick's voice and poking around would have awakened him by now. If it was a deeper sleep, a drugged sleep—

As Tom Seymour's friend, he had to find out. No physician could function for long on a morphine metabolism.

Once, from the landing, he called Dr. Tom's name, expecting no answer, getting none. He didn't have to turn a light on because light spilled from an open doorway at the head of the stairs. That would be the window he had seen outside.

He went up the rest of the stairs quickly and into what he assumed was Dr. Tom's bedroom, the assumption confirmed by Dr. Tom's body, supine on the king-sized bed, dressed except for shoes, waitcoat unbuttoned, Phi-Bet key on its chain, face gray, lips pinched and blue, fingernails blue, the rubber-stoppered vial of morphine sulphate empty on the night table, the hypodermic syringe on the comforter near one blue-fingered hand.

If Martinsburg had drifted into an inexplicable state of civic breakdown, if Garrick had himself slid into helplessness while Melody starved herself, this was different, this was something that could be handled, that he had to handle the right way for his friend. It was, he thought, as if the death of Dr. Tom had stopped the drift, stopped the glide, given him something to cope with that made sense not only rationally but morally.

He looked at the body again, and the horror of finding it diminished. Even the sorrow would come later. He had things to do first.

And things he must not do. Like picking up the telephone.

He could almost see the lead he would never write

for the Martinsburg *News. A self-administered overdose of morphine sulphate last night claimed the life of
Dr. Tom Seymour . . .*

Suicide? Accident?

No, death from natural causes. The body would be
found in the morning by Dr. Tom's housekeeper; the
verdict would be heart failure.

An autopsy?

Dr. Tom had no relatives in town, none anywhere
that Garrick knew of. Garrick himself, both as publisher of the *News* and Dr. Tom's close friend, would be
notified right after the police.

There'd be no autopsy. Garrick knew he could talk
Ned Revere out of it. Ned liked Dr. Tom too, and Ned
would be reasonable provided the evidence of what
really had happened was removed.

Garrick put the empty vial and the syringe in his
pocket. He went downstairs to the library, took the top
sheet from the pad. He wanted that, wanted to try to
make some sense out of it—two columns scrawled on
yellow paper in Dr. Tom's crabbed handwriting, his last
testament.

Garrick walked slowly along Conant Street. It was
cold, and darker than it should have been. Most of the
street lights were out, their bulbs shattered by stones, by
pellets from BB guns. Another new teen-aged sport, like
slashing tires.

A group of men approached as he neared the Commons. He kept walking, refusing to give way to the fear
that now was endemic in town, and then he saw the
baseball bats they were carrying. They fanned out, six
of them, near the spill of light from one of the few intact streep lamps.

"What're you doing out this time of night?"

"Let's have some identification, mister."

One of them said: "Say, wait a minute, it's Mr. Garrick from the newspaper. Hiya, Mr. Garrick."

Garrick did not approve of the implicit vigilantism.
He knew the men were well-meaning, but it was only

one small step from keeping the peace to taking the law
into your own hands.

"Busy night?" he asked mildly.

"Nah. Dull one."

"Then why don't you fellows go home to bed?"

The one who had recognized him said, "We found
some spic kids busting lights. Scared the hell out of
them."

Garrick saw heads nod. "How?" he asked.

"Whomped their asses with a ball bat."

"Better call the police next time," Garrick said, still
mildly.

Two of them spoke at once:

"There ain't enough police to go around."

"You got to teach them a lesson."

Garrick said nothing. It was true that the police were
spread dangerously thin these days, but a bunch of self-
appointed block wardens were apt to cause more problems than they solved. He'd better talk to Ned Revere
about that too. It looked like he'd be spending a lot of
time with Ned tomorrow morning.

"You heading straight home, Mr. Garrick?"

Garrick said that he was.

"We could walk with you if you want."

"No, that's okay."

When they were out of sight he walked along the
curb, found a sewer, dropped the vial and hypodermic
needle down it. He straightened and began to cross the
street.

A car came around the corner, tires squealing. Garrick was in the middle of the broad street by then, sidewalk behind him, grass and trees of the Commons
ahead. The car swerved toward him, headlights catching
him, holding him. He quickened his stride, and he
thought: Surely the damn fool sees me. A split second
later he was running for his life.

The car braked at the last instant, a panic stop,
scorching rubber, slewing to the left, front end dipping.
It stopped close enough for Garrick to touch the fender.
He went around to the door, yanked it open.

"Just what sort of damn-fool way to drive is that?" he shouted, and saw Ned Revere behind the wheel.

"Jesus, Rob! I could have killed you."

With the door open and the courtesy light on, Garrick could see Ned's big hands gripping the wheel hard, his knuckles white.

"You wander around at night like this," Ned said after a moment, shaking his head, "better wear some light clothing. I didn't see you until it was almost too late."

Garrick couldn't believe that. The headlights had been directly on him, had practically blinded him. But he couldn't believe the obvious alternative either—that Revere had wanted to run him down.

"Long son of a bitch of a day," the police chief said. "Maybe I was kind of half asleep at the wheel for that. Drive you home?"

Garrick declined the offer, as he'd declined the earlier offer of an escort. He wanted to talk to Ned, but this wasn't the time.

He watched the car drive off and walked the rest of the way home. Eve opened the front door before he could put the key in the lock.

"Rob," she said, coming into his arms, "thank God you're here."

20

They were in the kitchen, Eve talking while Garrick made coffee. Her face was pale, her voice thin, the words quickly spoken as if she wanted to get them out before she could change her mind.

Garrick listened without interrupting until she said, "And then it was like something struck him or shoved him back hard in the chair, struck him in the shoulder and—"

"What do you mean, something struck him?"

"He unbuttoned his shirt and . . . I don't know how to say this, Rob. Any way I say it, it sounds crazy. But I saw it. A big bruise all over his shoulder."

"Maybe he injured himself before you got there."

Eve shook her head. "No, I'm telling you I saw it changing! It was faint at first, and then an angry red blotch, and then all black and blue. . . . Oh God, Rob, what's *happening?*"

"Where's Dahlgren now?"

"He just sat there, staring right through me. I said something, I don't know what. He didn't seem to hear me. I touched his arm. It was like wood." Eve's hand was shaking as she passed her coffee cup. "Then he got up and started to attack me."

"You mean he hit you?"

"I mean he tried to rape me." Eve took an unsteady breath. "Not just a pass because he had a couple of drinks too many. Not like that at all. He started pawing me. He threw me down on the sofa. Then he looked at me like . . . well, by then he'd already dragged my skirt off, but it was like he was seeing me for the first time. Like I'd just come into the room. He backed away from me, rubbing the bruise on his shoulder. Then he said a funny thing. 'You're not the one, you're not Dominique.' I *think* that's what he said. Then he ran out. I don't know where he is. I only know something hit him and made him go wild like that. Something in the room with us. Something . . ."

Garrick knew Charlie had been heading for a nervous breakdown; tonight he'd obviously gone off the deep end. But what about the blow, the bruise?

He heard Eve say, "It wasn't just a bruise. It was like he was branded."

Garrick didn't understand what she meant.

"I mean it had a shape. Like it was stamped there. It looked like a shamrock."

"A what?"

"A shamrock. You know, like a three-leafed clover." Eve looked at Garrick over the rim of the cup, defiantly. "Okay, say it, why don't you? You think I'm crazy."

Garrick reached for her hand. "Easy," he said. "Hey, easy now, baby. There's got to be an explanation somewhere. We'll find Dahlgren, we'll—" He stopped. "What did you say?" he demanded. "The shape of the bruise, Eve?"

"I told you. Like a shamrock."

Or like a club in a deck of cards, Garrick thought.

Wordlessly he removed the yellow sheet of paper from his pocket, unfolded it, smoothed it on the table in front of Eve.

She read it slowly, then looked up. "Who wrote this?"

"Tom Seymour," Garrick said. "Right before he died."

"Right before he—he's dead?"

Garrick told her what he'd found, what he'd done.

Eve looked at the paper again. "Rob, I'm scared. I've never been so scared in my life."

By the time Garrick had brewed a second pot of coffee, Eve was calmer.

"Psychic attack," she said. "That isn't some kind of a medical term, is it?"

Garrick shook his head.

"It's black magic—like voodoo. You make an image of someone you want to kill, stick a pin in it, call on whatever demons you know."

"Haitian witch doctors. Come on, Rob," Eve said impatiently. It was as if their roles had been reversed.

"Tom Seymour was the most pragmatic man I ever met, and he was led to that conclusion. Or at least to giving it serious thought."

"And he died."

"So did Matt Hawley," Garrick said, his glance rising from the yellow paper to Eve's face. "Look, the things that've been happening these last ten days, taken one at a time they're not that weird. It's only when you put them together in one time, in one place. But Dahlgren's bruise is something else, something all by itself outside the realm of possibility."

"It happened. I saw it happen."

"I'm not arguing with you. And there's another thing. I told you what Matt Hawley said he'd seen the night of the accident. But I haven't told you what *I* saw—deep ruts out there that could have been made by wagon wheels."

"Could have been, sure, but—"

"How did the painting get there, Eve? It wasn't in the consignment from Bourg St. Martin. It just showed up when the kids went out there looking for some coins." Eve was going to interrupt, but Garrick went on, "Then what? Then we brought it home, and the next morning Melody lost her limp. And her appetite."

Garrick paused. "Everything started changing at the same time. Melody changed. The whole town changed. And the painting. First it was the faded spot on the wall. Then the face of St. Martin. It's like whatever's affecting the town is affecting the painting too."

Garrick looked at Dr. Tom's notes again. "There were a bunch of books on Tom Seymour's desk. He'd been giving a lot of thought to those psychiatric cases. He had an idea they might have been just the tip of the iceberg."

"You mean, how many people didn't turn themselves in? I was working on that idea myself all day, remember?"

"I think what Tom had in mind," Garrick said slowly, "was the possibility of a psychic attack on the whole town."

"On Martinsburg? Who on earth would want to put a curse on Martinsburg, assuming anyone could? Come on, Rob!"

"Did you know Columbine was interested in black magic?" Garrick repeated what Margriet had told him.

"Jean-Baptiste Columbine died almost three hundred years ago in France," Eve said patiently. "You don't believe in ghosts, do you?"

Garrick had passed the point where he knew what he believed. "What about his paintings? They're here, aren't they?" He pushed back from the table, stood up. "Eve, it scares me. I want to get rid of it."

"Melody's painting?"

He went into the living room, Eve following, and stared intently at the dark, somber canvas—the storm, the village brooding in the background, the Sieur de Ramezay as St. Martin in seventeenth-century dress, leaning down from his saddle, sharing his cloak with the beggar.

Abruptly Garrick got a chair, stood on it, lifted the painting off its hook and carried it to the low cocktail table in front of the sofa.

The Sieur de Ramezay now looked up at them, the arrogant expression totally gone from his face. The eyes were wide, the mouth parted almost in a parody of terror.

The beggar looked different. Younger? Boyish? Almost girlish, Garrick thought.

Then Eve gave a muffled cry. "Look—there's a third faded spot now."

Garrick saw it. Faintly, but it was there—a blurring, a lightening of the pigments on the wall of the church, a suggestion of pale red behind the dun-colored stone.

Garrick studied the second faded spot. He thought the pigments were paler than before. The window of a building, second floor. Garrick could almost see inside, the vaguest suggestion of a painting beneath the painting, caught in the eerie glow of the storm, the single shaft of sunlight.

He went into the den, returned with a magnifying glass. With it he could see nothing beneath the faded window. He moved the glass and brought the original faded spot, near the gateway to the village, into focus.

There *was* something beneath that. He knew it wasn't just the magnifying glass, knew the pigments had faded still more.

He could make out a steep stone staircase and four tiny figures descending, carrying something.

Enough of the overpainting remained so that the scene wasn't clear, but the figures had been executed in meticulous detail. Whatever they were carrying was heavy. The tiny figures stood poised to take a step, bracing themselves against the weight. A sack? A heavy cloth wrapped around something?

Suddenly it seemed to jump out at Garrick. He knew what they were carrying downstairs.

They were carrying a body.

A scene flashed before his eyes. In back of the *News* building, standing there with Ned Revere.

Hadn't the call come the night he'd seen the first change in the painting? He'd been talking with Eve about—about what? He couldn't remember. Revere's call had interrupted their conversation, and he'd reached the *News* building in time to see them carrying Matt Hawley out in a body bag.

And the second pentimento, the window? What waited behind that?

He brought it into focus with the magnifying glass again, saw the reflection of the lowering sky on the leaded glass, a tiny dazzle of the single shaft of sunlight glittering like mica, and inside dimly and then suddenly clear a four-poster bed and on the bed a human figure.

He flung the magnifying glass aside and heard Eve shout, "Rob, what is it?"

He had no recollection of crossing the room, returning to the painting, raising the heavy wrought-iron poker overhead, ready to deliver the first blow.

Then he heard running footsteps and Melody was there, pathetically thin in baggy flannel pajamas, hurling herself between him and the painting.

"Daddy! No! What are you doing? What are you trying to do?"

Melody crying, her face contorted, her frail body between him and the warning written in Dr. Tom's crabbed hand-writing.

Melody Garrick. Ultimately death.

He looked at the horror on her emaciated face.

He couldn't do it.

To do it would not be to destroy evil but to admit his own insanity.

It was, after all, only a painting.

Melody lay quietly in bed, the door to her room opening on darkness, on silence. She hadn't slept. How could she?

Her own father. The one person in the world she could trust, the one person she loved, and if she hadn't heard Eve shouting, hadn't rushed downstairs . . .

Why did he want to destroy the painting?

Why did he hate her?

He had to hate her if he wanted to do a thing like that.

He really did blame her for her mother's death, that was it, that had to be it. Putting her in boarding school, ignoring her, pretending she didn't exist, and then pretending everything was fine between them, giving her a false sense of confidence so that without warning he could take away the one thing that mattered to her, the one beautiful thing in her life.

"Melody?"

He stood in the doorway.

"I'm sorry," he said, his voice gentle, deceitful. "I'll try to explain it to you soon, doll."

"That's okay, Daddy." She just wished he'd go away.

His voice took on a wry tone, even more deceitful than the gentleness. "As soon as I can explain it to myself," he said. "Forgive me?"

"Sure. All right."

She'd have to put the painting somewhere safe.

Margriet Kelly—Margriet wanted to examine it, wanted to prove it was no forgery. Margriet Kelly loved the painting almost as much as she did. Margriet would protect it.

"Daddy," she said, "I've been thinking. You were right all along. In the morning I'm going to let Margriet Kelly have the painting."

He sat on the edge of the bed. She tried not to stiffen too much in his arms when she accepted his kiss.

"You're making the right decision," he said.

"I know that now, Daddy."

When he was gone, she shut the door and opened the Notebook.

Of all the nubile girls in the village it was the wainwright's eldest daughter Marta whom Father Vasili lusted after most. She was a slender, olive-skinned child with long, dark hair and a placid disposition. Some thought her simple-minded, and if absolute devotion to the religion of her people was evidence of that, then she was. Marta would chant her prayers over and over again in a high clear soprano, the light of her faith burning like twin candles in her luminous eyes.

—Paint her into your Black Mass, Gaddara told me.

—How can I? I protested. Her father won't let me.

—Do it from memory.

Slowly the new icon for the church took shape. I painted it on wood with the pigments I had ground myself, so pleased that my hand had not lost its skill that the act of painting assumed far more importance for me than the subject.

Not that I objected to the Black Mass. The lingering remnants of my faith were dead. If there is a magic in the mass of the Church itself, a magic as strong as Gaddara's, who is to say which is the good and which the evil?

It is the magical use of language, the speaking of words charged with supernatural power, that transforms the bread and wine into the body and blood of Christ. The words consecrate the host because they were spoken by Christ at the Last Supper and because they are spoken by an ordained priest who assumes Christ's person.

And if the priest were not in a state of Grace? It mattered nothing.

The fornicating, lustful Father Vasili, himself mired in sin, would speak the same words, and with time become Christ.

Even Judas Iscariot, had he been ordained, could have said mass, for he would have spoken the magical words not in his own person but in the person of Christ.

Good and evil are a hooped snake that bites its own tail.

And, in a way, I had been twice ordained. Hadn't Father Vasili blessed me in the commissioning of a new icon for his church? Hadn't Gaddara ordained me, after her fashion, by killing a black cock at sunrise, ripping out its tongue, heart, and eyes, grinding them and burying the powder, then chanting a mass for the dead to make the power of the demons of hell flow into my fingers? Hadn't she chanted nine times nine names of great power? Hadn't she from yellow candle wax fashioned a crucifix and then beaten it shapeless while whispering the filthiest words against the Most Glorious Virgin and casting the vilest aspersions on the birth of Her Son from the purity of Her womb? There is a power in blasphemy, a current of force in sacrilege.

And this soon belonged to *mon cors* (My horns? No.

Possibly a variant of *corps,* body—"belonged to me")
as I painted the Black Mass, the host a black triangle,
the chalice black, black candles lighting the altar, the
scarlet missal decorated with a black goat with silver
horns, on the priest's scarlet chasuble the silhouette of a
nude woman in black, above the altar a derisive Christ,
head down, laughing in His Passion. Gaddara even
burned the Black Mass incense for me—nightshade,
henbane, myrtle, thorn apple—while I worked.

The priest in the painting wore the bloated, dissi-
pated face of Father Vasili.

On the altar sprawled the nude body of a young virgin. She had the face of the girl Marta.

Gaddara looked, and approved.

—To fail to worship evil along with good is to fail to
understand the true nature of the universe, for the knowledge of good and evil belongs to the Divine. Magicians
know that. Illiterate priests like Father Vasili do not.
Had he understood evil instead of despising it inside
himself, he would have lived his normal span of years.

—I understand neither good nor evil, I told her.

Gaddara laughed.

—You soon will understand the power that can flow
from your own hand. Deliver the icon.

But first I had to hide the Black Mass with the icon
Father Vasili would see, a painting of the Crown of
Thorns. It was simply and swiftly done, the agony in the
eyes of Christ, the blood on his forehead, the jeering
Roman soldiers.

Father Vasili was pleased with the icon and hung it at
once. That same day he came rushing to Gaddara's
house, puffing and blowing, his black skirts flying, his
beard quivering with the quivering of his cheeks.

Gaddara gave him wine to drink, and when he regained his breath and could speak he told us:

—A miracle! A miracle has happened!

Such was his excitement that he forgot he had not
spoken to Gaddara for months, forgot he held her responsible for his fall from grace.

—It is a good miracle? Gaddara asked. She was amused.

—All miracles are God's handiwork, all are good, said Father Vasili passionately.

—And what is this miracle?

—I can see. My blind eye can see. I gazed up at the icon and all at once I could see as well with either eye. It is God's hand that guided the hand of Jean-Baptiste.

After he left, I asked Gaddara:

—How can that be? I thought the icon would destroy him.

Gaddara smiled the smile of a cat.

—Even a fool like Father Vasili should know a fall is all the greater the greater the height. Let the *giagnon* (here we go again) trumpet of his happiness while he may.

(Four pages missing. Four whole pages! And something's wrong with the binding here.)

. . . with his daughter Marta's body in his arms leading the people of the village across the plaza to the church.

Gaddara told me the child had been enticed by Father Vasili to an olive grove beyond the first range of hills above the village. That she knew this did not surprise me. Gaddara knew anything she wished to know.

What transpired was this:

Father Vasili used the child's simple, consuming faith to seduce her, saying he would instruct her in the mysteries of the metropolitans in distant Moscow. Before such words she was helpless and permitted him to strip off her garments and stroke the tiny buds of her *escors,* her *flanchet,* her *braon* (well, I can guess—that poor kid!) until her spiritual excitement became physical and she opened her legs to him.

He had *ragié* (??) in both wine and lust, and it was only after he had lain with her that he saw the danger. He said to the child:

—The glories I have shared with you today are for us alone, you understand that, don't you?

But Marta said in her naiveté: Can't I tell my

mother? She loves the Church as much as I do. She'll be so happy.

—Especially not your mother, Father Vasili said.

—But you know what a good woman she is, as you are her confessor. She chants her prayers fifty times a day.

—If you tell anyone, it is a mortal sin, said Father Vasili.

—You always preached that what we just did is a mortal sin.

Father Vasili said she was too young to understand.

—Oh, I am not too young. I've seen rams and ewes *reluire*.

—That's different, there is no religious ecstasy in that.

—It's the way they have babies. What we did is the way people have babies.

Father Vasili became nervous.

—You're imagining things. We did not do that. You are a foolish child. I was mistaken to give you the Holy instruction.

—You hurt me, Marta said.

—The Lord in His Passion felt pain.

A gold coin appeared on Father Vasili's sweating hand. He held it out to her tremblingly.

—If you promise to forget what we did, I'll give you this.

(Mildew here.)

. . . your money. I want to go home now.

(More mildew.)

. . . and he chased after her, catching her at the edge of the olive grove. Possibly he only meant to frighten her, but she was a frail child. He struck her once, and she screamed, and from behind he covered her mouth with his strong hand while she struggled to break free. Still she made sounds, mewling with terror as she tried to bite his hand. Then he bore her to the ground, coming down with his knee in the small of her back while his hand jerked her head up.

That much was an accident. Her neck snapped like a twig and she was dead.

A goatherd saw it happen. He ran, and Father Vasili ran after him, but the goatherd was swifter.

(More mildew.)

. . . into the church, where they placed the dead body on the altar. They had had trouble with priests before in this part of Serbia, Gaddara told me. One would think that if an Orthodox priest must marry, as he must, such trouble would be avoided, but it is otherwise. More than one priest has fled this country for his life. Father Vasili was not so lucky.

That the whole village marched silently into the church with the dead child's body may seem strange, and even seems so while I write these words. But I saw their faces, I saw the madness in their eyes, and afterwards I asked Gaddara about that.

—It is an ecstasy like any other religious ecstasy. They acted out the Black Mass for you.

—For me?

—You made them do it.

I followed them into the church, watched them place the body on the altar and light the candles. They never spoke, not even the wainwright. They gathered faggots of olive wood to set about the altar.

The wainwright touched fire to them with a torch, and the villagers fled outside.

I lingered a few moments, long enough to see the flames leap and dance around the body on the altar. Then I saw the icon.

The face of Christ in the overpainting had become the face of Father Vasili, but even as I gazed on it awestruck it faded and was gone.

Through it sprang the Black Mass.

The church was stone, like all our important buildings. The villagers knew the fire would soon die out, and in the sunlight in the square they waited.

After the smoke had cleared, I returned inside with them and smelled charred flesh.

The fire had not damaged the dead child's body, nor

even scorched her hair. Father Vasili, as naked as she was, lay over her, their two dead bodies forming a cross.

His face was barely recognizable. He had been burned black.

The Reverend Miles Pritchard awoke sweating, his mouth dry, his heart racing. He padded barefoot into the bathroom and drank two glasses of water.

"Miles?" his wife called.

It was just past three on the luminous dial of the clock on the dresser. Pritchard returned to bed.

"Talk about nightmares," he said, reaching for Janet's hand.

"Really, dear? You hardly ever dream at all."

"Hardly ever *remember* my dreams." Pritchard suppressed a small shudder. "Not that I'll forget this one soon."

"Want to tell me?"

"It was . . . weird, Janet."

"Or maybe take one of your pills and go back to sleep."

"I wonder what Father O'Reilly would say."

"If you took a sleeping pill?"

"If I told him I dreamed a Black Mass."

"A Black Mass! I'm not sure I even know what that is, Miles," Janet said.

"I wasn't aware I knew the details myself. Maybe I made them up. My subconscious. Anyway, there I was in a scarlet chasuble and my birthday suit under it. Inside an old stone church somewhere. A black chalice to hold the wine, the wafer a black triangle, the missal decorated with a black goat. It was all so *real,* Janet."

"Is that what a priest was supposed to use in a Black Mass?"

"I wouldn't know. That's what I used. Along with a black altar, black candles, and a crucifix hanging upside down. And then of course there was the virgin. As I told you, my dear, quite a dream."

Pritchard felt better talking about it. In retrospect it almost amused him.

"The Virgin Mary?"

"No, just your common, garden-variety virgin lying naked on the altar."

"Dear me," said Janet.

"Dear me, indeed," said Pritchard. "Apparently what you do in a Black Mass is, uh, defile the body of the virgin with the host. Or perhaps it's the other way around."

"You can skip that part, dear," said Janet quickly.

"It's what comes next that I'd like to forget. After the host, it seemed to be, uh, my turn."

"You can skip that part too, dear."

"Pretty little thing. Very . . . ardent."

"Miles," said Janet.

"Well, *that* wasn't the part I want to forget. I meant what came after that. Instant retribution, I suppose. It's nice to know my subconscious won't let me get away with a dream like that."

"What happened?"

Pritchard could feel the dryness in his mouth again, and the way his heart was racing. Retelling the dream no longer seemed amusing.

"The church caught fire," he said. "I couldn't get out. I could feel the heat, the flames. I could see my hands blistering and charring. . . ."

She held him hard against her. "Miles, Miles, you're shaking all over."

He couldn't help it. He could smell the burning flesh, see the virgin untouched by the flames that were destroying him in the dream.

From the Notebook of Jean-Baptiste Columbine

For two days and nights I could neither eat nor drink, though Gaddara tempted me with sweet wine and succulent meats. Once she opened a pomegranate for me, but the seeds swam in blood.

—Why do you turn your face to the wall, Jean-Baptiste? You knew what would happen.

—I did not know the child would die.

I became lightheaded with hunger, and my vision blurred. On the third day I had a dream so real that I was back in Bourg St. Martin, living again the horror of my final time there, seeing again the death of my wife, watching the dragoons rape our child Annique, rushing through the streets with her to the doctor, who would not help us, and to the priest Gavrillac, who tried to betray me. I went again in my dream to my false friend the Sieur de Ramezay, and again that almost cost my life. I watched my true friend Rivoire die, and I fled to the gates, but the watchman would not open for me. I saw the Sieur de Ramezay's face, and his blond lame child who lived, who would be a woman now while my Annique was long dead. It all seemed more real than it had the first time.

—*Mariole*! I screamed, and Gaddara tried to comfort me.

I needed no comfort. I knew what I would do, and the knowledge filled me until nothing else was there.

The next day Gaddara told me: Tita and the gypsies are back.

(Three quarters of a page missing.)

. . . then take these three books, Gaddara said, if you are really fool enough to go. She was vexed with me.

—Why shouldn't I go?

—Good and evil are a wheel that spins; they are one, not many. A sorcerer may spend all his days trying to understand the wheel. Incomplete knowledge is worse than no knowledge at all, Jean-Baptiste. I know what it is you wish to do, but you are not ready.

I am ready, I told her.

—You only think so. Once I knew a practitioner of the black arts who put a curse on the man who had stolen his wife. The man was his brother, and the magician no more adept than you. The curse went awry.

The gypsies were waiting, but in spite of my eagerness to leave, I was curious.

—What happened?

—The curse struck their father instead, killing him before either of them had been conceived.

I grew confused.

—But you said you knew him.

—I knew him until the curse went awry. I did not know him afterward.

I said that was impossible, but Gaddara shook her head and looked at me pityingly.

—You have not mastered the wheel of good and evil, Jean-Baptiste. Nor can you dominate time and distance, and one who is inadequate risks being dominated by them. Take these books. Perhaps they will help you.

—What are they?

—The three great *grimoires*. This one is the *Key of Solomon*. It was written in Aramaic not long after Christ died, and was translated into many languages. The Inquisition of the Roman church proscribed it more than a hundred years ago.

That *grimoire* was printed in French. The second one she gave me was in Latin. The *Grimoire of Honorius,* she told me.

Then, saying nothing, she gave me the third book. It was bound in black leather, the title stamped in red: *The Black Pullet*. I opened it and saw the mistake at once, on the title page. The year of publication was MDCCLX.

—Is this a joke? I asked.

—I assure you it is no joke.

I laughed uneasily.

—In the year 1760 I'll be long dead and buried. Unless the date is in error, this *Black Pullet* hasn't been written yet.

—Of course not, Jean-Baptiste. You might say I went to great lengths to get it.

—That is no more possible than the man whose father . . . You are trying to confuse me.

—Confusion is the state of the world. An adept ma-

gician, like God, restores order. An inept magician brings chaos. Stay a few years longer, Jean-Baptiste. I will try to teach you.

But Tita and the gypsies were waiting, and I knew what I had to do.

Janet slept on her side, facing him, her haunch a plump mound under the covers. He moved restlessly, and she stirred. He moved again, and her breathing became shallower, less even. He lay still, trying not to wake her. No reason she should lose a night's sleep because he had a nightmare. It wasn't exactly his first bout of insomnia. She always slept like a baby. Then he would look at her and love her and resent her.

Like now. Six-thirty, a steady rain falling. Should have taken a Nembutal earlier. A few hours of drugged sleep. Too late now. He'd be fuzzy and querulous all day. So he lay there, trying not to move, trying not to disturb Janet's sleep, resenting her, remembering the virgin in the dream, supine upon the altar, long blonde hair hanging free over one side, legs parted to defile the host or be defiled by it, certainly to be defiled by him.

The virgin in the dream had been Melody Garrick.

That part he hadn't told Janet.

He had dreamed about her before, twice—no, three times—in the past couple of weeks. Hadn't told Janet about those dreams. Hadn't told Rob. No one. Be easier for a Catholic. Things like that always were. A small act of contrition and you could forget it. Sixteen years old, for God's sake. And you dreamed that kind of dream about her, a dirty old man's dream, waking in the night aroused. So finally this time you imposed a punishment on yourself. Immolation in a nightmare.

Wonder if Father O'Reilly has dreams like that. How much can a priest suppress, anyway? Pretty good life, O'Reilly had once said. A man wants three things. Security. Love. Sex. Most men get none of them in sufficient measure. A Catholic priest's lucky. Two out of three—security of the Church, love of God, so he can do without sex quite nicely.

Congregational minister's something else again. Old Calvinist tradition still hanging on. Church took a long time to get liberal. Witch trials, way back. Blue laws, in your own lifetime. Frivolity was never a strong point with the Calvinists, with the Huguenots. They fought it, and if you fight that sort of thing long enough you'll wind up neurotic. The Protestant syndrome. Jews too, because if they were persecuted so thoroughly, generation on generation, they must have done something wrong. Collective guilt becomes individual neurosis. But not the Catholics. I'd hate to be a psychiatrist trying to make a living in a Catholic country.

I do believe I'm getting sleepy. Deep thoughts, my friend, will always do that to you. Minister's automatically an intellectual to his flock, which is just as well. Pious fraud is more like it. But I suppose you've done this town some good. Old Dr. Tom for the body, you for the soul, and it's funny because Tom's the intellectual, not you. Wonder what's troubling him. Looked like hell at lunch, and then that sudden change, not Dr. Tom Seymour at all.

Not Miles Pritchard at all, if you dream that kind of dream about Melody Garrick.

So sleepy.

And the dream returning, the Black Mass, the black host to be defiled, the virgin awaiting him on the altar, the villagers gathering kindling outside—

Bathrobe, slippers. Janet still sleeping. Himself still sleeping, sleepwalking. Know the house well, can walk through it in your sleep, bumping into nothing. Downstairs, third step down creaks, always has. Door from kitchen to garage. Don't even have to go outside. Good thing. Listen to that rain, will you?

Gasoline can's heavy, but you don't have to go far. Back through the kitchen, the library, the door to your office and the church and the flames enveloping her but not burning her, the face looking up at you, the face of Melody Garrick, but of course the altar is empty, and the pews. Footsteps silent on the stone floor, cold through the thin soles of the slippers, and here come the villagers now, with eyes like glass and not making a sound, ghostly communicants in a Black Mass where it is not Christ born again eternally but Christ hanging derisively upside down while the priest dies.

You are not going to do this.

It's a dream.

Well, a nightmare, sure, but you're still in bed and in an hour or so it will be fresh orange juice, you'll squeeze it yourself while Janet, dowdy and comfortable in a housecoat, fries the eggs and the bacon for the meal you are never going to eat because you're not still in bed but sleepwalking for the second and, obviously, last time in your life.

For a moment he was almost awake, screaming inside himself, No, stop, please, please stop, there is no reason to do this, you'll sit up sweating in bed and Janet will say it's a bad dream, but in the next moment he was no longer awake, not that kind of awake, except for the instant when he could smell the gasoline as he un-screwed the cap, sloshing the gasoline all over himself and standing before the altar as he calmly with a neat economy of motion struck a match.

"That's not as funny as it sounds. Arh, or came

21

Garrick awoke to the sound of rain rattling against the windows, pounding steadily on the roof. He hadn't slept much. It would be one of those days. He'd have to get through it on nervous energy, on too many cups of coffee.

He put the electric percolator on, then shaved, dressed quickly, looked in on Melody. She was sleeping, her fist against her cheek like a baby.

When he got back downstairs Eve was at the stove, scrambling eggs.

"You're up early," he said. "Sleep okay?"

She turned for his kiss. "Like the dead." She looked very young, her coppery hair framing her freckled face as she smiled up at him. "Now, in the clear light of day—" she said.

"You mean that psychic attack stuff?"

"I feel a little silly about it. There's got to be some other explanation."

He said nothing.

"Doesn't there?"

"Well, I'm not going to run it under a banner headline in today's *News*, if that's what you mean."

"But you still think it's possible?"

"As you said, the clear light of day. I don't know what I think. Tell me the painting didn't change."

"Oh, it changed all right." Eve scooped the scrambled eggs onto a warm platter and poured coffee.

"And you did see that bruise on Charlie Dahlgren's shoulder."

"I saw it." Eve's face was pale, her freckles more

pronounced. "I don't want to think about it. If frightens me, Rob."

So much, Garrick thought, for the clear light of day.

He said: "Well, yeah. You can't just accept the supernatural. It goes against everything you ever learned—five hundred years of Western civilization. But what's the supernatural anyway, except something that doesn't jibe with our own ideas of the natural? In New Guinea during the war there were natives living in the Stone Age who'd never seen an airplane. Then we came in, bulldozed a field, and the planes started to land, bringing magic things like guns and radios, clocks and jeeps, refrigerators. After the war we took it all away, and the natives got religion. They built something out of wood that looked like an airplane and they put it on the abandoned airfield and they prayed to it. If they prayed hard enough they believed the gods would return. In a C-47 cargo plane."

Eve shook her head. "That isn't the same thing, Rob. They were trying to go forward. If you accept things like curses or astral bells or a painting that's . . . evil, it isn't going forward, it's going back, all the way back to the Stone Age when gods hurled thunderbolts and demons lived in every tree and rock."

"Maybe it's going where the evidence leads you," Garrick said.

"Evidence of what, Daddy?" Melody stood in the doorway, dressed to go out.

"Nothing, doll. We were just talking."

"Is it too early to take the painting to Miss Kelly?"

"She gets in at nine," Garrick told her, relieved that Melody hadn't changed her mind. "I've got to see Ned Revere. Eve'll drive you, all right? Want some scrambled eggs?"

Melody came to the table, obediently took a forkful from the platter. She washed it down with a glass of water, like medicine.

"Will you be coming to the Armory later?" she asked Garrick.

"I'll try to."

"I'll tell Miss Kelly."

Ned Revere dropped a cassette into the player and, as the first bright notes of Mozart's *Concerto for Flute and Harp* sounded, swiveled his chair toward the window. His shoulders were hunched, his uniform blouse a starched, tight fit over his powerful torso.

"Jesus, Rob, you put me in one lousy position." He rubbed the back of his neck and waited for Garrick to say something.

Surprised, Garrick asked, "Well, what would you have done? It doesn't hurt anybody this way, Ned."

"Not until you told me. Now it does. Now whatever I do, it's the wrong thing. Goddamn it, I'm a cop. What makes you think I'll help you cover up a—"

"Suicide?" Garrick cut him off. "We're talking about the possibility of suicide, not murder. And it's only that, a possibility. It could have been an accidental overdose. Who does it hurt if the death certificate says heart failure?"

Revere turned his chair, shut the cassette player. "You threw the stuff away. Okay, maybe I can see why you had to do that. But why'd you have to tell me?"

"Because I'm no doctor," Garrick said. "If there was going to be an autopsy I didn't know if they'd find traces of morphine. I had to tell you."

"One more thing dumped in my lap when the whole fucking town's coming apart," Revere shouted.

"He was your friend too, Ned," Garrick said, trying to keep his own temper in check in the face of Revere's unexpected anger.

"You wanted to dump it in my lap and watch me squirm. At least have the guts to admit it."

Revere's face was red, his voice hoarse, his assessment of Garrick's motives almost paranoid.

He didn't look, or sound, like Ned Revere at all.

"The obit goes in today's paper. Death from heart failure. You can take it anywhere you want from there,

Ned," Garrick said slowly. "But if you rake mud over Tom Seymour's grave it's going to cost you your badge."

In the instant before Revere swung at him, Garrick thought, Now just why the hell did you say that?

It wasn't what he'd meant to say at all. You don't make that kind of cheap threat to a close friend, no matter what he says.

The words had just come out.

Garrick caught the blow on his forearm and shoved the police chief away from him.

"We better both cool off, Ned."

"Cool off, shit. From now on you want to come in here you better call for an appointment a week in advance. Now get out of my sight."

Monsieur Taitbout came slowly down the steps of the Armory holding an enormous black umbrella low over his head with both hands to keep the wind from taking it.

"I am on my way to the newspaper to see you," he shouted at Garrick, who was beginning to climb the steps.

When Garrick gestured toward the doors above and behind him, the little Frenchman shook his head emphatically.

"Not while that woman is there, Mr. Garrick. This is why I am on my way to see you. I have booked my flight to Paris."

A sudden gust of wind took the umbrella. Monsieur Taitbout lurched after it down the steps, Garrick catching his arm. The Frenchman's glasses had fogged over and he stared sightlessly at the driving rain.

"Is Melody here yet?"

"Your daughter and that ridiculous forgery of a Columbine, yes. And the Kelly woman insisting it is authentic when even a first-year student would know this is impossible. A mockery, monsieur. She makes a mockery of our profession."

Garrick had come straight from police headquarters,

and Monsieur Taitbout's agitated state matched his own. He pointed across the Commons to Nick's. "Tell me about it over a cup of coffee?"

Taitbout nodded dolefully. "Very well, but it will make no difference. My decision is definitive."

Ten minutes later they sat at a table on the glass-enclosed terrace outside Nick's. At this hour, and in this weather, they were the only customers.

Garrick only half listened while Taitbout explained, as he had the day Melody found it, why the painting could not be more than thirty years old. "And perhaps a good deal less," he said, sipping his coffee. "Perhaps, for all I know, the varnish is barely dry. When a man ages, his hair turns gray or falls out, his teeth fall out, his skin wrinkles, *entendu*? Certain ineluctable signs of age. It is the same with a painting. Blanching, *craquelure*, bloom, flaking. Ineluctable signs, my dear Mr. Garrick, and they are not apparent in this forgery. A fact that M. A. Kelly is as aware of as I am."

"Faded spots?" Garrick asked suddenly.

"Eh?" Monsieur Taitbout thumbnailed his mustache and cocked his head to one side.

"I said faded spots. Aren't they a sign of age too?"

"Well, of course, those too," Monsieur Taitbout said in a very soft voice. He was staring down at his coffee cup. "The passage of time can cause transparencies in the oil medium which we call pentimenti. The artist's initial work, even his charcoal sketch, may become visible. Or sometimes one discovers that the canvas was used for an earlier painting, then covered with a later one. An example of this—"

"What about the pentimenti in the painting Melody found?"

Monsieur Taitbout pursed his lips. He started to say something, then changed his mind.

"Well? What about them?"

Monsieur Taitbout adjusted his glasses low on the bridge of his nose. He blinked. He removed his glasses and polished them with a napkin. "It is strange you should mention those, monsieur," he said at last. "As I have said, certain ineluctable signs of age. My eyes are not what they once were." He managed a faint little smile, and Garrick suddenly liked him. "I thought they were—how do you say?—playing tricks on me. At first I saw no pentimenti, and then . . . now even these eyes can see them. The one attempt the forger made to artificially age his painting."

"You couldn't notice them at first," Garrick said, "because they weren't there."

"That is not possible, monsieur. I assure you it was my eyes."

"Except that I saw it happen too."

Monsieur Taitbout looked at Garrick for the first time. He shook his head. "My eyes," he said, and tapped a finger against his temple. "And if not my eyes, then here. I thought it was in here. And therefore of course I could not bring it to the attention of M. A. Kelly. But you saw it too."

"Yes."

For a long moment the little Frenchman did not speak. Then he sighed and said: "Monsieur, is it possible for one to have cognac with his coffee at this hour in the state of Connecticut?"

The cognac was ordered and delivered to the table. Monsieur Taitbout belted it down. "What we both saw was impossible. You understand that?"

"I understand what you're saying, yes."

"And I must now tell you that what is beneath seems as genuinely the work of Jean-Baptiste Columbine as what is above. Considering the apparent age of the painting, that is impossible too."

"Are you certain about the age of the painting?"

"Absolutely certain, monsieur. And yet . . ."

Garrick waited.

"No forger is that good."

Again Garrick waited.

"I believe I shall have another cognac, monsieur. Before I cancel my booking to Paris."

Margriet Kelly was adjusting a reflector on a lamp

clamped to the edge of the table, lowering it until the beam of light was nearly parallel to the canvas.

"*Bien,* we are in time," Monsieur Taitbout said to Garrick. "She is just about to examine the painting with raking light. Unlike flat light, it reveals the slightest occurrence of flaking, cleavage, those ineluctable signs of age which—"

"More important in this case," said Margriet, "the shadows can indicate the presence of underpainting."

"If there is any," Monsieur Taitbout said.

The narrow beam of light slashed the painting horizontally, falling across the wall of Bourg St. Martin.

"Absolutely no flaking. Absolutely no cleave," Monsieur Taitbout said. "Absolutely less than thirty years old." He almost sounded disappointed, Garrick thought.

"It's bumpy," Melody said. "Look, you can see bumps all along there."

"A ridge," Margriet said. She moved the lamp sideways.

"And there," Melody said, "like there's something under the painting, making it higher there."

"Indeed," said Monsieur Taitbout. "The pigments of *another* painting. It is evident that the canvas was used more than once."

"And," said Margriet, "from the extent of the ridging—look, here and here—I'd say for two complete paintings."

Margriet moved the lamp again.

"Hold it," Garrick said.

Midway along the narrow beam was the two-story house, the window he had seen, the single shaft of sunlight striking it, the vague suggestion of something beneath.

Either it had faded more or the raking light showed more clearly what Garrick thought he had seen.

A room. A bedroom, the canopied bed executed minutely, painstakingly.

"An interior scene," said Monsieur Taitbout, bending over, peering at the canvas. "Hardly a pentimento at all."

"But he painted the window over it," Margriet argued. "And sunlight reflecting off the glass. The question is whether—"

"Hold it," Garrick repeated. Margriet had been about to move the lamp.

A tiny figure lay on the four-poster bed. Garrick could feel the back of his neck prickling.

"That wasn't like that before," Eve said. "You couldn't see the bed."

"You couldn't even see inside the room," Melody agreed.

"Will this raking light do that?" Eve asked.

Margriet shook her head. "Not ordinarily with pentimenti. You'd have to use infrared photography."

Melody said it before Garrick could. "Unless it's changed somehow since I found it. Can that happen?"

Garrick knew what Margriet's answer would be, or even Monsieur Taitbout's. He said, "Put the light on the church, will you?"

Margriet moved the lamp higher on the painting. The stone wall of the church seemed transparent now. Under it was red, not the uniform suggestion of redness Garrick had previously seen, but a redness that Columbine had captured in a flickering instant. A fire.

All right, Garrick thought. They all saw the painting before, more than once. This wasn't there. They'll have to admit that much, won't they? A solid stone wall, the pigments thick to show its massiveness. Now a wall like glass, and a fire raging behind it.

He heard Monsieur Taitbout's hushed voice. ". . . as if, in one regard, the painting had aged three hundred years right before our eyes."

Garrick waited for someone to refute that now. He almost hoped that Margriet could.

She said nothing.

"Like Columbine painted a cross section of the village and then painted the village over it," Melody said.

"That seems quite possible," Margriet agreed, "though I can't imagine why he'd do it."

Melody scowled, bit her lip. "Well, what if he was experimenting with magic, and he—"

"Mademoiselle," Taitbout interrupted her, "it has not been established that this is the veritable work of Jean-Baptiste Columbine. Far from it."

"What were you saying about magic?" Garrick asked Melody.

"Oh, nothing. Only that Columbine, you know, got pretty heavily into it. Didn't he, Miss Kelly?"

Margriet nodded. She had shut the tangential lamp and, its colors less vivid under the overhead light, the painting seemed to Garrick somehow less inimical.

"That's all I meant," Melody said quickly. Garrick sensed she was backing off from something, as if she didn't want to share it with anyone who doubted the painting's authenticity.

"Mr. Garrick?"

It was the Armory custodian. "Paper calling you, Mr. Garrick."

Garrick took the call in the custodian's small office just off the entrance.

"Rob? What a goddamn thing." He recognized the voice of Howie McGrath, the day rewrite man. "Both of them the same morning. Christ."

Garrick thought of Dr. Tom at once. He almost asked who the other one was.

"Dr. Tom Seymour and Reverend Pritchard, they were both found dead this morning," McGrath said, and numbly, Garrick told himself he somehow should have known.

22

Margriet was adjusting the bellows of the enlarger when Garrick joined her in the basement darkroom of the Martinsburg *News* Building. The small, windowless room was cluttered with old-fashioned equipment that Garrick had never seen the need to replace.

"You look all in," Margriet said. "We could skip this."

"No, that's all right," Garrick told her. "How are you making out?" His fatigue was more emotional than physical. He'd spent hours reworking his obituaries of Dr. Tom and Miles Pritchard, not that he'd been able to do much for the minister. If a man douses himself with gasoline and lights a match, it can't come out any way but suicide. The only question that couldn't be answered was why: Miles Pritchard was as unlikely a suicide as anyone Garrick had ever known.

Except for the painting. Except for the pentimento on the wall of the church, the red of flame beneath it.

Faded spots in a painting found under mysterious circumstances by the daughter of Martinsburg News *publisher Robert Garrick today predicted the death by suicide of the Rev. Miles Pritchard, minister of the First Congregational Church, as earlier pentimenti had predicted the deaths of Matthias Hawley and Dr. Tom Seymour. Mr. Garrick could not be reached for comment in his padded cell in the psychiatric ward of Martinsburg General Hospital.*

". . . working from sixteen-millimeter closeups of the three pentimenti," Margriet was saying. "High-speed film under raking light, so the definition ought to be okay even after they're enlarged. It better be, because I drew a blank with X-rays."

"Didn't you more or less expect that?"

"Well, forgers generally do use white lead in the ground to make their work X-ray proof."

Garrick wasn't sure whether he felt disappointment or relief. "Then it is a forgery?"

"Forgers generally use it, and Columbine almost invariably *did*. So we're right back where we started. Still, with these enlargements . . ."

As Margriet talked of texture, of the individuality of brush strokes, of using pigment analysis later to establish whether the palette was Columbine's own, Garrick knew he was reluctant to see the enlargements. He was almost afraid of them.

"It isn't necessary, though," Margriet said.

"What? I'm sorry."

"You *are* all in. You've had one tough day, haven't you?"

"I'll survive," Garrick said, angry with himself. "What isn't necessary?"

"Analyzing the pigments. It would only confirm what we already have. Brush strokes are as reliable as fingerprints. This was the work of Jean-Baptiste Columbine, believe me. Never mind the apparent age of the canvas. I'd be convinced even if the medium was still wet."

"How come?"

"If a forger tries to duplicate an artist's brushwork, he had to do it painstakingly. And that's self-defeating, because the spontaneity of the master isn't there and you can see the hesitation. If this were just a painting in the *style* of Columbine, I might have doubts. But here, where it's faithful to the sketch in so many—" Margriet had been examining one of the enlargements closely. "I've got to be seeing things," she said.

Garrick joined her at the enlarger table, where she had set the three prints out in a row.

"The one in the middle, Rob."

Neither of them spoke for a while; there was nothing that had to be said. The enlargements said it all.

The wall of the church had faded completely. It had become—*become*—an interior scene.

Flames flickering at the altar, and a tiny figure of a priest in a chasuble a deeper red leaning over something on the altar, something almost hidden by the flames. A body?

Above the altar hung a crucifix, upside down.

As the painting, Garrick remembered, had hung upside down that first morning at home, when Melody had come downstairs not limping.

Garrick picked up the enlargement. "That's how Miles Pritchard died," he said. "He doused himself with gasoline and lit a match. In church this morning. At the altar."

Margriet turned into his arms, her hands on his chest, her head against his shoulder. "That letter. That old letter of Columbine's."

"What about it?"

"When he was writing about black magic, remember?" Her voice was throaty, urgent. "He said that the artist could learn from the sorcerer. And then he said something about a fire in a church."

"Listen," Garrick said, "I want you to tell me everything you know about Jean-Baptiste Columbine. His life in Bourg St. Martin, exactly why he had to leave, where he went, what he—"

He felt her straighten in his arms before moving away from him. For an instant he saw the fear in her violet eyes, but then it was gone. She smiled thinly. "You don't really think that's the explanation, do you? That was just talk," she said, and even her voice sounded different, as thin as her smile. "Of course you see things you couldn't see before. That's why I made the enlargements in the first place. Nothing mysterious about that. As I expected, they confirm the authenticity of the painting."

"Come on. That's not what we were talking about." Garrick thrust the three prints at her. "We were talking about this. Dr. Tom dying like this," he told her, showing the print of the building with the see-through window. "And Miles Pritchard dying like this."

"Killed by a painting? Please, Rob. Really."

"Well, damn it, you were thinking the same thing a minute ago."

"Was I?" She smiled thinly again, walked past him toward the door. He wanted to grab her, shake her, force her to admit it.

How could she change her mind like that?

Bewildered, he went out after her, shut the door, watched her striding along the corridor toward the stairs.

He never heard the explosion. He was only aware of something shaking him, picking him up, and hurling him across the scuffed asphalt tiles of the corridor.

"What am I going to do with a guy like you?" Ned Revere asked. "Let you out of my sight a few hours, and look what happens."

Garrick was seated on the one comfortable chair in his office, submitting impatiently to the ministrations of a gangling young man from the rescue squad.

"That ought to do it, Mr. Garrick," he said, running a second strip of adhesive tape across the gauze pad on Garrick's lacerated elbow. The analgesic ointment was beginning to take effect. Garrick moved his arm experimentally. It was stiff, and he knew it would get stiffer. His right knee throbbed with pain.

"We still ought to X-ray that," the gangling young man said.

Revere agreed. "Let them run you down to the hospital."

"No. I'm okay."

"Well, just to make sure."

"I said I'm okay."

Revere came close, staring into his eyes. "Dizzy? Nauseous or anything?"

Garrick shook his head irritably. He hated being made a fuss over. The door to the office was shut, but he knew half the paper's staff waited outside in the hall, the half that wasn't down in the basement peering into the shambles that had been the darkroom. Margriet sat next to him smoking a cigarette. She'd been too far from the darkroom for the force of the explosion to reach her. She put the cigarette out as Revere said, "It was under the sink. In a can, or some kind of heavy container open at the top. Sink took most of the blast, but the whole room's a mess. A few seconds earlier and they'd have carried you out of there. In pieces. Who has access to the darkroom?"

"The door's never locked," Garrick answered. "Staff photographer, that's Larry Applebaum. But some of the reporters shoot their own stuff and develop it too. Hell, Ned, even some of the high-school kids use the darkroom. Photography club—fifteen, maybe twenty members."

Revere made a face while Garrick pointed out, "It doesn't have to be someone who ordinarily uses the darkroom. I told you the door was never locked."

"Well, I'll want names. The reporters who take their own pictures, the members of the club."

"Ask young Craig Donaldson, he's their president."

Revere chewed on that a few seconds, then said, "Donaldson's been blowing stumps out at his place with dynamite."

"Come on, Ned," Garrick said. "Craig Jr.? Why would he want to—"

"Why would anyone want to?"

"You're sure it was dynamite?"

"I don't know what the hell it was. Anybody can make a bomb. And kids can read about it in those underground newspapers, step-by-step instructions. Plumber's pipe filled with gunpowder, or a couple of sticks of dynamite. A percussion cap. A crude timing device. You could do it with a five-and-dime alarm clock. Maybe the bomb squad from Hartford will be able to tell us what it was. I'm just guessing. You know anybody with a grudge against you? Maybe even one of those nuts who keeps writing letters to the editor but you won't print them?"

Garrick shook his head. "It isn't that we didn't have any warning," he said. "How many places did the bomber call?"

"Doesn't have to be the same guy. A harmless crank makes some calls and it puts a bug in someone else's ear. Sometimes it works like that. But I'm just guessing there too. Bombing's not exactly a common crime in Martinsburg."

"What is?" Garrick asked.

Revere looked perplexed for a moment, then nodded. "Sure, you've got a point. We used to get nothing but traffic infractions and weekend drunks. Now we've got every crime in the book except homicide. It's like the whole town's become a disaster area. How can a place get jinxed like that?"

The gangling young man said, "Well, if you're sure you don't want me to run you down to the hospital . . ."

Garrick shook his head and the man opened the door on faces and a babble of voices, and left.

"Rob? About this morning." Revere looked uncomfortable. "Forget it, okay? Sometimes a guy gets up on the wrong side of the bed."

"Okay, Ned. Sure. I'm sorry too."

He hoped Revere didn't catch the note of impatience in his voice. There was nothing more to be accomplished here. Whether or not Revere found the bomber wouldn't explain what was happening to Martinsburg.

Eve was sitting on the sofa, shoes off, a book on her lap.

"Hi," Melody said as she came in.

Eve put the book on the cocktail table. Melody read the title upside down. *The Cry of the Dove: A Life of Jean-Baptiste Columbine.*

"Where'd you get that?" Melody asked. She felt jealous, as if Eve had taken something away from her. "They didn't have it in the library here."

"I sent to New York for it. It just came in the mail. They didn't have anything in the library on him."

"They had a few books. I took them all out. Is that

one any good? Does it tell anything about . . ." Melody's voice trailed off.

"About what?"

"Nothing. I just . . . nothing."

"Moreau's a marvelous biographer."

"He is? Maybe I'll read it when you're finished."

"Five hundred and some pages of small print still to go," Eve said.

"Can I see it?"

Eve held the book out, and Melody turned quickly to the contents page. Nothing about Gaddara in the chapter heads. She flipped through to the index—no Gaddara. She handed the book back.

"It looks okay." Melody smiled.

"It ought to. A lot of people think Moreau's the best biographer of the twentieth century."

"Really? Even if he leaves things out?"

"What kind of things?" Eve asked quickly.

"Just things. You know."

"Things you read in those other books?"

Melody nodded.

"I guess that makes you Martinsburg's leading expert on Jean-Baptiste Columbine. Give me a for-instance."

"I can't think of any right now. What does *Wanderjahren* mean? That's German, isn't it?"

"What it sounds like. Wander years," Eve said.

"That's what I thought, but I wasn't sure. Can I look at it again?"

Melody found the *Wanderjahren* chapter, skimmed its pages.

. . . journeyed to the East with a band of Manouche gypsies. Where and how long they traveled remains a mystery. It is probable that Columbine's interest in the occult began during this interlude, for the Vouet letter was written not long after his return to the West, where he settled for a time with the gypsies outside the market town of Coevorden in Drenthe.

No Serbia, no Gaddara, no Black Mass. It was all speculation on what living with the *manouches* around the turn of the eighteenth century might have been like.

The next chapter, the next-to-last chapter, was called *At Home in Drenthe*. Melody skimmed it quickly too. Almost pastoral existence . . . Dutch toleration of the gypsies . . . effect of the *grimoires* on Columbine. Then:

> . . . *traveling alone that winter to La Rochelle, hoping to hear news of his son Philippe, the sickly child who had been convalescing on an aunt's farm in the Charente-Maritime that night so long before when Marie and Annique were brutally murdered by the dragoons. But Philippe had some years earlier sailed from La Rochelle to Armsterdam and eventually to Ireland, a route taken by many Huguenots during the years of persecution.*

> *Thus one can imagine Jean-Baptiste's pleasure when, on his return to Drenthe, Tita informed him that she was expecting a child. It almost seemed that he could begin again, the years stripped away, the torment forgotten. . . .*

"I didn't know he had a son," Melody said.

"Columbine?"

"A son that went to England or somewhere." Melody turned back a page. "What does *akelei* mean?"

"It's Dutch for columbines."

"How many languages do you know, anyway?" In spite of her impatience to get back to the Notebook, which she hoped she could finish this evening, Melody was impressed.

Eve smiled. "To speak? Just English, really, and sometimes I wonder about that. But you know me, I'm a bug on derivations of names. Did Columbine change his name to Akelei in Holland?"

"No, it was something about his son."

"Did *he* change his name?"

Melody's impatience got the better of her. She shut the book, put it down. "I just happened to see it in a footnote. If the son had children and all, and what the family name might have become. Well, I've got some homework to do."

"See you at dinner? I'm making filet stroganoff," Eve said.

"I'll take a snack upstairs."

Melody went to her room thinking: How about that? The name could have become Kelly.

23

From the Notebook of Jean-Baptiste Columbine

. . . for their fine Belgian Percherons more than the
wagon, but Tita was their *phuri dai* and finally they
consented.

The morning I left, she said, You're no longer a
young man, Jean-Baptiste. Must you go?

I told her I was far from *nonpoant*. She looked at my
gray hair and the empty sleeve of my tunic.

—It's a long way.

—La Rochelle was farther.

And what did that journey accomplish?

—My son is safe in Ireland, I learned that much.

—Your daughter is here. Our daughter. She needs
you, Jean-Baptiste. Why must you take the painting to
Bourg St. Martin?

Her words startled me, and I asked how she knew I
would take the painting there.

—Because the day after you completed it, you said
you were going. Tita looked quickly away. I told her
she was lying.

—Because I can see certain things, not so clearly as
Gaddara can, but nevertheless. Again Tita glanced
away. When her gaze returned to me, in the dim light
her face looked catlike.

—You must not go, she said, and her voice was
deeper, huskier.

I patted her arm, whether resssuringly or condescendingly I wasn't certain. I had learned the gesture
from Gaddara.

—Gaddara came to me in my dreams last night, Jean-Baptiste. She said that I must stop you.

That was only a dream.

—It was Gaddara speaking to me. I know, because once before, years ago, she came and spoke in my dreams. Zurka was drunk that day, and he beat me. In my dream that night, Gaddara commanded me to leave the wagon. When I returned in the morning I found Zurka dead. The interior of the wagon looked as if . . .

(Most of a page rotted away.)

. . . smaller and smaller, standing in the dust with the child in her arms, and then I flicked the reins and the road curved past some willow trees, and I could see them no more.

Mariole! I was finally doing it, the painting in the wagon, the four huge Percherons carrying it every day closer to Bourg St. Martin.

All the magic Gaddara had taught me, all the lore I had found in the *grimoires,* all the hatred that consumed me flowing through my fingers to the painting.

I hoped to leave the canvas with the family of my friend Jacques Rivoire, who gave his life for me. I knew that his widow, if she still lived and if she had not fled like so many Huguenots, would *conjoir* me.

And what would happen to her, after I left the painting? I would not permit myself to dwell on that. How could I tell her to flee for her life, unless I told her why?

. . . all in the canvas, the carter who would not open the village gate, the captain of dragoons Lemaître who had raped Annique, the doctor who would do nothing to stop her bleeding to death, the priest Gavrillac who betrayed me.

. . . things I loved most, the smells of the oil and turpentine, the feel of the brush in my hand when I began to do the underpainting, as if the façades of the buildings had been cut away in one stroke by a giant knife, so that I could execute the details as meticulously as a Breughel or a Bosch. . . .

. . . that I loved . . .

(These pages at the end of the book are almost falling apart. Sometimes they crumble if I just touch them. Like right there. Does it say "to destroy something you hate with something you love"? That's what Gaddara always used to tell Jean-Baptiste. And this part isn't French at all, it's Latin. *Quod superius est sicut quod inferius et quod inferius est sicut quod superius ad perpetranda miracula rei unius.* Whatever that means!)

. . . when the Sieur de Ramezay stands helpless while his lame daughter Dominique suffers and dies, then my revenge will . . .

To paint him, then, as "St. Martin Sharing His Cloak with a Beggar" was the crowning touch. The patron saint of all France, the most beloved for the most hated, I feel even Gaddara would have appreciated that. And their faces below, in the underpainting . . .

. . . Christ of the Crown of Thorns becoming the face of Father Vasili. I saw that happen with my own eyes. This time I have made it happen.

colder

muddy from the autumn rains

familiar

as the landscape lifted toward rocky escarpments

urgency seemed to impart itself to the steaming horses   stride increased until they

control the careening wagon with only one

(I'm writing this part just as it appears on the page, or what's left of the page.)

The pencil slipped from Melody's fingers, trembling now with excitement. It's the same painting, she thought, the lost painting of Jean-Baptiste Columbine. It's *my* painting. It isn't in Bourg St. Martin *then*, it's here in Martinsburg *now*.

Tell someone? But who would believe her? Surely not Eve. Her father? Maybe. But he hated the painting, he'd just try to destroy it again. Margriet? Would Margriet understand? She knew the painting was genuine, despite that silly Monsieur Taitbout, didn't she? She knew it was real even if it didn't seem old enough.

If anybody believed her, it would be Margriet.

Melody was almost afraid to turn the page. Maybe the rest of the Notebook would be all but obliterated by time, by decay, like the last couple of pages. Maybe she'd never learn what happened.

. . . blinded me, two shafts of light piercing the darkness, in the pelting rain, just as I approached the crossroads north of Bourg St. Martin.

. . . worse, for with the sudden appearance of the shafts of light I heard a roaring sound, a frantic bellowing, terrifying in the night.

It came closer, and behind the lights I saw something enormous, a great boxlike thing larger than a dozen wagons, festooned with baleful red eyes. It was like a dragoon (??No, here dragon means "dragon"!!!), but they exist only in legends, and this was horribly real.

The horses went wild with terror, rearing and then plunging on. The wagon swayed perilously as I tried to rein up, but my one hand lacked the strength.

Toward us raced the vision of Hell, the great shafts of light impaling us, the body of it gleaming red with the light of those baleful eyes, the wind-driven rain bouncing off its flanks like hailstones.

Then the thing flashed by and I saw the smoke billowing behind it, smelled the brimstone, felt the heat of. . .

. . . as suddenly as it had come. The two lead horses whinnied and reared again, the wagon wheels slewed in mud, and I knew we must overturn. (Matt Hawley's truck??? Is *that* what happened?)

. . . two wheels off, one of them close by and one I found in a ditch farther along the road.

Of the vision of Hell I could see nothing. It had vanished like a *flamerole*. But there were deep tracks in the mud, like tracks mill wheels might make.

My head ached fiercely as I hobbled back to the wagon. It lay on its side in the mud, the steaming horses standing in the traces, their legs trembling. The rear axle had been split like kindling wood.

And I? My limbs were lead, my vision swam, I felt as if I had come through an *ignise*.

I barely had the strength to climb into the rear of the overturned wagon. A few hours of sleep, I thought, and then I would take the painting the rest of the way on foot.

I stumbled in the darkness, crawled across the side of the wagon that had become its floor.

My heart leaped suddenly, and I felt a terrible fear.

What if the painting had been damaged?

I groped my way past the curtain and into the forward compartment where the gypsies keep their icons, where I had placed the canvas. I found a candle, flint, and tinderbox. It was a laborious business with just one hand, but finally the flame flickered and held.

The painting had vanished.

(Most of a page gone.)

. . . nowhere . . . vanished as the vision of Hell had vanished. As if the vision of Hell had taken it.

I did not sleep that night. Gaddara's warning came back to taunt me. I could not do the thing myself.

Mariole! Would I have to paint it all again? I knew I would find no peace until I did.

. . . the wagon where it lay and set out with the horses on the long road to Coevorden, traveling by night, stealing food where I could. . . .

(It's practically all mildewed here.)

delirious with fever

on Tita's face

milsoudiers, Jean-Baptiste, and they are no more than *roquarts* now

nothing of the vision of Hell

in the mirror of an old man

only Tita, for
they loved her as much as they

strong enough to take short walks along
the canal beyond the fortifications. One clear cold day
early that winter, bundled to the ears

Skim ice had already appeared on
the canal, and soon it would be

strange and moody si-
lence   How could her eyes be violet, like the eyes of
Gaddara?   movements of a cat, could I ever forget? I shook her, but still the voice was not Tita's voice.
Deeper, huskier.

—You are such a bungler, Jean-Baptiste, she said.
Somehow Gaddara had come to me in the person of
Tita. Gaddara, who had killed Zurka over a vast distance. Gaddara, who had given me a *grimoire* that had
not yet been written. Why shouldn't she come to me
now? I could accept that more readily than I could the
vision of Hell.

I told her of the vision.

—Of course, I know all that, Jean-Baptiste.

—Then tell me where to find the painting.

The violet eyes gazed into mine, Tita's eyes but not
Tita's. She would not tell me what I wished to know.
Instead she spoke these words:

—Magic is for the select few, Jean-Baptiste. The less
adept lose their way. The magician must master all
things, must become God in man. But the inept magician? He is like a bumbling God.

I could not speak. The God Gaddara spoke of was
not the God I had forsaken so long ago. He was God
and the Devil in one, like the wheel of good and evil
that is one thing and not many.

—Now it falls on me to right the wrong you did. I
must go there.

I asked her where.

—Where you took the painting.

—To Bourg St. Martin?

—No, not Bourg St. Martin, she laughed.

—Then where?

—The other place. Where the forces are stronger, the blood of the Ramezays pulling you like a lodestone pulls iron, where there is another Ramezay with a lame daughter.

—They have left Bourg St. Martin?

—Oh, Jean-Baptiste! They are only gone for a while. To Paris. They'll return. That isn't what I meant.

I knew of a certainty then that I would paint the canvas again, though I did not say that.

—You understand so little. But you amuse me, my Jean-Baptiste. You always have. And now you have forced me to undertake the greatest adventure of all.

Then she spoke musingly, as if to herself:

—But I shall find no one close in blood to me. Who then? A Ramezay? Or perhaps a Columbine? Yes, that would be best, to set his power against my own.

I told her I did not understand, and she looked at me blankly, her eyes changing, her face changing as she clung to me.

She was Tita again.

We returned to the encampment. Later that afternoon, while Tita sang to our daughter an old romani song about a dancing bear, I stretched canvas over a frame and began to cover it with white lead.

Melody shut the notebooks and sat on the edge of her bed, staring at the dark window. Was it night already? She always lost herself in the Notebook, became unaware of the passage of time. She had lived a life in those pages, a life born anew in her translation of them. Now it was over—the last page, the last line, the stained supple covers of the book had surrendered all their secrets.

Had Columbine finished the second painting? Had he delivered it to Bourg St. Martin before his death?

Melody went to the window. The rain had stopped

but the pavement still gleamed wetly in the glow of the street lights.

Rivoire Street. Named so by the early Huguenot settlers because it went down to the river? But *rivoire* wasn't the word for river, was it? Melody tried the Cassell's dictionary. The word troubled her, and not just its meaning. She didn't know why.

It meant hammer. Riveting hammer. It had nothing to do with—

It was the name of Columbine's friend, the one who was killed when Columbine escaped from the priest Gavrillac's house. Jacques Rivoire. Like, say, Jack Hammer in English. She didn't know anyone named Hammer in Martinsburg. Maybe the name had died out. A lot of old names did. It was just left as the name of their street.

Unless, after almost three hundred years, it had changed in some way. What was that called again? Eve had told her once. An orthographic change, that was it.

Melody decided she would ask Eve about it. She wished her father was home. She wanted to talk to someone, wanted to get her mind off the Notebook, wanted to push the tingle of fear further back inside her. Bibi Tita's warning, her last day in Bourg St. Martin. *Don't go back. Stay with us. Be our little blond-haired Romi.* The other Tita, speaking in the Notebook with Gaddara's voice. *Where there is another Ramezay with a lame daughter.*

But that didn't make any sense. She wasn't a Ramezay, was she? Some kind of reincarnation then? A lot of kids at school were into reincarnation these days. Melody didn't believe in it, but it was a fun idea to play with. In an earlier incarnation I was ———. And then you'd fill in the blank as the spirit moved you. I was Alexander the Great or Cleopatra or Benjamin Franklin or Madame Curie.

I was the lame daughter of the Sieur de Ramezay, and I had wheat-blond hair and a friend named Annique who bled to death after the king's dragoons raped her. So Jean-Baptiste Columbine hates me, and he hates

my father, and he's going to get his revenge three
hundred years later.

Silly. No way.

Still, for the first time Melody wished Bibi Tita
hadn't given her the Notebook, wished she hadn't found
the painting. Wished Bourg St. Martin and Martinsburg
weren't sister cities.

She went downstairs. Eve was in the hall putting on
her white trenchcoat.

"Oh, I didn't want to disturb you," she said. "I left a
note in the kitchen. At seven-thirty you cut the steak
into strips and pan-fry it rare, in case I'm not back."

"Sure," Melody said. "I know how to make filet stroganoff. Where are you going, anyway?"

"There's some kind of a rally down at the Commons.
Those vigilantes or minutemen or whatever they call
themselves."

"Eve, I was wondering," Melody said. "You know all
that stuff about names. Rivoire, that's got to be French,
doesn't it?"

"Rivoire? Oh, the name of this street. It means—"

"I know. A hammer for rivets. Before they had rivet
guns."

Eve looked impressed. "That's right. Your French is
really coming along."

"What I was wondering—it used to be a name in
French, a surname. Didn't it?"

Eve nodded, looked more impressed. "That's right."

"Well, did it just die out here, or what?"

"No, it didn't die out. Old names have a way of hanging around in New England. But there was an orthographic change."

"That's what I figured when I . . . that's what I figured."

"Why don't you take a guess?"

"Rivoire? Gee, I don't know."

"Maybe if I gave you a hint. He's a friend of your
father's."

"Really? Rivoire? I still don't—" Melody clapped a

hand to her cheek. "Sure, how dumb can I get? It's got to be Revere—Ned Revere."

"And what would you like to bet he doesn't even know it?" Eve said with a smile.

Melody placed the knife and the butcher's steel on the work surface near the sink and hurried to the front door.

"Who's there?"

"It's me, Craig."

She wondered why Craig wasn't home eating. His father had a thing about promptness and in the Donaldson household seven o'clock meant dinner.

"You on a diet too or something?" she asked.

"Is anybody home?"

"Nope. That's why nobody answered the door when you rang."

It wasn't much of a joke, and Craig didn't laugh. He didn't even smile.

They went into the kitchen, Craig unzipping his parka.

"Don't I even get a little kiss?" Melody said.

Craig shifted his weight from one foot to the other. "Listen, are you sure nobody's home?"

"What's the matter with you, anyway?" Melody asked, picking up the butcher knife and sharpening it on the heavy rod.

"Nothing."

"Sure. Anybody can see that."

"I said nothing's the matter! I've just got to talk to you, that's all."

Melody had to talk to somebody herself, and when she'd opened the door to Craig she wondered why she hadn't thought of him earlier. She had to tell somebody about the Notebook, about Bibi Tita's warning. No matter how wild it sounded, Craig wouldn't make fun of her; he liked her too much to do that. Just telling him would make her feel better.

But now it looked like something was bothering Craig as much as the Notebook was bothering her.

He sat down at the table. He didn't say anything.

"I thought you had to talk to me."

"Melody, listen, I—" Craig swallowed hard, and then he began to cry.

Melody cradled his head against her chest, stroked his hair, and felt like crying herself. Craig was usually so easygoing, always smiling and cheerful, all she ever had to do when she was feeling down was talk to him.

"Hey, come on, hey now. Whatever it is, it can't be that bad."

Craig got up, went to the sink, doused his face with cold water.

"Sure. Of course not. What I ought to do is take this knife and slit my throat."

She came up behind him, her arms going around his waist. "Don't say dumb things like that. Don't even *say* them."

He dried his face with a dish towel. Melody rumpled his wet hair. "Greasy kid stuff," she said, and that drew a shaky smile from him.

Just when Melody thought he was ready to talk, ready to tell her what was bothering him, the phone rang. She went into the living room and picked it up. "Hello?"

"Melody?" It was her father. "Better tell Eve not to hold dinner."

"It's filet stroganoff. It doesn't take long to make. So if you want us to wait—"

"No, that's all right. I'm at the Armory with Margriet. We'll send out for something." After a pause, Garrick said: "Could you let me speak to Eve?"

"She's not here."

"Where'd she go?" Garrick sounded anxious.

"Practically right outside the Armory. There's some kind of meeting on the Commons."

"On second thought maybe I'll make it home for dinner after all."

"What's the matter, Daddy?"

"Nothing serious. Might be better if you weren't alone, that's all."

"I'm not alone. Craig's here."

"Is he? In that case, why don't the two of you come on over to the Armory?"

"You mean right now?"

"Sure. You'll want to be here anyway."

"How come?" Melody asked.

"Margriet's going to try to remove the overpainting."

"Oh, wow," Melody said. "We'll be right over."

After she hung up, Craig asked, "Did he say anything about the explosion?"

"What explosion?"

"Somebody planted a bomb at the newspaper."

"At the *News*? God! Was anybody hurt?"

Craig shook his head. "But they could've been. You have to be crazy to do a thing like that."

Melody looked at him, and she knew. She just knew, even before he said:

"I couldn't stop myself. I . . . couldn't . . . stop . . . myself."

24

Sergeant Whitlock sat behind the wheel, chomping on a dead cigar, Ned Revere at his side, First Selectman Alvin Waugh fidgeting in the seat behind them. They were parked on the north side of the Commons, in front of the Congregational Church, watching the crowd grow.

The radio squawked; Revere heard the dispatcher send two cars out to the Strip. Looters had broken the windows of Ames's Discount Center and were carrying out TV sets, kitchen appliances, hardware. Revere picked up the mike. "No shooting," he said. "Clear them out if you can. Otherwise let them walk away with the stuff."

Al Waugh leaned forward, placed a hand on Revere's shoulder. "We can't handle it, Ned. They're all over town."

Revere did not reply. It had been going on since nightfall. Mobs roaming the streets, rocks shattering plate-glass windows, indiscriminate looting, and three fires he knew of that looked like arson. Revere rubbed his eyes, a gesture more of defeat than weariness. Forty cops, six prowl cars, no riot equipment—he knew Al Waugh was right.

So did the noisy mob crowding the Commons. A thousand people anyway, Revere figured, and more every minute. They had baseball bats, golf clubs, two-by-fours. Revere thought more than a few of them were carrying handguns.

"Who's that joker?" Whitlock asked.

Across the Commons someone had climbed on the roof of a car. The beams of half a dozen flashlights pinned him against the autumn-bare branches of a maple. He was wearing a billed cap and raised both arms over his head.

Revere opened the glove compartment, took out a pair of field glasses. He focused them on the man standing on the roof of the car. "It looks like Vito Mauriello," he said. Mauriello, shop steward at the textile mill, was active in local politics.

Whitlock asked, "Wasn't his brother the guy that got knifed at Nick's?"

Revere nodded, watching Vito Mauriello raise a bullhorn. "Now just where the hell'd he get that thing?" he said.

Suddenly the front seat of the car moved, as if Whitlock had slammed back against it with all his weight. "Jesus!" Whitlock shouted. He bent forward, one hand to his chest. Then he opened the car door.

"Hey, Cal, what is it?"

Whitlock did not answer. He walked across the street toward the fringes of the mob, joined them as they crowded closer to Vito Mauriello, standing on the roof of the car on the far side of the Commons.

Mauriello's voice boomed out in the darkness.

You're goddamn right it's our town, Charlie Dahlgren told himself, listening to Vito Mauriello's speech. Charlie stood near the car, anonymous in windbreaker and jeans. You're goddamn right we can't let them get away with it. I know spics, you give them a hand and they'll chop off your arm at the elbow. Charlie could feel the weight of the service revolver tucked into his belt under his windbreaker. He knew he would use it before the night was over. He wanted to use it. He could almost feel it kicking back against his hand now, could almost see the muzzle flash in the darkness. Show those spic bastards.

Charlie heard the wail of fire sirens. The sky glowed red north of the Commons, behind the Congregational Church where Chief Revere's car was parked, corn popper flashing. Charlie couldn't hear everything Vito

Mauriello said. The bell—that goddamn bell was driving him nuts.

The mob surged away from Vito Mauriello's car, flowed across the Commons, splintered into smaller mobs that raced toward Conant Street, toward Bank, toward Rivoire, brandishing baseball bats, golf clubs. Vito Mauriello, carrying a shotgun, led a group past Charlie. He made sure his service revolver was secure in his belt and ran with them.

Garrick had been among the last correspondents to leave Phnom Penh, his final overseas assignment. The ugly sound of the mob now, the wail of sirens, the frenzied rushing through the dark streets distantly aglow with fires, the mindlessness of it all, the final terror when the structure of a society breaks down—all of it now reminded him of that last night in Cambodia as he walked quickly back to the Armory.

Melody wasn't home. No note. Nothing. He had left his own note, in case she returned, telling her to stay inside, to lock the doors, to open them only to him or Eve.

He looked at the solid ugly cut-stone facade of the Armory, thinking, Maybe I missed her. Maybe she's there now.

Make her be there now.

Eve was inside with Margriet, both of them standing near a trestle table. The frame had been removed from the painting; a length of white silk covered the canvas.

"Any luck?" Eve asked.

"She's not home."

"Maybe we'd better wait there for her anyway."

Garrick considered that alternative. He knew mobs, and he had seen enough of this one. If it wasn't out of control now, it would be shortly. A house, any house, could be broken into. The Armory was an anomaly—a small fortress.

"I'll go back in case she shows up," he said. "You stay here. Call me if she comes."

"All right," Eve said.

Margriet turned from the silk-covered canvas toward them. Her deep violet eyes were wide, her voice husky as she said:

—I must go there.

Eve glanced at Garrick, who shook his head.

—Where there is another Ramezay with a lame daughter, Margriet said.

Garrick grasped her shoulders. In her eyes he was sure he saw a fleeting look of bewilderment as she said, ". . . provided it works. We'll know in a couple of hours. The overpainting should adhere to the silk when I lift it—theoretically. I've never actually done it before."

Garrick and Eve watched her brush a sharp-smelling liquid onto the white silk, heard her say, her voice normal now, "The solvent shouldn't damage the pigments if I've got it right. What it *should* do is work its way down to the layer of varnish between the paintings and soften it, a little at a time. Three applications, and you have to dry the canvas after each one." She turned and smiled at them, a perfectly normal smile. "The man who developed the technique says it's only a bit more complicated than brain surgery."

Eve walked Garrick to the door. "Rob, what's wrong with her? Did you see her face? What was she talking about? It was like she—"

Garrick said suddenly, "Ramsey!"

Eve just looked at him.

"That night I couldn't recall the name, my great-grandmother who owned a farm here? I'm sure of it—her name was Ramsey."

He thought, *Where there is another Ramezay with a lame daughter.*

Eve gripped his hand hard. "Find her, Rob. You've got to find her."

Half an hour earlier, Melody and Craig were walking along Rivoire Street toward the Commons, Melody holding his hand, all but tugging him. They could hear the crowd ahead of them, hear an amplified voice booming in the darkness.

"I can't," Craig said. "How can I tell him?"

"You've got to tell him."

"Sure," Craig said bitterly. "I can just hear myself. 'Mr. Garrick, I thought you'd like to know I took a stick of my father's dynamite and one of those percussion caps and an alarm clock, and I—' " Craig's voice broke. He pulled his hand away from Melody and stopped walking. "Please don't make me do it. Please."

"Craig, you've got to. Daddy can—"

"He can't do anything. Nobody can do anything. I'm going crazy!" Craig shouted. "What are you hanging around me for? I'm some kind of a stupid homicidal maniac. Maybe . . . maybe I'll try to kill you next."

Melody reached for his hand again, but Craig pulled away and ran into the middle of the street. "Keep way from me if you know what's good for you!" he cried, and then Melody saw men running toward them from the direction of the Commons, shouting, carrying bats and golf clubs.

For one terrible instant Melody thought they were going to attack Craig. But they streamed around him and past him, and Craig ran after them.

Go to the Armory? Melody thought.

What good would that do? Craig needed her.

The mob had slowed to a quick walk, heading straight down Rivoire Street toward the river.

25

Ned Revere stood in front of the First Selectman's big, cluttered desk as Alvin Waugh hung up the phone. It was just after nine o'clock.

"Well?"

"Governor's not sure," Alvin Waugh said.

"What the hell does that mean? She's *got* to send the National Guard. I don't even have a police force anymore. They're running with the mob."

Waugh stood, went to the window, slanted the Venetian blind down. Two cars were overturned in the street below, one of them Revere's. The Commons was deserted.

"She's sending a Colonel Ballard," Waugh said.

"Sure, I know John Ballard. C.O., Third Battalion. I thought you said she wasn't sure."

"She isn't. Ballard's coming down in a staff car." Waugh adjusted the knot of his tie, scratched his jaw. "To, as she put it, assess the situation."

"Shit," Revere said. "He won't even get here for almost an hour, and then he'll want a guided tour. Can't they at least start to mobilize? The way they're going, they won't be here till morning." Revere grimaced. "Martinsburg going up in smoke and we have to have a lady governor."

Both men stood at the window and saw the steeple of the Congregational Church silhouetted against the pulsing red glow in the night sky. Even with the window shut they could smell the smoke.

The collar of his windbreaker turned up against the

cold wind that blew off the river and across the park, Charlie Dahlgren watched a dozen men rocking a car at the curb, heard them shout when it overturned.

"I want the García kid," Vito Mauriello said.

What Vito Mauriello wanted seemed perfectly normal to Charlie. The García kid had knifed his brother, hadn't he?

"I'll blow his balls right off of him," Mauriello vowed. Then he cradled the shotgun more comfortably under his arm and spat on the sidewalk. "Only if I know those yellow bastards, he's probably halfway to the Massachusetts border by now."

Charlie said nothing. Any other Huguenot would do just as well, he thought.

Craig moved back quickly, three awkward skittering steps, as the car went over on its side with a crash. It reminded him of clearing the stand of timber with his father, the sputtering roar of the chain saw, judging which way the tree would fall and then getting out of the way fast. It reminded him in a way of a football game too, when Martinsburg High scored a touchdown, because the men were whooping and hollering like that now, like the crowds in the grandstand, whooping and hollering so much that they couldn't hear the big guy standing in front of the apartment building until he let go with one barrel of the shotgun to quiet them.

"Let's go get us some spics!" he shouted, and that sounded like the high school too, like the head cheerleader bellowing through his megaphone, urging the team to greater efforts, all in the spirit of good clean fun, like dynamiting stumps with his father and not letting himself think what else he had used the dynamite for.

Craig followed the crowd to the sidewalk. "You're kind of young for this, ain't you, kid?" the big guy said.

"I can take care of myself."

He felt someone grasp his arm—Melody. He broke away from her and followed the big guy into the lobby.

Glass shattered behind him as someone swung a bat at the plate-glass door.

Someone blocked her way. "Melody," he said, his voice urgent. "You don't belong here."

Relief flooded her. It was Charlie Dahlgren. Charlie could take care of them; Charlie would know what to do.

"You've got to stop him. Craig, he—"

Charlie wasn't listening. He said, "I'm taking you home."

Colonel John Ballard, Commanding Officer, Third Battalion, Connecticut National Guard, sat alongside his driver in the staff car as it raced west on U.S. 44 toward the intersection with State 62. The night was clear and cold, the sky overcast, the pavement dry. Ballard could see white patches of ice on the road shoulder.

Major Hockaday, his G-2, leaned forward from the back seat and asked, "What's this Waugh like, anyway?" He knew Ballard had been raised in Martinsburg, still had family there.

"Al Waugh? Well, a bit of a worrier."

"False alarm then?" Hockaday asked.

"Hard to say. Waugh's a fairly cautious man, conservative, but he tends to get anxious. It could be anything from a full-scale riot to a pep rally."

Ballard was glad that Governor Stresa hadn't ordered him to mobilize on the basis of one phone call. If the rioting hadn't reached the critical stage, the sight of a National Guard convoy rolling into town might make things worse, not better.

Ballard saw the amber warning light ahead, swaying in the wind. If Waugh was a cautious man, so was he. The battalion's rolling stock, trucks and jeeps and a half dozen armored personnel carriers back in Hartford, could start moving fifteen minutes after he sent word. He'd already called ahead to the state-police commander, French County; twenty state troopers had reached town by now to augment the city police.

Ballard hoped they could do the job. Martinsburg was a small enough city so that they'd know the locals. Many of them had likely grown up there themselves, as he had. The Guard was something else again. The reaction to it was usually reflex hostility. No matter how well his men were trained in riot control, no matter how coolly they played it, they would still be regarded as outsiders, almost like an invading army. And of course if things got out of hand once the Guard moved in, both the locals and the media would blame Colonel John Ballard.

"Know your way around town?" he asked the driver.

"No, sir. I only been to Martinsburg once or twice."

"You just follow Forty-four straight in," Ballard said. "Château's on the Commons."

Hockaday chuckled in the back seat. "Have a hard day, John? Did you say 'château'?"

"Did I?" The amber warning light was closer now. Ballard could see the steel girders of a small bridge ahead of them. The road was deserted.

Suddenly Ballard felt uneasy. "Town Hall," he said. "I mean the Town Hall."

The uneasiness gave way to fear. Ballard wished the car wasn't careening along at seventy miles an hour, wished they were in Bourg St. Martin already, a warm fire on the hearth in the great hall of the château, good red wine and a joint of beef shared with his friend Armand de Ramezay, the dragoons already billeted in the village. . . .

For a few seconds Colonal John Ballard, sitting ramrod straight now, wondered if he were going insane. Then he heard Hockaday shout "Watch it!" and felt the slick smooth sideways slew of the car as it crossed the bridge, wheels losing traction on ice, fishtailing, straightening, girders rushing by, swinging toward them, crunching a fender, shattering glass, the car tilting on two wheels, thumping back on all four, clear of the bridge, hitting more ice, the road shoulder this time, and skidding again, slower now but still out of control, flipping over into a gully, flipping again, the shoulder strap of the safety belt rigid across Colonel Ballard's throat.

Sometimes, especially when she was intent on the task at hand, Margriet was in control. Then that other thing, that thing inside her, would recede, would almost seem to go away.

Sometimes they argued inside her, Margriet and— and who? Her voice soundless inside her, and still she could hear it, her voice but deeper, huskier.

—You can destroy it. You have to destroy it.

"No, I can't. I cant."

—If you left the solvent on too long?

"No! It would eat through the varnish. The under-painting would be damaged, destroyed. I can't do that."

—You don't wish to, naturally. You're a Columbine.

"*It's* a Columbine, you mean."

—You could use a palette knife. Why don't you pick up that knife? It's so simple, really. The work of a few seconds. Slash the painting, Margriet.

The palette knife was in her hand.

"Margriet?" She heard Eve call her name.

The thing inside her receded. Margriet put the knife on the table, placing it carefully beside the silk-covered canvas.

—If you destroy it, I'll go away. You'll forget I was ever here. Wouldn't you like that?

Margriet's hand moved toward the can of solvent.

How could she destroy the canvas? Jean-Baptiste Columbine was her life's work, his lost painting the greatest art find since that Rembrandt turned up in an English country village, Margriet's opportunity to remove the overpainting the chance of a lifetime.

—Wouldn't you like that?

Margriet picked up the palette knife and hurled it across the room.

"Help me," she cried, going to Eve. "You've got to help me."

Major Hockaday's left wrist was swollen and blue. Blood from a gash on his scalp trickled into his eyes.

The car had settled upright a hundred yards off the road. Hockaday found a stick, used it and the tail of his shirt for a tourniquet on the driver's arm. He was unconscious, forearm shattered, arterial blood pumping black.

Colonel Ballard was dead.

Hockaday loosened the tourniquet, tightened it again. Then he tried the car radio. Miraculously, it was working. He put it on the state-police band and reported the accident.

Garrick saw the note he had left for Melody on the hall table, the knife on the work surface in the kitchen, butcher's steel next to it, the slab of steak on the cutting board, a pot simmering on the stove. She must have gone right out after his call, dropping everything, eager to join him at the Armory.

How long ago had that been? Almost three hours. It was less than a ten-minute walk down Rivoire Street to the Commons.

Garrick picked up the phone on the second ring. Craig Donaldson, Sr., said he'd been trying to reach him all night. Young Craig had gone out before dinner, hadn't returned. Did Garrick know where he was? Did Garrick know that Al Waugh had called the Governor and asked her to send the National Guard? Craig Donaldson sounded as concerned and helpless as Garrick felt.

He hung up and tried the ground floor again, hall, living room, dining room, kitchen, study, not knowing what he was looking for, hoping to find something.

Call the Armory? No point in that; Eve would phone him the minute Melody got there.

He poured Scotch in a glass, drank it straight, glanced at the bare wall above the hearth. He went upstairs slowly, his right knee stiff and painful, still not knowing what he was looking for.

Melody's room, the door shut, barring her teen-aged secrets from the rest of the world. He went in. The room was tidy, the bed made, none of the usual teen-aged clutter. Melody was as neat about her room as she was about her person. Even the books in the shelves under the window were neatly arranged in Melody's own order, paperbounds on the upper shelves, hard-cover below, fiction alphabetically by author, nonfiction by subject matter.

Except for the two books lying on the bed, the only note of disorder in the room. One looked like an ordinary school notebook, ruled and bound in mottled cardboard. The other was a dark, slim leather-bound volume with no printing on the cover.

Garrick felt the supple, stained leather of the unmarked book, opened it at random. The pages were brittle, yellow with age, mildewed. Not printed. Handwritten in a difficult script. He recognized a few words in French.

He turned to the first page. That was easy to read and even easy for Garrick, whose French was rudimentary, to translate.

Le Cahier de Jean-Baptiste Columbine.

Where in the world had she got hold of it?

He picked up the school notebook and saw in Melody's handwriting: **From the Notebook of Jean-Baptiste Columbine.** He had read only a couple of lines when the phone rang again.

He got it in his own bedroom, knowing it had to be Eve, sure that Melody was at the Armory with her.

"Rob?"

"Is she there?"

A pause. "No, not a sign of her. I'm sorry, Rob. I guess I shouldn't have called, but—"

"No, that's okay," he said. "What is it?"

"Margriet. She's worse—hysterical. She just sits there crying, begging me to help her."

"Help her? Help her do what?"

"Just help her. I don't know what. She—"

"Hello?" Garrick said. "Eve? Eve?"

He hung up, waited a few seconds, put the receiver to his ear. No dial tone. The phone was dead.

Garrick could almost take that in stride—the mobs prowling the streets, looting, burning, the phone company was no more immune than anything else, not if King Louis unleashed his soldiers like mastiffs kept too long in confinement. The Maréchal de Marillac had warned him, hadn't he?

Garrick sat for ten seconds without moving, the ten longest seconds of his life.

Then he returned to Melody's room, opened her notebook and began to read.

26

Ned Revere drove slowly past the Southern New England Telephone Company building. Smoke poured from the gaping doors, the shattered windows. That would be a bad one, Revere knew—if the Volunteer Fire Department didn't get there soon, the building would be a gutted ruin.

Revere reminded himself that the fire department, like the police; was out of commission. He was driving the last remaining patrol car, and he'd seen abandoned fire trucks on Bank Street, on Conant, and out on the Strip. Now, at eleven-fifteen, the rubble-strewn streets were almost deserted, the fires still burning out of control. All the looting that could be done, had been. The mobs had gone elsewhere; only an occasional pedestrian hurried furtively along the streets. Downtown Martinsburg was indoors behind locked doors, licking its wounds like a dying animal in a cave.

Revere reached the Commons, drove past the Town Hall, past the Congregational Church and the Armory. Flames silhouetted the spire of the church. The entire block behind it was burning and if the wind shifted, the church would go too. Revere rubbed the back of his neck, a weary gesture. Hadn't he seen the church burning? Then he remembered the night of the snowstorm, a quiet night, but he'd been expecting the worst. He'd gone outside, imagined the church spire burning like a torch against the dark sky, almost hoping insanely it would happen.

He drove along Rivoire, past the Garrick house, saw lights in all the windows, a light outside the front door.

A state-police car came toward him, dome light flashing, headlights dipping off and then on high beam. Revere braked to a stop, waited while the other car pulled up alongside.

"What an awful damn thing, Ned." He recognized the beefy face under the campaign hat—Captain Tomlinson, state-police commander in French County.

Revere nodded bleakly. He was beyond feeling anything. It had been like driving through a movie set of a city destroyed in an air raid.

"Guard's on the way," Tomlinson told him. "Word came fifteen, twenty minutes ago."

"Just a little bit late," Revere said, still not feeling anything.

"They couldn't help it. Ballard never got here. Car went into a skid on the Frenchman's Creek bridge. He was killed instantly."

Revere accepted that too, as he had accepted the rest of it, the indiscriminate arson that had hit the phone company but not Connecticut Light and Power, that had leveled some blocks but left others untouched, the looters running wild in some neighborhoods, ignoring others, the Commons an oasis in the rubble.

"You got anything on casualties yet?" Tomlinson asked.

"I don't even have a police force," Revere told him. He remembered Sergeant Whitlock climbing out of the car, joining the mob. Cal Whitlock hadn't been unique. As far as Revere knew, he was the only cop in Martinsburg still on duty—if patrolling the ruined streets to no purpose could be called that.

Tomlinson didn't understand. "Spread too thin? Yeah, I can see that."

Revere didn't bother to explain.

"Listen, we've got hot coffee over at the Town Hall," Tomlinson said. "Sandwiches. Why don't you come on over?"

"Thanks. Maybe I'll take you up on it later." Revere felt suddenly confused, as if there was something he had to do but couldn't recall what. He wished Tomlinson, with his good intentions and the look of commiseration on his beefy face, would leave him alone.

"We'll be there all night."

"Sure, Fred. Thanks."

They drove off in opposite directions, Tomlinson toward the Commons, Revere toward the river.

He made a left on Ironbound Road, a right on Elm Street past the junior high school. It stood untouched behind the chain-link fence of the athletic field, bypassed by random violence, motiveless destruction. When all this ended, Revere knew, no one would be held accountable, no one *could* be held accountable, not Vito Mauriello haranguing the mob, not most of forty cops running with the mob. Mauriello was a symptom, not a cause; the uniformed men were just following orders, the King's orders, the Maréchal de Marillac's.

Blame the King and Marillac? The village meant nothing to them. If its cobblestones ran red with blood, that was only a political accident. Their decision to send the dragoons had been pragmatic, a simple move on the chessboard of history, not a betrayal of their people.

But the Sieur de Ramezay, safe behind the walls of his château—hadn't he encouraged the looting, the burning, the raping? If anyone was responsible, it was Ramezay.

She slumped exhausted against the chain-link fence of the junior high school as the police car went slowly by. She even lacked the strength to worry about Craig anymore. She just wanted to curl up somewhere, anywhere, and sleep. Except for Charlie, she couldn't have taken another step. He would take care of her, see that she got home safely, she knew he would.

They began to walk along Elm again, Charlie holding her arm, half supporting her.

If he wanted to take her home, Ironbound was the shortest way, but they crossed it, kept walking straight ahead. Elm Street went on forever.

"Where are we going?"

"It's not much farther."

"This isn't the way home."

"My place is closer," Charlie said.

Melody didn't mind where he took her. Anything was all right as long as she could sit down somewhere, lie down somewhere.

Charlie opened the gate of a picket fence, led her along a path that went around the side of a two-story house.

The Armory. Her father. He'd be worried out of his mind.

"Could we call my dad first thing?"

She heard the jangle of Charlie's keys in the darkness. She could imagine a soft bed inside and stretching out on it, shutting her eyes and making the world go away.

—Well, does she live here or doesn't she, this model of yours? I would like to meet her, Charlie said.

Melody tried to scream, but all she could manage was a choked little sound, a sob of total despair.

Craig was right behind Vito Mauriello when he ran up the stairs to the roof of the apartment building, right behind him when he pushed the metal door open and sprinted across the roof to the elevator housing, right behind him when he found Angel García cowering on the other side of the square brick structure.

Except for his labored breathing, Mauriello never made a sound. He just swung the stock of the shotgun sideways at Angel García's head, García ducking, shotgun stock shattering against brick. Mauriello hit him once in the face with his fist, swinging again as García started to go down. Craig knew Mauriello wouldn't stop until he killed García. He grabbed Mauriello's arm, tugging him off balance, giving Angel García a few seconds to make a run for the stairs.

But by then a dozen men had burst through the doorway to the roof and Angel García, turning in the other direction, was quickly trapped against the edge, eight stories above the street.

Eve wished she hadn't given Garrick something else to worry about. Now, half an hour after she phoned him, there was nothing wrong with Margriet. She was totally in control of herself, so absorbed in her work that Eve doubted she knew what was going on outside or, knowing, would have cared. Something of that attitude had rubbed off on Eve herself. The Armory was a sanctuary, its thick stone walls shutting out the madness of the night. Eve wanted to see the paintings come apart almost as much as Margriet did.

She watched Margriet brush a strand of hair from her face, her lovely dark eyes sparkling with excitement. "Assuming I've got it right," she said, "that's it. In a minute or so we ought to find ourselves with two Columbines instead of one."

"I'm still not sure exactly how it works."

Margriet sighed. "That makes two of us. I've never tried it before. I'm not even sure I've got the solvent right. Mostly toluene, but just how much propyl alcohol, how much acetone—"

"No, I mean how do the paintings come apart?"

Margriet was carefully lifting a corner of the stiffened silk with the palette knife. "If all I've done is dissolve the varnish, and I *hope* that's all I've done, the overpainting adheres to the silk, the underpainting remains on the canvas." Margriet carefully slipped the knife under another corner of the stiffened silk. The solvent had turned it all but opaque, hiding the painting.

"Here goes," Margriet said.

Garrick shut the notebook and shut something of himself away in its pages, something he knew he would never get back—his belief in a sane and ordered world, in the truth behind the labels we call science, in a clockwork universe, its secrets attainable, its dark mysteries revealed by the patient probing light of man's reason, mysteries no longer—all that refuted now by what he had read in these pages, in Melody's earnest translation, in the way the pieces came together, Bourg St. Martin then, Martinsburg now. . . .

He went to the window, gazed out at the darkness, the faint red glow, his own reflection on the glass.

What in the world was he thinking of? Things like that didn't happen, had never happened, never could happen.

Melody losing her limp as Father Vasili had regained his sight, Dr. Tom dying in place of the nameless Bourg St. Martin physician, Miles Pritchard for the priest Gavrillac, Matt Hawley . . . where did Matt Hawley fit in?

It was insane.

Tom Seymour's notes on psychic attack, the bruise on Charlie Dahlgren's shoulder, Melody starving herself.

Where there is another Ramezay with a lame daughter.

The painting—too new, no signs of aging, in the Armory now, Margriet using the tools of science to reveal what lay beneath.

Matt Hawley's vision of the four huge horses. Percherons. *Milsoudiers.*

The pentimenti—one for Matt Hawley, one for Dr. Tom, one for Miles Pritchard.

The Sieur de Ramezay as St. Martin, fear replacing the arrogance on his face.

Ramsey. His great-grandmother's name.

Bourg St. Martin then, Martinsburg now . . .

He struck the reflection of his face in the glass, shattering it. He ran downstairs and outside, saw a police car pulling to the curb.

"Rob?" It was Ned Revere.

Four blocks to the Commons, the Armory, just seconds in Ned's car.

Ned was pointing at him. Pointing something at him.

He saw flame spurt from Ned's hand, heard the crash of the gun, the whine of the bullet past his ear.

He ran. The gun crashed again, three more times in the darkness as Ned Revere came after him.

Melody's eyes were tightly shut.

I'll feel nothing, he's not doing this, he didn't bring me here to do this, he's not crazy, he's not an animal throwing me down on the floor, he's Charlie Dahlgren, shy and polite Charlie Dahlgren and he wouldn't, please, oh please don't, Charlie, please, I don't want you to do it, please Charlie.

The mistakes of Jean-Baptiste had to be rectified, of course, but the Columbine woman was resisting her. The love of painting was too strong in the blood, as if Jean-Baptiste, like herself, had walked the dark unknown astral path of his descendants to that place and that time.

What place? What time?

Across the sea, across a void of many generations, to where the language was a kind of English. Was the town, burning now, its people under a spell of madness, Bourg St. Martin also?

Vision was not clear. One did not leave the astral plane entirely. One saw phantoms, caught glimpses of strange and fearsome things—roaring vehicles that moved under their own power, others hurtling like cannonballs through the sky, voices sent over long distances in an instant.

Were they, in that far place, all masters of the black arts, vanquishing nature, soaring above angels, finding the unity behind the chaos of the universe? Had they all found the path to the Godlike power she coveted?

Perhaps she would have had trouble with any agent she could have chosen there, perhaps the Columbine woman was no stronger than the rest.

But the power would destroy them eventually— Nineveh in ruins, Tyre, Sodom, Babylon with its hundred gates smashed. She saw the time to come, how many generations later? The darkness, the flames, the great cities dust.

It might have been her imagination.

She returned, fluttering like the wings of a trapped bird, beating against the stubborn soul of the woman who was a Columbine.

27

Margriet held the two loosened corners of the silk in her hands. All she had to do was pull it slowly away, and the hidden painting would be revealed.

She couldn't do it. She wanted to drop the corners of the silk, pick up the palette knife, slash the canvas.

No!

"Margriet?" Eve looked at her anxiously. "Are you all right?"

The silk still in her hands, the palette knife on the table, the voice, her voice and yet not her voice, so faint inside her that she couldn't hear the words—

It was gone. The voice was gone.

Carefully, so as not to damage the painting adhering to it, she drew the stiffened silk away.

He could hear Ned's footsteps pounding behind him. Fifty yards? Less?

Had he locked the door? Had Eve? If the door was locked, he was dead.

He raced up the stairs, heaved himself against the door, was through it, leaning against the inside, turning the lock, then running past the office, along the corridor to the great hall of the Armory, its many windows dark, the hall brightly lit, Eve and Margriet at the table.

Margriet was stripping back the silk. Eve smiled at him. "Talk about timing," she said, and he flung her aside, flung Margriet aside, the silk coming away with her, grabbed for the palette knife, heard one of the windows shattering, saw Ned Revere there, the gun in his hand, one leg over the sill.

Saw his own death on the canvas, St. Martin's face not the Sieur de Ramezay's but Garrick's own, the beggar a child, a girl—Melody.

Margriet fought him for possession of the pallet knife, shouting soundlessly, her voice lost in the single, enormous, resonant tolling of a bell, Dr. Tom's astral bell, and then he was stabbing at the canvas with the palette knife, stabbing and slashing, back and forth, right to left, pigments cracking, flaking, crumbling.

The floor swayed under his feet, tilted. He heard a distant rumbling sound, like far-off thunder.

The room shook.

The rooftop shook, the first shock hurling Craig against Angel García, the second almost sending them together over the edge.

Vito Mauriello was down on one knee, right in front of them, close enough to touch. He got up slowly, the shotgun with the smashed stock still in his hands.

He stood there for what seemed a long time, or maybe, Craig thought, that was what it was like right before you died, everything slowing down, waiting.

Then he heard Vito Mauriello say, "Are you kids all right? What was that, anyway, some kind of earthquake?"

Melody thought the floor tilted, jolted her. Shook Charlie off her.

She lay there, afraid to move.

Then she heard footsteps. Something covered her, something scratchy and warm, a blanket against her bare skin.

What was she doing undressed, anyway?

She opened her eyes and saw him, kneeling next to her in a robe—Charlie Dahlgren.

She remembered the apartment house near the river, Charlie in front of the door, the mob rushing in, Craig with them, Charlie taking her home.

Only she wasn't home. She didn't know where she

was. She'd never seen this room before. Maybe it was Charlie's place.

By the time she had dressed, she no longer remembered being undressed.

Charlie brought two cups of coffee. It was a pretty nice room. They sat at the table under a travel poster.

"I couldn't get your dad," Charlie said. "There's something wrong with the phone."

"He's at the Armory."

"Drink up," Charlie said. "I'll take you there."

"You make pretty good coffee, you know? Got anything to go with it? I'm starving."

The canvas on the table was a total loss, varnish dark, blistered, flaking, long jagged cracks crisscrossing it, almost as if someone had slashed the painting with a knife.

Had he done that? Had he come running in like a madman, grabbing the palette knife, attacking the painting because Melody's—what, her book?

He no longer remembered, and in another moment forgot that he did not remember.

Margriet stood with the stiffened silk in her hands, blotches of color, flakes of pigment clinging to it.

She was crying softly. "I couldn't do it," she said. "The solvent, or the amount of time—I've ruined them. I've ruined both paintings."

Garrick felt a surge of pity. Poor Margriet—such a plain and dowdy girl. Of course her work was her whole life. Of course she was all broken up.

Outside, Garrick heard the rumble of traffic on Commons Avenue South. Ned Revere came back from the door.

"National Guard," he said. He even sounded chipper, despite the night of terror, the mobs prowling the streets, the looting, the burning, as if somehow he knew it had ended. "Ever occur to you that the National Guard and the Red Cross have something in common? They're always just a little bit late."

Garrick thought he was being unfair, but didn't argue the point. It had been a rough couple of weeks for both of them—close friends dying, and that inexplicable crime wave. No wonder Ned was a little cynical.

He saw Ned open the flap of his holster, take out his service revolver, raise the barrel to his nose.

"Did I fire this damn thing? When the hell did I do that?" He thumbed the cylinder away from the frame. "Four cartridges missing. I don't get it."

Varnish

28

Melody opened the door and leaped into Garrick's arms. It was a warm day early in April. Garrick's face was deeply tanned, Eve's covered with even more freckles than usual.

"Hey, use some of that energy to help with the suitcases, why don't you?" Garrick suggested.

Instead, Melody hugged Eve too. "Hi, Mother," she said. "Am I supposed to ask how the honeymoon was? He's pretty old for a newlywed, you know."

"The honeymoon," Eve said, "now that you ask, was spectacular."

They went inside, Melody carrying one of the suitcases.

"Soft sands and coral beaches," Melody sighed. "Trade winds blowing at night, whispering through the fronds of frangipani and—do they have frangipani there?"

"I wouldn't know," Eve said dryly. "I didn't get to spend much time looking at the flowers."

Eve was all right. She really was neat. She wouldn't be bad to have as a stepmother at all.

"Turn around, young lady," Garrick said. "Uh-huh, that's what I thought. Something of a tummy there."

"It's just the way I'm standing. I am *not* fat."

"I didn't say you were."

"Craig says so."

"Well then—" Eve began.

"But Charlie says I'm not."

"That must get pretty complicated," Eve told her.

"Not really. I just like them both for different reasons. Daddy, Mr. Waugh's been calling all morning. It's something about a bond issue for the new civic center, he said."

Garrick headed for the phone.

"Can't it wait until after lunch? I found the most marvelous new recipe for chicken. You bake it in a clay pot to seal the juices in. It's almost like the way the gypsies make hedgehog."

"Hedgehog?" Eve said dubiously.

"It's delicious, the way Bibi Tita used to make it."

"What's the matter?" Garrick asked her. Melody looked pensive.

"Oh, nothing. I just remembered. There was a little book she gave me. It meant a lot to her. She really wanted me to read it."

"And?" Garrick asked.

"I lost it. I can't find it anywhere."

Pete Kalem looked at the painting. The old woman who ran the antique shop had allowed them to take it outside to see the colors better in the bright sunlight.

"What do you think?" he said.

"I really like it, hon," his wife told him.

His wife. His bride of two days, he still couldn't believe it. But here they were in Paris, and in a few days they'd drive down to Bourg St. Martin for the rest of their honeymoon. The Kalems came from Martinsburg, had both spent a summer as exchange students four years ago in Bourg St. Martin.

"Sure, but she'll ask some price, I bet. Claiming it's an Old Master."

"It looks old enough, hon."

"Genuine masterpieces aren't found in antique shops on—what's the name of this street again?"

"Rue St. Martin," Linda Kalem said. "Can't we buy it, hon? Please?"

Pete Kalem stared at the painting, at the figure on horseback in the foreground, his face arrogant as he leaned from the saddle, cloak unfurled to shield a man dressed in rags from the storm. Pete didn't care about that part of the painting much, but the background was something else, the background he would know anywhere.

It was Bourg St. Martin, high on its crag, looming almost like the prow of a ship through the storm, the lowering clouds pierced by the single shaft of sunlight.

The old woman came out, and they haggled over the price. It was less than Pete had expected her to ask, but certainly not cheap.

Still, Pete had to smile. The woman sensed an ally in Linda, and soon was working on her as only a French shopkeeper could.

"Five hundred's too much," Pete said, and the old woman came down to four-eighty with a look on her face that said the sky was about to fall.

"Oh, Pete," Linda said. "We've got to. It's Bourg St. Martin, isn't it? Until that summer there you hardly knew I existed."

"Four-eighty's pretty steep."

"It's our honeymoon. It's where we practically met."

"We won't even have room for it in the car."

"I'll make room."

"A month from now you'll be sorry we ever bought it."

Linda pretended to address the passing crowds of Parisians. In French yet. *"Eh bien,* where's the man's sentiment? Where is his romance? Where is his feeling for the woman who—"

"Hey, cut it out," Pete said. "Everybody's staring at you."

"Buy the painting."

"Four hundred," Pete told the old woman. She said that would be like selling her granddaughter for four hundred francs.

They settled on four hundred fifty.

It was worth it, Pete knew. It was worth it just looking at the smile on Linda's face as she said:

"I can't wait to get it to Bourg St. Martin, Pete. I'll hang it right over the bed."